GUARDIAN OF ANGEL

by
Lanie Mores

To: Juliana
Enjoy the journey!

♡ Lanie Mores

Guardian of Angel
Copyright © 2019 by Lanie Mores

Tellwell Talent
www.tellwell.ca

ISBN
978-0-2288-1246-3 (Hardcover)
978-0-2288-1245-6 (Paperback)
978-0-2288-1244-9 (eBook)

Of sisters and best friends:
For Karen—my real-life Taryn and constant cheerleader,
Steph—our *sestra*-hood was never dull, thanks to you,
And for my three amigos—always.

No one who, like me, conjures up the most evil of those half-tamed demons that inhabit the human beast, and seeks to wrestle with them, can expect to come through the struggle unscathed.
– Sigmund Freud –

Prologue

Darkness, emptiness.
A passage of time.
For me, but a fragment of a second.
For you mere mortals where time is a factor,
Decades have passed since the fateful day
That Milena and Renner first met.
Theirs, a perfect love.
Until my meddling corrupted it,
Turning it sour before the sun had set.

When they first met in the smoky pub,
Renner was instantly hypnotized by Milena's exotic beauty.
Not yet aware of her gift.
Scoffing at her abilities once discovered,
A scientist, not believing in such nonsense.
Without scientific evidence proving psychic abilities exist,
Then they did not.
It was as simple as that.

Or, so he thought.

After witnessing her powerful gift firsthand
The possibility could no longer be denied.
Disbelief quickly turned from curiosity, to interest,

Snowballing into obsession.
If psychic phenomena did exist,
Then there must be a scientific explanation for it.

I followed him, I guided him,
As he researched the topic.
Disappointed by the lack of studies on the phenomena,
He set out to do studies of his own.
His discoveries—life altering.

Aided by the Guardian Angel Spell at the old abandoned chapel,
He finally discovered how psychic abilities occur.
Developing a blueprint to create these abilities in humans,
Genetically altering a part of the human brain
Connecting them to the supernatural realm,
With the ability to borrow the powers available therein
From other-worldly entities.
Unbeknownst to Renner,
It would really be the other-worldly entities
Who held all the control.

Finally, a way to exert my immense powers on Earth
In a physical sense.
Not only confined to the subconscious,
But able to manipulate others at my whim.
The concept tantalized me, tantalizes me still.
Spurring Renner on to continue down this path of selfish ambition.

There were sacrifices along the way.
Not for me, so much.
For me they were like mere trifles, inconsequential.
But, perhaps for Renner they were…more difficult.
Turning on Milena, for one,
Causing him an element of turmoil.

But with my help, those feelings easily blocked. Ignored.
Then there was Paul,
And my other loyal followers from the chapel,
The old crone that performed the Guardian Angel Spell.
They are here with me now.

In the Sea.

They see me as easily as I see them.
They know me, for who I am now,
Slicing through me with accusatory glares
Wrought full of anger, betrayal, and fear.
There was no reward for them.
They are simply spectres now, harmless to me,
Floating by filled with unrequited malevolence.
What did they think awaited them here?
Sunshine and lollipops?
They made their choice.
It's too late for them now.
Stuck with me in the darkness.

And Renner, what of his fate?
Not my spawn, but my formidable pawn.
Not dead yet, but his destiny awaits him.

Soon, back to the darkness, my friend,
Soon back to me.

—Father of Lies

PART I

Chapter 1

Tomas – 1984

Tomas Scholz sits upon a throne beside his father above the stones of fire. Surrounded by splendour, he bursts with pride as all bow down and honour them, bestowing gifts of great riches: precious gems and stones—sardius, topaz, diamond and onyx—silver and gold, and the rarest of artifacts collected from all over the many realms. This destiny, although not yet achieved, awaits him after this world has passed away, or so the shadow has promised.

In time. He must be patient.

A three-toed woodpecker, normally a quiet, shy, little bird, hammers out a tune on a nearby dead spruce, redirecting Tomas' thoughts away from his daydreams and back to the matter at hand. Carrying the device with painstaking care, he reaches a clearing in the mountains. This flat fold of land has been carefully selected for the job, unchartered territory, a place no man has previously travelled. The device is light despite its enormous potential for destruction, light enough for his nine-year-old hands to carry.

The wind swells in unpredictable gusts sending uprooted weeds and debris to tumble across the dry landscape. It is not ideal weather to test out his experiment, on the contrary, but he is impatient, insistent. If it were anyone else attempting this feat they would be prudently dissuaded, encouraged to wait for more opportune conditions. The summer had been a dry one, and the arid conditions mixed with the gales of wind are a recipe for disaster.

But Tomas is not like other children. His abilities are powerful enough to defy even the wind.

Besides, Tomas is too excited to see how it finally works, unable to wait a moment longer. Adrenaline almost palpable as he flits and floats across the glade despite his clubbed foot, preparing for the initial trial of the weapon he has designed and built all by himself.

He is a genius. Wisdom doesn't grow on trees; it is inherited. Or prepared in a lab. Both methods are responsible in Tomas' case. Born of Renner's sperm, he has inherited the genes for brilliance, but his earthly father further manipulated Tomas' genetic structure to enhance his potential for genius. In this Renner has been successful.

Just a child, Tomas is already capable of recombinant DNA technology and minor medical procedures. Always the perfect pupil. Always eager to learn more. Technology and inventing advanced weaponry are his preferred hobbies, skills that come to him naturally, and had he been allowed to go out in public to submit these innovations for patenting, he would earn millions, perhaps billions. But they *are* billionaires and have no need for more money. And he is not ready to go out in public, to be exposed to the world—the world not ready for him yet. For Tomas' talents don't stop there.

Surpassing his higher level of intelligence are his supernatural abilities, having both fathers to thank for this gift. By the shadow entering Renner's body that fateful night in the abandoned chapel, his DNA changed, which was then passed on to his offspring. These changes increased the development of DMT produced by the pineal gland and the subsequent presentation of supernatural abilities, the like of which have never been seen in humans. Renner had also manipulated Tomas' genes, splicing them with favourable animalistic traits to increase his special abilities. The final product is a boy who has powers that are both profound and intense. Unrestrained. In this Renner has also been successful.

Tomas is a telepath, able to read other people's thoughts and desires with great ease. Most impressive are his telekinetic capabilities, able to teleport any object, from the size of a grain of sand all the way up to a massive Gothic castle to any location he so desires. Able to transport his own body.

But impressive though this is, Tomas is not perfect. None of them are. Flaws remain in Renner's recombinant DNA techniques, glitches he still struggles to correct with each series of experiments. There is always an element of trial and error when it comes to experimenting in new unexplored areas, but he has faith he will overcome these limitations and the supernatural abilities that all the offspring display prove he is on the right track.

Tomas is the most handsome of them all if you could call him handsome. Hair, worn long and unruly. Taller than most nine-year-olds, he is more muscular as well but not a giant like some of his brothers. He prefers to wear mostly jogging pants, jeans, T-shirts, and sweaters for there is no need to dress up here. No one to impress. His eyes are as black as pitch and empty. Dead embers.

Born with a cleft palate, Tomas underwent corrective surgery as a young baby, but Renner being untrained in cosmetic procedures, the repair didn't go as well as planned. Tomas can feed and communicate much better than he would have without the surgical procedure, but a resultant lisp when speaking words that contain the letter s has Tomas training extensively to articulate his words. The lisp now more of an extended, exaggerated s sound. The speech impediment isn't as bothersome as the thickened scar tissue between his nose and upper lip. Tomas plans on visiting a real cosmetic surgeon who will correct the botched effort his father performed and eliminate the scar—when he is older, when he is permitted to venture out into the real world. He also has a clubbed right foot that gives him a mild limp. These deformities are considered minor compared to his brothers'. So, he has little to complain about, this he knows.

His brothers, on the other hand, have not fared as well. The flaws in Renner's experiments far more evident. The deformities more intensive, requiring massive reconstruction, the likes of which do not yet exist. Tomas is already working diligently on this limitation, inventing his own brand of prosthetics that will help the remainder of his triplet brothers—his womb-mates—and other siblings to help them be more aesthetically pleasing to the eye or at least less abhorrent while simultaneously helping them to channel their own gifts. Augment them.

But again, in time.

Tomas' preparations slowly come to completion. He lopes across the field through tussock grasses and stunted shrubbery to the location he has deemed most beneficial for his test. He stops amidst a patch of denser grasses and wildflowers, adjacent to a stand of tiny gnarled aspens. Mounds of rhododendron underbrush proudly display their yellow and white puff ball-shaped flowers tinged with pink and lavender.

Soon their beauty will be extinguished.

The sound of a river rushing at highs speeds can be detected from this vantage point, an important proponent for this experiment to function smoothly.

He looks over to see if the shadow—his other father, the one that matters most—is watching, desiring his praise. A moment of insecurity?

But, the moment of weakness is short-lived. As soon as Tomas senses approval, he commences, extending his right arm towards the surrounding rhododendron mounds and dry grasses. Clumsily, he fastens the contraption to his extended right wrist with plastic straps and buckles. The weapon, a flame thrower, is like no other. It is controlled by Tomas' mind alone, lacking buttons or switches, with nothing to turn it on or off, no dials to increase or decrease its power, except by his mind's will.

Abruptly he stops, eyes fastening on the shadow as the sound of a woman's scream pierces his mind. The sound is heard through his gift, although the actual source is not much further than their location, yet still safely out of harm's way. Their eyes make contact, full of mutual understanding. It is Milena, once more in the throes of labour.

"It will be a boy," he tells the shadow.

"Yes, yes, I know," the shadow responds.

They are all boys, so it is a natural conclusion. However, Tomas knows this on another level, knows it for a fact as the baby's thoughts can already be heard, although he is not yet born. "He is different," Tomas adds, before returning to his task without further explanation.

A shiny, black crow bursts out of the shrubbery and furiously flaps its wings, escaping barely in time, somehow anticipating the fire that will quickly follow. Tomas telepathically transmits a message to the weapon to eject a far-reaching rope of flame from its tip, and the contraption immediately obliges, bathing the mountain glade in fire. He slowly spins in a circle creating a ring of fire around him, the flames dancing and rising as if in adoration and worship. The intense orange from the fire's light is reflected in his black eyes as if tiny flames have been sparked from within the lifeless black embers.

"It works!" he exclaims. "Father, can you see it?"

The flames continue to rise.

And rise. And rise higher still, the flames licking and lapping at Tomas' face and body and limbs. Searing, melting, binding. Until flame and skin become one.

Chapter 2

Angelika – September 2002

Not your typical day in the life of a teenager but a typical Monday for Angelika. Up at the crack of dawn. The room kept dim to encourage a soothing atmosphere. Another person to care for before taking care of herself.

Sabina, Angelika's grandmother, sat stiffly in her wheelchair looking at the reflection in the mirror without recognition—of herself, or of her granddaughter, it was difficult to tell. This was not unusual ever since the Alzheimer's had advanced; her condition rapidly deteriorating over the last few months.

Angelika stood behind her grandmother combing her thick, black tresses streaked with silver, the stubborn curls springing back to their original position after each stroke of the brush. Part of their daily routine.

"*Babka*, it's me, Angel. Remember? Your granddaughter?"

She hated the nickname Angel—preferring Ang for short, which is what all her friends used—but her grandmother had always called her Angel. She thought the use of her grandmother's pet name would jog her memory and put her at ease.

It worked. The elderly woman's withered body relaxed within the soft powder-blue robe she wore, and the furrow in her brow disappeared. Angelika's heart broke daily as her grandmother's health rapidly declined. Ever since her grandfather died of a massive coronary last December, his wife seemed to lose her spark, her zest, and like the statistics predicted, it looked like she would perish within a year or so of her soul mate's passing.

Angelika accepted the role of caretaker, a natural and easy decision, although it was proving to be her most difficult journey in her seventeen years of life. But it was a small sacrifice to pay. Her grandparents not only meant the world to her, but they were also her legal guardians.

"Your father was only a boy himself when he came to me one day to tell me Sophia was pregnant. He didn't know what to do," Ang's grandmother had told her a long time ago when she was a little girl.

"Who is Sophia?" she had asked innocently.

"That's your mother, dear," Babka had replied. "She was practically a child when she became pregnant, and quite an immature one at that."

Up until that moment, she had always thought of Babka and *Dedko* as being her parents. She was still too young to realize what their titles meant, instead, that she was the offspring of their son and his trampy girlfriend. What a revelation.

"Of course, Dedko and I knew they couldn't possibly take care of a baby, so we quickly took her in after she was born. That was your sister, of course. It would be another year before you were born. I guess they didn't learn the first time. Perhaps it was our fault, not letting them take on any responsibility, but then you wouldn't be here with us, so I think it worked out in the best way possible."

Once the two girls were legally adopted by their grandparents, both their biological parents fled the small town of Thunder Bay. Their father followed his heart to California, remained unemployed, covered himself in leather and tattoos and bedded more women than he could name. Their mother turned to heroin, contracted Hepatitis C and wasn't faring well, last Ang heard. A couple of real winners.

Reflecting on her childhood, although resentful at first, she was now glad her parents realized they couldn't care for two kids. Having her grandparents raise them was a blessing. They were the most awesome individuals she could ever know—warm, caring, loving, and always supportive. It boggled her mind that her older sister could so easily leave town, abandoning Ang to care for Babka alone. But Ronnie was always a bit selfish.

"Time for breakfast?" Ang asked Babka, who managed a slight nod. She placed the boar-bristled brush back in the top drawer of the antique vanity—the vanity and a four-poster bed, the only two pieces of furniture that remained in Babka's room, the rest removed for easier wheelchair access.

Angelika wheeled the heavy chair into the kitchen—thankfully, Babka's room was situated on the main floor, so she could easily move her around without having to navigate stairs—and slid the woman's emaciated legs under the kitchen table.

"Toast and orange juice?" This was Babka's usual breakfast so, after another slight nod, Ang popped two slices of whole wheat bread into the toaster and grabbed two glasses from the cupboard. She tumbled a Donepezil tablet into the palm of her hand, the only medication Babka was still taking, although its effectiveness in delaying the progression of the debilitating disease was questionable. The doctor insisted she continue her course of treatment, regardless. Choking, however, was becoming an issue as of late, and Ang wondered how long her grandmother would be capable of taking the pills. And, what then? How long would Babka have left?

The phone rang, stopping her mind from travelling that path of pessimism, a path she often roamed, and instead grabbed the cordless out of its cradle.

"You have to go to the bank and deposit more money into my account!"

"Well hello to you too, Ronnie," Ang responded to her snarky sister's demands. "If memory serves me correctly, I deposited five hundred dollars two weeks ago."

"Yeah, well it's gone. It's expensive being on your own. But you wouldn't know anything about that. You're only in high school."

Ang white-knuckled the receiver. "The accountant said we need to follow a budget, which includes five hundred a month for you, besides your tuition and residence fees. We're already way over that for you this month. Dedko's inheritance won't last forever, you know."

"Don't be a such a bitch. Just do it!"

-click-

No "How is Babka doing?" No "What's new in your life?" Just demands. Typical Ronnie. And another unwelcome ball for Ang to juggle. She wished that she wasn't placed in charge of finances now that her grandparents weren't able, but she was clearly the best choice. If Ronnie were in charge, she would bleed them dry in months.

The doorbell binged, signalling the arrival of Maria, the neighbour. It was a school day—Ang was in her last year at St. Paulina High School—so Maria was coming to hang out with Babka while Ang was away. The two women had been close friends for years and, both widowed, they had grown closer over the past year until Babka's mind slipped away. Now Maria acted not only as companion but also as day nurse as she had recently retired from a nursing position, well qualified for the job.

Ang swung open the back door, which opened into the kitchen, and welcomed Maria. The older woman was the picture of a healthy senior, clad in a purple velvet tracksuit, perfectly curled, shoulder-length, auburn-dyed hair, and a pink stain on her lips and cheeks.

"How are my two favourite ladies?" she asked with a broad smile.

Ang stepped aside to allow Maria into the warm kitchen. "Besides another *cheerful* call from Ronnie, it's a decent morning so far. Babka's fairly alert, and we're getting ready to have breakfast. Thanks again for watching her today. I owe you so much. Are you sure I can't pay you for your time?"

"Don't be ridiculous. Babka's my friend, and ever since Reginald died, I've felt bored...lost. Sabina gives me a sense of purpose. Spending time with her is my pleasure. Besides, you don't know how randy she can get when you're away. She's still a hoot."

Ang snickered. "I'm sure she is. Well, we truly appreciate it," she added but felt guilty having to rely on her so often. "Can I make you some toast?"

"I'll have a coffee, hon. Thanks," Maria replied, settling into a chair beside Babka at the kitchen table.

A small television sat idle on the Formica kitchen counter. Ang flicked on the news to check the weather forecast—to see if she would need her brown, leather jacket or a simple sweater today—while continuing with her breakfast ministrations. The weather report had recently concluded, so she would have to wait another ten minutes for it to repeat. Leaving the television on to drone in the background, she prepared her own morning meal: two eggs sunny side up and a bran muffin.

As Ang brought Maria her steaming cup of coffee, a news alert drew both women's attention to the television.

"Another woman was reported missing this morning in the downtown Toronto area. Leah Toppin, 27-years-old, 5'8", with long brown hair and green eyes, was last seen by her neighbours one week ago," the female news reporter announced on the television. "Her husband is also missing, Robert Toppin, 6'1", short brown hair, goatee, with brown eyes. Investigators are treating the disappearance as suspicious and suspect foul play. The neighbours notified police concerning the couple's disappearance after noticing mail and newspapers piling up in their yard. Their house was completely ransacked, police reported after searching the missing couple's home. There are currently no leads. If anyone has seen this couple or has information regarding their possible whereabouts, you are requested to contact the authorities immediately. This is the third missing person's case this month alone involving women between the ages of..."

Ang quickly cut the feed. "Disturbing news tends to agitate Babka. Besides, I was only interested in the weather report."

"I just came from outside. It's freezing. How's that for a weather report."

"Actually, quite helpful." She would go with the leather jacket.

"Weird, how all these women have started disappearing again. Wasn't it around the same time last year when eight women vanished without a trace? I wonder if it's a serial killer."

Ang made the watch-what-you-say-around-Babka eyes at Maria, who merely shrugged.

"I know you worry about your grandmother, but she's still a tough cookie in there."

Babka smiled. Did she understand?

Unexpectedly, the doorbell chimed. Man, they were popular this morning. Ang whipped open the kitchen door to let in her closest friend in the universe, Taryn. They had been BFFs since first grade and unwaveringly ever since.

"Hey, buddy. I have the best news!" Taryn bounced past Ang and made herself at home, grabbing a piece of toast off Babka's plate.

"What's up?" Ang encouraged, grabbing her own breakfast and depositing it on the kitchen table.

"You'll never guess what I heard!"

"Go on. I'm all ears," Ang pulled out a chair between Maria and Babka, sat cross-legged, and ran a hand through her layered, blond hair, listening expectantly.

"This weekend, there's going to be a huge bonfire and camping party out at Cushing Lake and everybody is going to be there. Including Josh."

Josh was this cute, albeit slightly geeky boy Ang had a puppy dog crush on but hadn't gotten the nerve to speak to yet. A bit of a geek herself, she was probably the shyest seventeen-year-old in existence, so it was difficult for her to put herself out there, to risk vulnerability and possible rejection.

If it weren't for Taryn, Ang's social life wouldn't even exist. Only because her bosom buddy was continually brainstorming new ways to push her out of her comfort zone—her protective shell, so to speak—did she have a life outside of caring for Babka and attending high school.

Taryn was the opposite of Ang—super bubbly, loved partying and socializing, and didn't give a rat's ass what other people thought of her. She was quirky and edgy, a real unique individual, and only because of this was she omitted from the "popular crowd." Best thing was that she didn't care. She had Ang.

She often wondered why Taryn would want to be friends with someone as boring and awkward as herself. But her bestie always insisted that she had a distorted image of herself, and instead was naturally beautiful with her sexy, tousled long hair, almond-shaped hazel eyes, and tall, slim body. Ang secretly thought she was saying that to make her feel better, boost her self-esteem. It did help, though—Taryn was like her own personal cheerleader.

"I was thinking we could drive up at five o'clock since it takes an hour and a half to get there, which still gives us enough time to set up our tent before the sun sets," Taryn explained, already determined Ang was going. It was nearing the end of September, and the sun set quite late in their geographical neck of the woods, usually around eight o'clock in the evening. That gave them plenty of time to reach the campsite and settle in before dusk.

Ang rejected the muffin she had been munching, dropping it onto her plate. A tight churning acid bloomed in the pit of her stomach. A total social phobe, being around so many people, particularly Josh, made her instantly sick with anxiety. Especially because they would be staying the night. Taryn must have picked up on this because she quickly added, "We'll have to pick you up some liquid courage before we go, eh, buddy?"

"I'm going to pretend I didn't hear that," Maria piped in, the girls forgetting she was present and listening. The legal drinking age in T. Bay was nineteen-years-old, so they would have to be creative in scoring some alcohol, but it wouldn't be the first time. They had their ways.

"You're going to force me to go, aren't you?" Ang asked Taryn, already knowing the answer.

"Of course. Come on, I'll give you a ride to school. We can discuss the details on the way." And, with that conclusive statement, she slipped out the door and headed to her vehicle left idling in the driveway.

Oh, crap. Another uncomfortable evening when she would so rather be watching a movie at home with Babka, a massive bowl of warm, buttery popcorn on her lap. But Taryn was determined, and when her mind was set, there was no changing it. Besides, they had some amazing times in the past. Maybe this would prove to be one of those cases? Since she hardly had a choice, instead of squandering her energy getting out of the party, she decided to focus on what she was going to wear.

Josh was going to be there, after all.

Chapter 3

Veronica (aka Ronnie)

A song of love, of courtship. A song foreshadowing tragedy.

Veronica lost herself in the music. The rich, passionate vibrations from the violin strings wound their way through her entire being, her vulnerable soul captivated and taken prisoner.

Strings caressed, playfully plucked, then caressed once more coaxing her down the path to her memories, distant and warm. Her eyes closed, head leaning back against the couch cushions as she paid heed to the rhythm of her thoughts.

She was only eight years old the first time she saw Tchaikovsky's *Swan Lake*, and "Danse Russe" quickly became her favourite piece from the romantic Russian ballet. She remembered that day perfectly, like you do when you have an experience that transforms your life forever.

The hum of excitement, like an undercurrent of electricity, ran through the crowd as they gathered in line to be admitted to the performance at the Community Auditorium on Paul Shaffer Drive, a building of gold and glass. Anticipation and wonder bubbled up inside Veronica, this being her first live theatre production.

Clad in her fanciest Sunday dress, a shimmering pink gown with ruffles on the skirt, she took her seat among the other young girls with their mothers, holding her breath in expectation for the heavy velvet curtain to rise. She wasn't there with her mother, though, as she didn't know where her mother was during that time, and for that matter hadn't known for several years. Instead, she was with her best friend, Lana, and Lana's mom, Valerie.

When the performance commenced, Veronica watched in awe as sleek, Swan-like creatures in feathered tutus floated across the stage. Pointed toes kicked and flicked with knife-like precision, every move perfectly executed. Bodies bent and flew around the stage in ways that defied the laws of physics. Veronica felt entirely small as she stared up at the mystical story unfolding before her. A fantasy brought to life. As the ballet dancers took their final bow and receded off the stage, she knew she wanted to be like them. Her dream to be a performer was born.

This final thought brought her back to the present. At least one hour had passed since Veronica started studying. Opening her eyes, she stared back down at the heavy Theatre Research and Development textbook cradled in her lap with frustration. The title was as dry as the book's contents. Re-reading the first paragraph of Chapter One what felt like a thousand times, she still hadn't a clue what it said. Not that the content was too complicated for her to understand—she simply couldn't concentrate.

Dressed in comfy fleece sweatpants, a faded, grey T-shirt with sparkly pink skull and crossbones tightly stretched over her ample chest. A pumpkin spice candle flickered on the end table beside the cream-coloured couch. Classical music played softly in the background. This was all to set the perfect mood, the perfect ambience for studying—to facilitate the learning process and create some new neural pathways in her stubborn brain.

None of it was working.

Maybe I need a break, she thought, even though she had made little progress. Releasing a huge sigh of disappointment, she sprang off the couch like a tightly coiled spring, worked out the kinks in her legs from sitting cross-legged far too long, flicked the light to a brighter setting and continued into the kitchen to grab cranberry juice from the refrigerator.

Six weeks had lapsed since Veronica moved up to Red Deer, Alberta to attend college in pursuit of her dream to become a performer, more specifically, a screen actor. With classrooms packed full of hundreds of bodies, it was easy to get lost in the throng and simply flow from one space to another with minimal social exchange. She was becoming an expert at small talk but sorely missed the deeper conversations and relationships with her friends she had left back home.

Also missed was the attention and adoration she had garnered in her quaint high school, from males and females alike, as a result of her stark beauty and overly dramatic personality. She kept reminding herself to give it time, that she would be noticed soon enough. Not only by the students but by the collective net of humanity.

Believing it was her sole purpose and destiny to become a performer, she surely fit the part. Blond hair worn long, with a natural wave and shine, eyes a dark ocean blue, skin a light tan, also tight and pore-less, and lips of the bee-stung variety that usually required a saline injection by a skilled cosmetic surgeon but came naturally to her. Exercise had always been a part of her daily schedule, which included running, resistance training, and yoga, keeping her body taut and flexible. Dancing, singing, acting, you name it, she could do it. Cry at the drop of a hat? No problem.

Yet, she realized one key element was missing. The tortured, dejected and controversial quality was lacking that most true artists possessed. Why, even Tchaikovsky's life and death were shrouded in mystery and controversy, with rumours that he was forced to commit suicide after shaming his family.

Although Veronica's life was not completely free from hardship and complications, it wasn't all that bad. So, tortured she was not, but successful she would still be, because she had perseverance and self-assurance on her side. Some had the gall to call her egotistical and narcissistic, but she ardently disagreed. No, she was just self-confident and believed that those people who doled out the criticism were merely jealous of her beauty and many talents.

Like Ang...especially Ang. She was pissed at their earlier exchange and only hoped the brat would follow through and deposit the money into her bank account. There was a slightly used Balenciaga motorcycle handbag for sale that she had to get her hands on. After all, she had an image to uphold.

A sharp rapping at the door startled Veronica out of her reverie, causing her to slosh scarlet juice down her chin.

"Who the hell is that?" she wondered aloud, not used to having anyone drop by unannounced. Hastily, she replaced the plastic cap on her juice and returned it to the fridge. Wiping the red liquid from her chin with a dishtowel, she then plunked it on the kitchen credenza in a crumpled heap. Once she reached the door to her apartment, she peered through the peephole that revealed a man with an exaggerated stature in both height and musculature, but that's all she could discern from the limited view as he stood facing back towards the street. He had a wheeled cart of books balanced against his leg and a clipboard clutched at his side. A salesman?

Veronica unlatched the chain and unlocked the deadbolt from her apartment door, opening it to a gust of fresh air with the slight undertone of rotten foliage from the cool, autumn night. Her loft, a few blocks off campus, was part of an independent apartment complex with four separate units in the building, each having its own external entrance. The wind gusted once more loosening orange and gold tinged leaves from a nearby oak tree, sending them on a wild dance through the darkened sky.

The man turned towards her. "Hello, ma'am. How are you this evening?" he said in a hollow, flat voice, each word over-articulated, the s's prolonged. His eyes were small holes in a putty-like face, devoid of all warmth and emotion.

Veronica immediately felt on edge. Did people actually sell door to door anymore? He didn't strike her as the salesman type either. Thick shoulders and biceps bulged beneath his brown corduroy coat, and his tight blue jeans left little to the imagination. The deep baritone of his lifeless voice was anything but personable and convincing.

And his face. She couldn't stop looking at his face. It was all wrong, the way the light from her apartment lay flat against his skin, the lack of wrinkling around the eyes and mouth as he spoke. A puckering around the dense moustache and beard coating his lip and chin. The way the skin tone didn't quite match up with that on his hairline and neck. The contacts he wore were dark green.

The man continued with his spiel, despite the lack of response from Veronica.

"The Red Deer Book Club offers a collection of books to meet the needs and tastes of its members. We include fiction, non-fiction, documentaries and encyclopedias. We also have a magazine subscription list at prices far below the store prices." The rehearsed speech was paused for a moment, no doubt the blank space in his memorized dialogue sheet where the customer can respond, but Veronica felt temporarily unable to speak. Tongue glued to the roof of her mouth that had gone completely dry, she stood there frozen. She hoped her mind was overreacting, but she couldn't shake the feeling that there was something wrong with this man. He was creepy, and her internal instincts were on high alert.

Never open the door to strangers, she heard her grandmother's voice in her mind, a rule she had taught her a thousand times. Why hadn't she listened?

"Sorry, I'm not interested," Veronica finally croaked as her tongue came unglued, but she could hear how feeble the words sounded.

The man continued in a monotone, ignoring her statement. "For as low as $9.99 per month, you will be shipped a different selection each month and can review it for seven days. If you do not wish to keep the selection, you can return it at no cost to you." He took a giant step towards Veronica, causing her to step backwards while handing the clipboard to her as if she was going to sign the form. The door softly clicked shut behind him.

He was inside her apartment.

Her scalp tightened and prickled in fear. A hot sweat crept up her back and neck, dampened her armpits. Still, the man droned on as if his behaviour were perfectly normal, now talking about methods of accepted payment, but Veronica paid no attention. Her mind was reeling, trying to figure out how she would get out of her place if the man chose to attack, seeing that his massive form now blocked her only exit.

"I'm sorry, sir, but I said I'm not interested. I would like you to leave now," she spoke in her most assertive tone, thrusting the clipboard back at him, but a slight waver belied her fear.

Without breaking his dialogue, he reached behind his back, withdrawing something from his jeans pocket.

Oh God, he has a gun, she silently assumed. In a full-blown panic, realizing her fears were founded, she threw the clipboard at the salesman's head, lunged sideways and tried to squeeze behind him in hopes of opening the door and escaping, but he was too quick. With Goliath-like strength, he grabbed her by the throat with his free hand and pinned her like a rag doll against the door. The item from his back pocket materialized in front of her—not a gun but a soaked rag—which was thrust firmly over her nose and mouth. The pungent odour from the unknown liquid had warned her to hold her breath before her clean oxygen supply was cut off, and she began thrashing her body violently to dislodge the hold he had on her, but his vice-like grip held firm.

A large Oriental vase teetered and then crashed onto the floor in jagged pieces, a victim of the struggle as Veronica's leg kicked out, missing the attacker and connecting, instead, with a small wooden table in her foyer. Desperate to escape his steel hold, she reached up and raked her nails across the man's face. In horror, she felt a large chunk of it tear free into her hand. The top part of his beard now hung down in a flap over his cheek. Pink, mottled skin was exposed beneath the fake epidermis, most likely from a severe burn. The scarred skin cracked open, and tendrils of smoke escaped the fissures, along with a hint of orange hiding beneath like magma peeking through the Earth's crust.

In shock, she inadvertently gasped, accidentally inhaling the fumes from the toxic rag. Unable to hold her breath any longer, she took a few more ragged breaths, choking as her throat tightened in resistance.

She gaped at him, wide-eyed, his face still completely devoid of emotion, despite their struggle.

Her vision started to swim, threatening to consume her consciousness, black spots floating like waves in a turbulent ocean. A rush of nausea overwhelmed her. Then everything was hot, and spinning—she felt like she was falling, her body suspending on nothing.

And then he smiled.

Her world went dark.

Chapter 4

Gavin

The potted begonias, bright cherry red in sunlight, were now stained deep mahogany by the thickening roll of clouds unfurling across the sky. The morning continually growing darker, not brighter as it should as Gavin gazed upon the twelve hundred square foot bungalow with the maple siding and attached garage. Had he been visible to the naked eye, Gavin could easily have been mistaken for a stalker, standing at the base of the Lockstone driveway, staring at the home, waiting patiently.

Tall, muscular, statuesque, attired in distressed jeans, white T-shirt and black leather jacket, his appearance was like that of a model or celebrity. This was the image he chose.

The clouds continued to thicken, and then transformed into a distinct shape—an undulating hand reaching over the bungalow, gripping the roof with black arthritic knuckles, coming to rest there with a heavy message of foreboding.

It would happen soon.

Inside, they were still oblivious, sleeping soundly, warm and content in their beds. Not aware of what was soon to occur. *This will shatter their world.* It always did. But, what could he do? This was the way of things, not up to him to change.

But he didn't have to like it.

In fact, Gavin hated this part of his job with every immortal fibre of his being. He couldn't help but get attached to his clients, especially after spending so much time with them. Knowing them intimately, caring for them and loving them. There had been so many clients that he had lost, too many to even count, but every time they passed away, it still pained him deep within his heart. The ones taken too early were the most painful to bear.

At least Hansuke Yokoyama, Gavin's current client, had lived a happy, long, fulfilling life. At the age of ninety-five, he was leaving behind a strong, intelligent wife two decades his junior, two adult children born late in their marriage who were both successful in their respective careers, and one grandchild, Arata, a boy of four years who, as if on cue, came bounding out of the house, the screen door slamming shut behind him. He stopped, looking lost and confused, amidst the darkening blossoms that Hansuke had planted earlier that summer. Searching frantically, knowing something was missing.

His eyes locked directly on Gavin. *Does he see me?* Gavin wondered. Sometimes the wee ones did. But then the black-haired boy's gaze shifted, and he slipped back inside the bungalow, the adults inside unaware of his brief escape.

And then it happened.

Gavin remained unnoticed at the end of the driveway as the silver Nissan Pathfinder pulled to a stop in front of the Yokoyama home. A portly man with silver hair the exact shade of his vehicle emerged from the Pathfinder and lumbered with head lowered to the front entrance. He hesitated, shook his head slowly from side to side. Finally, after the good half of a minute had passed, he rang the doorbell.

Sadako Yokoyama answered the door in rumpled pyjamas, and her son, Chimon, walked protectively up behind her to see who was calling so early in the morning when the rest of Sapporo was still deep in slumber. Chimon and his son, Arata, had spent the night, keeping Sadako company while Hansuke was in the hospital.

The portly man spoke, Gavin unable to hear his exact words, although he didn't have to hear...he knew what was coming.

Sadako's face crumpled in anguish and tears instantly streamed down her face. Turning towards her son, she buried her face in his neck. Her son was attempting to fight back the tears, putting on a brave face as the portly man continued to speak.

It was the doctor who was delivering the news in person because not only was he Hansuke's doctor, but he was also the Yokoyama's next-door neighbour and longtime family friend. He felt it was the right thing to personally deliver the heartbreaking news that Hansuke had passed away during the night from complications due to double pneumonia. He had been admitted to the hospital only as a precaution the night before. Nobody had been by his bedside holding his hand as he expelled his final breath. Except for Gavin, of course, but he was unable to have physical contact with his clients, and the old man would have been unaware of his presence; however, he still granted him comfort and peace as he died.

Gavin didn't need to stay during the mourning phase, to watch helplessly as the family tried to cope through the roughest time of their lives, but he always chose to stay—at least for the initial blow. He needed to see the whole job through to completion, though it was only until the client passed that he was obligated to stay.

He would have a new assignment soon enough.

Until then, he reflected back on Hansuke's life, remembering every detail whether insignificant or profound—the day he was born as he cried out for the first time, when he broke his arm at the age of five while wagon racing down a steep hill with some other young boys, the day he met his future wife, their marriage, and the days their kids were born, even the few times where the marriage was strained and almost fell apart. Through all these times, Gavin was there. The memories resurged in his mind as if they had occurred a few hours before, they were so clear and real. This was part of Gavin's grieving process.

The doctor returned to his Pathfinder and pulled into his own driveway next door while the family retreated into their house, no doubt to prepare to go to the hospital and pay their final respects to their loved one. Gavin felt as if he could move on now. He performed a short prayer and blessing over the family, again unnoticed, and then left to talk to his boss who would be waiting to hear the details and close the file on Hansuke's case. As sad as he was in saying goodbye to him, the old man's spirit was now in a better place, and Gavin was eager to see what awaited him for his next assignment.

★ ★ ★

Gavin materialized at his boss's office door, the quatrefoil patterned gold gleaming bright and sterile. Tapping the cold metal with his knuckles two times, the third tap met with air as the office door flew open. His superior, Matthew—he had no last name like all the other members of the congregation—was overly agitated as he signalled Gavin to enter the office. The scene was all wrong. His boss's desk, normally spotless and ordered, was buried in paperwork as if he had been rushed, searching through documents fanned out in all directions. More reams of paper were stacked in precarious towers on the floor or leaning up against the walls. But it wasn't the office itself that signalled to Gavin of trouble brewing, rather the worry that darkened Matthew's emerald eyes. Knuckles white from firmly gripping a file, sweat beading his brow—all very unlike his boss. Turning towards Gavin, he paused as if unsure how to begin.

"Gavin, we have your next case," he spoke in a grave voice. This much, so far, Gavin had expected. Entering the cluttered office, he waited to hear the rest of what Matthew had to say, his blue eyes wide and wary.

"Before we can officially assign you this case, we need you to promise us a few things."

Gavin nodded, feeling his body tense in anticipation. This was getting weirder by the moment.

"This case is abnormal—different from any you have received in the past. We need your utmost cooperation and trust in this matter. When you accept the assignment, we command that you conduct it to the best of your abilities while abstaining from asking any questions regarding its unconventional nature and speak of this with no one." His intense stare unnerved Gavin, and he stuttered in response.

"Yes—ah, yes sir. Of course, sir. What exactly is the assignment, sir?" It was always difficult to commit to an assignment for which you had no prior knowledge, what the possible dangers were, what the repercussions could be—but Gavin was dedicated to his position. He would do whatever was asked of him. Besides, he was expected to follow all orders, and only a few colleagues had disobeyed in the past, letting their egos, jealousy, and desires cloud their behaviour and judgment—they were brutally punished and cast out by the Big Boss himself. There was no worse punishment than that.

"You will be guarding a young woman, following her very closely. If you notice anything amiss—I mean anything, even if you believe it may be trivial—you report back to me immediately." Matthew was firm, the intensity in his eyes boring right through Gavin.

This case was, indeed, odd. All assignments were from birth until death when protecting a client. He wondered what had become of this woman's former guardian. She, without a doubt, must have had one. Every human did.

But this wasn't the first oddity that Gavin had noticed in the last while. Several of the guardians seemed to be "missing." At least, he hadn't seen them lately, couldn't feel them with their special mental link, and now with the onset of this new case, he feared something more sinister was at hand.

Gavin grabbed the file from Matthew's outstretched hand, noticing a slight resistance from his boss in letting it go—as if he was reluctant to part with it, reveal its secret—and proceeded to flip it open. The front page was an animated photograph, vivid, in fluid motion an image of an attractive young woman with long, blond hair, bright hazel, almond-shaped eyes, high cheekbones, large red lips, and a lean figure. He watched her in real time. She was stretched out on a plaid loveseat watching television, a human pastime he never did understand and, quite frankly, thought was a devastating waste of the precious time they had on earth. After staring for a few moments at the photo, he concluded that she was not only attractive but rather stunningly beautiful in an understated way. A name was typed at the bottom of the photo—Angelika Juris—and in brackets, the pronunciation of the last name, *Yuris,* as if he would ever be able to talk with her, have to utter her name.

Words stuck in Gavin's throat. Unsure what questions were appropriate for him to voice after Matthew's clear warning kept him speechless. Yet, he needed to know more.

"You start immediately. I'm assuming all went well with Hansuke's case, and you wrapped things up accordingly."

Gavin nodded in the affirmative.

"I expect a formal report summarizing the case for his file no later than tomorrow. You can leave it on my desk."

They both glanced at the chaotic desk covered in paperwork.

"On second thought, leave it in my mail slot. I haven't had time to organize things in here. A lot has happened, and I'm afraid I must cut our meeting short. I'm needed elsewhere. In fact, I'm already late. You'll let yourself out?" And without waiting for a reply, Matthew fled the office and disappeared down the hall.

Gavin remained stunned in Matthew's office, unsure of his next step. Matthew had vacated the room so urgently rushing off to where? An important meeting? His boss's demeanour was so different. Normally calm, cool and collected, organized in all aspects, it was disconcerting to see him under so much stress and pressure. What could be the cause? Gavin observed the photo he still held, his new assignment. The girl, curled into a fetal position, was fast asleep in front of the illuminated television screen. What part did she play in this newfound chaos pervading the organization? He reflected on his conversation with Matthew, brief as it was, and feared he didn't have enough information to adequately protect the pretty girl who was entrusted to him. Compelled to find out more information, he struggled with his promise not to ask any questions.

But perhaps if he did his own investigation, in the most discreet way possible, of course, he wouldn't be violating his promise. Didn't he owe it to the young girl? Besides, his sense of curiosity was piqued. First, he would find out where Matthew had hastened and figure out what his boss was up to, what his emergency meeting was all about. It could provide him with clues as to what had gone awry in their consistent and predictable world. A casual type of surveillance—surely nothing for which he would be reprimanded.

Gavin hurried out of the room in the direction Matthew had taken moments before. The long golden hallways were deserted, his footfalls echoing much louder than he liked.

Matthew had another office space where he preferred to conduct his private work, so Gavin headed in that direction assuming it would be the ideal place to start. Once at the door to the office, Gavin pressed his ear against the cold, hard steel and tried to ascertain if there was any movement, any sound from within. At times, he thought he did hear a sound—faint shuffling, muted voices—so he crouched behind a verdant weeping fig plant in an alcove across the hall and waited. Unsure of what he was waiting for.

Was he overreacting to his boss's nervous demeanour and the odd new case he was assigned? Or, was his gut instinct correct… that the foundation of their world was weakening, becoming unstable and in danger of complete and utter collapse?

Chapter 5

Ang prayed all week for it to rain on the day of the camping party—or better yet, for some freak blizzard to hit, rendering everyone housebound. Although not a common occurrence for early October in Thunder Bay, it was a farfetched possibility she had been clinging to.

But when she woke up on Saturday morning, she was blinded by the brilliant bright sunlight streaming through her second-floor bedroom window, the rays fragmented by a giant maple tree outside creating a spattering of dark shadows to play across her face like butterflies trapped in a jar.

Throwing off her down-stuffed comforter, she slipped fuzzy, pink socks over ice-cold feet. Her toes were frigid, a chronic nuisance. Babka used to say it was because she was too skinny, that she didn't eat enough, but, shamefully, she knew her lack of circulation was more due to laziness than to an inadequate diet.

After brushing her teeth and a quick face scrubbing, she studied her features in the circular mirror above the sink. Fresh, clean, with a bit of a natural blush to her cheeks, she appeared much younger than she felt. But her eyes held the truth, she could see it there clearly...the worry, the fear, the guilt. An adult trapped in a teenager's body.

Why couldn't she be like other teenagers? Taryn, at this point, would be bouncing off the walls, bursting with excitement, counting down each millisecond until the party tonight. Surely, most of the other party goers were doing the same. Packing their coolers, tents and sleeping bags into their vehicles, calling each other to decide where they would meet out at the campsite, hoping to score the best spot to set up their tents, figuring out what they were going to bring to eat, drink or smoke. But, not Ang. She was too busy battling the anxiety that welled up in her chest, clouded her mind, and paralyzed her socially.

"What the hell is wrong with me?" This was a sentiment she had harboured deeply for at least a year now. Yet, upon reflection she realized she had been this way much longer, stemming back to early childhood as she would hide behind her older sister, Ronnie whenever they were out in public. Her sister had no issues with public displays; in fact, she relished each moment that the public's eyes were upon her.

Why can't I be like that? Ang contemplated. *We share the same DNA. You would think some of that boldness and flair for entertaining would be present deep down inside me somewhere.* But, if it was there, it was apparently inaccessible.

Another issue feeding her anxiety involved leaving Babka overnight. It was always difficult for Ang to leave her grandmother, but Taryn constantly argued that she needed a break, needed some time to act like a teenager to refuel her tank so that she would be better able to care for Babka over the long term. Ang had to admit that there were times she felt overwhelmed, pulled in too many directions. She did need rest and the chance to act like a teen—able to loaf around with her pals without any immediate responsibilities.

Reminding herself that now was one of those times where she had the opportunity for freedom, some "friend time," she wandered back into her bedroom and picked up the phone. After dialling Maria's number and listening to the phone trill over the line, Maria finally picked up on the fourth ring.

"Hi, Maria. Can you give Babka a ride to hospice around 2 p.m.?"

"Yes, of course, sweetie. Going to the big camping party at Cushing Lake?"

"Yup. We'll be back by tomorrow evening. Can you bring her back home on Monday afternoon, after I'm finished school for the day?"

"Sure, that would be fine. I hope you were both joking concerning the liquid courage. You'll be responsible, right?" Maria was like a mother figure to Ang over the past few months, nobody else there to pick up the reigns. Her protectiveness warmed Ang's heart.

"Obviously. You have nothing to worry about," Ang promised before hanging up the phone, fingers crossed. Just a small white lie.

Ang shuffled downstairs and peeked in on her grandmother who was fast asleep. Studying the mound of flower-covered sheets, Ang searched for the gentle rise and fall, signifying the old woman was still breathing, holding her own breath because, at first, the covers were still. But, after a few panicked moments, an audible sigh drifted out of the small shape on the bed, filling Ang's ears with its glorious sound. Relieved, she tiptoed out of the room, letting her grandmother enjoy a few more moments of slumber. Perhaps, it was in her dreams that her memories dwelled, where she could finally connect with them again. See her beloved Dedko.

Delaying the inevitable long enough, she shuffled back up the stairs to her bedroom. It was time to pack for the grand adventure. Her stomach flip-flopped again at the thought.

★ ★ ★

Hunkering behind the weeping fig, Gavin continued his surveillance of Mathew's office. Occasionally, he detected sounds issuing from under the crack of the door—voices raised in anger or concern, he couldn't quite tell—but then again, there would be silence. He ran a hand through his thick auburn hair, eyes trained on the silver door, so he wouldn't miss anything.

But nothing happened.

After a while, he grew bored. Feeling a little silly, let alone guilty for spying, he was in the process of abandoning his hiding spot when he heard footsteps approaching from down the hall. Sliding further behind the plant, he prayed the leaves and flowers of the shrubbery concealed him completely. Held his breath.

The footsteps intensified and gradually mutated into the form of a man—tall and muscular like himself but with long, golden hair and azure eyes. This was the form *he* chose.

It was Philip, another member, yet he was not a part of the Crystal Foundation where Gavin was employed. What was he doing here? Was he also invited to the mysterious meeting in Matthew's office?

Philip glanced around suspiciously, his gait fast and purposeful. Marching straight past Matthew's door, he came within touching distance of the fig plant, behind which Gavin crouched. Then he rotated right and continued down a vast hall leading to the restricted wing—the only employees allowed in that area were a clearly defined handful of the higher-ups. Philip and Gavin were not included on the list. What was Philip up to?

Gavin recalled Matthew's orders; he was to report anything suspicious to his supervisor immediately. But he still wasn't sure what Philip was doing. Maybe he was here under his own orders, on perfectly legitimate business. Until he was *sure* that Philip was breaking the rules, he would abstain from troubling Matthew any further. His boss was stressed out enough. For now, Gavin had no choice but to follow Philip, and figure out his purpose for being in the forbidden wing. If, and only if, he detected erroneous behaviour, he would report back to his boss.

Gavin shadowed Philip while trying to remain unseen. It was distressing for him to go down the forbidden wing—the rules that they were expected to uphold weighing heavily on his mind. But his gut feeling was that Philip was up to no good, so he choked down his guilt, trusting his instincts, and stalked Philip down the gem-encrusted hallway with every intention of reporting his findings to Matthew as soon as he knew more. That was his duty.

Philip floated down the hall with a strong sense of purpose, Gavin following silently behind, trying not to get distracted by the glory surrounding him—rubies, opals, sapphire, onyx, gems of all sizes and shapes embedded in the walls and flooring so that everything around him sparkled, a sight he had never witnessed. Tears streamed down his face, but he quickly brushed them away, refocusing on Philip, who had paused in front of cathedral-sized doors made from acacia wood, intricately adorned with hammered gold cherubim on its surface—the forbidden doors to the crystal room. As no one was allowed access to this area, except the higher-ups, there were only rumours as to what lay beyond those mystical doors. Gavin lingered behind the corner of the adjacent hall, cautiously peering around it to monitor Philip's next move. Surely, he wasn't daft enough to enter.

But, enter he did.

Appalled, Gavin almost called out to him. Begging him to stop. But he had to see where this was leading. If he interrupted him now, he probably would never know of Philip's intentions, assuming he wouldn't be forthcoming in explaining his strange actions. As Philip opened the massive doors, a fierce, blue beam of light cast down the hall, nearly reaching Gavin's hiding spot. With one more cursory glance around him, Philip slipped inside the forbidden room.

Without a moment to spare, Gavin crept to the doors but faltered, not knowing what awaited him on the other side. Would Philip see him as soon as he entered? Was anyone else inside the room? What would he say he was doing there if he was caught? He pondered these questions but realized Philip was the one who would need to explain his rebellious behaviour. Gavin was only doing his duty.

Summoning the courage God gave him, Gavin cracked the door open barely wide enough for him to squeeze through, again casting the blue light down the hall, now only a sliver. The door snicked closed behind him. Once inside, he was completely blinded—the blue light, all-encompassing and brilliant, seared his eyeballs. He feared as he stood frozen and unseeing like a deer caught in headlights that Philip was before him, and his position would now be exposed. Blinking profusely to no avail, he stood paralyzed until his eyes finally adjusted to the magnificent light. Distinct shapes emerged, and he was able to discern his surroundings.

The room was sparsely furnished, with a small desk, a collection of massive alabaster sculptures and a dazzling wall of light. And then he saw a small figure crouched down in front of the far wall, which was the source of the light itself. The entire wall glowed and pulsed vibrantly as if it were alive, heaving and flowing. It stirred a deep emotion inside of Gavin—like he was witnessing a divine creation. The room smelled of burned ozone like the smell that lingers in the air after a lightning storm.

Not yet discovered, Gavin sought shelter. Tiptoeing over to the grouping of sculptures, he realized they depicted Michael leading the angels to victory against Lucifer and his followers. A proud moment. He tucked himself behind the hindquarters of a horse sculpture, part of the war scene, and peered beneath the detailed legs of the statue that allowed a clear view of Philip's form doing something to the wall. But what exactly was he doing? Gavin's vantage point was too remote. He appeared to pull at the wall several times, the glow itself moving with his hands, rippling and swirling away from the wall, and then pushing back towards it, within it. Then, abruptly, Philip spun around and briskly walked back to the doors. A peek out into the hallway must have indicated the coast was clear since he disappeared out of the room faster than the bat of an angel's wing.

Gavin was unsure of his next move. Should he follow Philip back into the hall, see what else he was up to? Or should he figure out what he was doing at the wall of brilliant blue light?

He vacillated between the two choices but in the end, whether it was due to gut instinct or simple curiosity, Gavin chose the latter. Most likely finished his suspicious errand, following Philip would be futile, would shed no more clues. It was the wall that held all the answers, Gavin was certain. But, as he cautiously approached the illuminated wall, his vision became overwhelmed by its vivid pulsing luminescence, and he worried the light would consume him. Fear took hold, that awful beast, and held him firm. Maybe he should abstain, report back to Matthew, and let him deal with Philip's apparent breach of the rules? But again, after a few moments, his eyes adjusted, and with that, his fear dissolved. He would investigate himself.

Up close, he could see now that the wall was composed of billions of blue crystals in tube-shaped forms, resembling that of two test tubes melted together to form a capsule, completely containing a brilliant vaporous sapphire liquid within. Tentatively, he withdrew one of the tubes, examining its smooth shape, completely lacking any opening. It was cool to the touch. A label was affixed to the tube he held—a name—Bradley Kutcher. The liquid swirled within, like life's pure energy source, and he knew now with a certainty that the rumours he heard were true. The crystals within this room contained the life energy of all the humans on Earth. God's breath of life originally breathed into Adam, and subsequently all of mankind. He replaced the tube and retrieved another, this one labelled Olivia Rogers. The tube was half empty. He wondered if the amount of the light indicated life span as the previous tube had been three-quarters full.

Then, he had a brilliant idea. He could find the tube for Angelika, his new client. The only problem was how to find the tube out of the billions of crystals before him. Were the crystals arranged in any specific order?

Opening the file he still held, he studied the animated picture of the beautiful young woman with the blond, tousled hair and sparkling hazel eyes full of life, presently yanking items out of her closet and tossing them onto her bed, and as he did so, the wall began to move. Startled, he looked up. The wall abruptly stopped.

Could it be that simple? Again, he studied the photo and concentrated on the picture, repeating her name in his mind over and over. His efforts succeeded for the wall again shifted, forwards and sideways like a massive writhing waterfall struggling against hurricane winds, and then slowly it glided to a stop. Gavin reached out a shaking hand and grabbed the tube directly facing him. He rotated the tube until the label could be read.

Angelika Juris.

It was Angelika's, and to his horror, the light was almost extinguished with only a faint blue glow at the tip.

Before he could stop himself and consider the possible ramifications of his actions, he began searching for a crystal full of the sapphire light, grabbing at the wall until, finally, he found one that was completely infused with the blue energy. He deftly swapped it with Angelika's. He placed the two capsules back into the opposite receptacles from which they came. After a few seconds, he again pulled out Angelika's tube, and it was now filled with bright blue swirling light. Although this is what he was hoping for, he couldn't help but feel another stab of guilt, instinctively knowing that the other tube was now almost empty, but his desire to protect his new client was so strong that he left the tubes as they were.

Voices approached increasing in volume. For the first time, he noticed a slim door in the corner of the room, masked by shadows. The voices were rapidly getting louder, coming directly from behind the previously hidden door. If he lingered any longer, he would be caught. Suddenly, self-conscious of his actions, he realized he couldn't report back to Matthew after all.

Gavin hurried to the massive doors where he initially entered, peering outside into the hall as Philip had shortly before. Also finding the way clear, he left the forbidden room, hoping he hadn't made a grave mistake.

★ ★ ★

At 4 p.m. on the dot, a loud horn beeped from the front yard of Ang's home. Peeking out of her bedroom window that overlooked the street, she saw Taryn decked out in one of her crazy outfits, today channelling the '90s. Jet black hair highlighted with blue streaks, fastened into Princess Leia buns over her ears. Black tights, an oversized Misfits T-shirt, and a knee-length black cardigan. Army boots finished off the ensemble. Not quite camping wear but typical Taryn-wear.

Ang, the practical one, had settled on a more conventional style of camping attire—blue jeans, Ed Hardy sweatshirt over a plain white T-shirt, sneakers, and a waterproof lime-green jacket. Even if it was warm during sunlight hours, the evening would be cool, despite the warmth from the bonfire. She had packed her favourite Lululemon rainbow-patterned toque and woollen mittens just in case.

Ang flew down the twisting staircase, skidding down the last three steps, flung open the front door and hollered, "I'll be right there." Silently, she repeated the mantra, "I can do this… everything will be fine…this is good for me," as she hustled into the kitchen to grab her backpack and cooler. The cooler was chock full of sausages, hotdog buns, marshmallows, bottled water and mix for their drinks. She was struggling to get the heavy cooler out of the door along with her other belongings when Taryn ran over to lend a helping hand.

"Oh my gosh, I am so excited," Taryn exclaimed, grabbing one handle of the cooler and walking adjacent to Ang as they ambled towards the open trunk of her blue SUV.

"I wish I could join you in that." Ang knew as soon as the words escaped her mouth that she would put a damper on her friend's high spirits.

Boy, I can be a real stick in the mud sometimes, she thought.

"Well, our next stop is the liquor store, and I brought my fake ID, so soon you will be feeling totally peachy."

They had decided to purchase some Blue Curacao—not quite the typical camping beverage, but Ang wasn't much of a drinker and couldn't stand beer, or any of the hard stuff. Besides, it was both of their favourite. *Blue Hawaiian's, here we come.*

Testing their fake IDs a few times at the liquor store, they had met with success. But a few months before when they tried getting into one of the local bars, a bouncer cast them out, their false identifications confiscated. Luckily, the authorities hadn't been called. But that didn't stop the two teens from trying again. A little more handiwork on their part and new ID's were crafted but remained untested. Ang was, as usual, more than a tad worried. As they headed towards the Arthur Street Liquor Store, Taryn attempted to assuage Ang's fears.

"Why don't you let me do all of the talking."

"Well, that goes without saying," Ang replied.

Taryn gave Ang a once over. "Actually, maybe you should wait in the car. You look like you're going to piss your pants. You'll give us away the second you enter the store."

Ang would have liked nothing more than that. To stay in the car away from the danger of being caught. But that would have violated their unspoken "friend code."

"I can't make you do it alone. If you get busted, then we both get busted together."

"The problem is I'd rather not get busted at all. The state you're in right now, well...you have guilt written all over you." Taryn pulled into the parking lot and switched off the ignition. Turning towards her bosom buddy, she stared straight into her eyes.

"I can do this," Ang returned her stare, trying to sound convincing.

"Alright, if you insist," Taryn replied with a sigh of resignation. "I hope I don't regret this."

The girls clambered out of the SUV and tried to avoid the odorous wino perched against the rectangular orange-brick store. He was begging for donations to support his life-shattering habit. Buried in oversized soiled clothing, a foul-smelling dirty blanket draped over his form, he spoke to them from a toothless mouth. Ang almost expected green vapour trails would accompany his breathy speech.

"God bless you today, beautiful ladies. Do you have some change to spare for a poor soul, such as me?" he begged in a gravelly voice, sans vapour trails.

Taryn whispered to Ang out of the corner of her mouth, "Don't make eye contact," while simultaneously turning her head away from the beggar, allowing such a wide berth around the homeless man as they walked towards the building that she practically squished Ang into the railing of the entrance.

But Ang couldn't resist. She gaped, captivated, staring at the wino's wrinkled, sallow face, his sunken, lifeless eyes. She didn't mean to stare like he was some circus show freak on public display but stare she did. As he realized the girls weren't going to throw any hardware his way, his face contorted, filled instantly with rage. Vulgarity poured forth from his toothless maw. Cursing the girls' ignorance, disrespect for the poor and hungry. He flipped them the bird. Ang remained captivated, wondering how this man ended up this way. Was it the drink that drove him out onto the streets scrounging for change? Or was he one of the many individuals suffering from a mental disorder and due to the shortage of mental health care in the city was forced to wend for himself? The threat of the Thunder Bay Psychiatric Hospital shutting down was always present, the rumour circulating for years, and if that happened then there would be more homeless people like this man, unable to care for themselves, roaming the streets, helpless.

As Ang continued to stare, his ranting ceased, and a sudden change came over his eyes with a clarity that wasn't there before, and a stark look of warning. "Don't go," he uttered, and he grabbed her arm. His eyes now beseeching.

Ang froze with mouth wide. What did he mean? Don't go away from him, leave him behind? Or…don't go camping?

Freaked out, Ang yanked her arm free and trampled over Taryn through the turnstiles to get into the store as fast as possible, away from the old wino.

"Hey, keep your cool, remember?" Taryn whispered authoritatively.

One of the cashiers glanced in their direction but quickly returned to the patron at her till.

Ang had goosebumps. "Did you hear that man out there?"

"Yeah. I heard a bunch of words I can't repeat in front of my mother. He's crazy, totally bonkers! I told you not to make eye contact."

"I guess you're right." Ang pushed the strange warning aside and attempted to regain her composure.

The two teens walked with focused purpose to the aisle housing the liqueurs, grabbed a bottle of Blue Curacao, and then stood in line for the cash register. Two patrons later, it was their turn, Ang practically hyperventilating.

The cashier, a victim of the "hairband" days, squinted up at them through blond, teased bangs and heavy, black eyeliner.

"Can I see some identification?" she demanded in a deep, smoker's rasp. She glared at Taryn unblinking, although how she kept her eyes opened beneath all her makeup was a feat against gravity. Nicotine stained fingers reached out expectantly.

Without any hint of her youthful age, besides her outfit that reeked of adolescence, Taryn confidently thrust her altered driver's licence into the cashier's hand. The woman scrutinized it, ran her finger over the area where the birth date was typed. Ang held her breath until she thought her lungs and brain would burst.

"Do you have an Air Miles card?" the cashier continued, returning the driver's licence to Taryn who retrieved it exuding pure confidence.

Ang exhaled a whoosh of anxious breath. That was it. They were home free.

Taryn paid for the precious package and with brown paper bag in hand, they left the store and climbed back into Taryn's SUV. Ang now barely noticed the wino slumped against the brick building; his collection bucket still empty.

"Woohoo! See Ang? You worried for nothing. You have to have a little more faith." Taryn tossed the brown paper bag into the back seat and revved the SUV to life.

"That *was* pretty impressive."

"Now, let's blow this pop stand."

Ang felt a glimmer of excitement—the good kind—replacing some of the dread she had been constantly suppressing. Maybe this wouldn't be as bad as she thought.

Taryn made a left onto Arthur Street and continued to head straight until Arthur Street converted into Highway 17 West, following a heavy stream of traffic. There were numerous Thunder Bay folk heading out of town for the weekend, taking advantage of the warmer autumn weather.

Taryn had burned a disc of mixed songs—upbeat dance tunes, pop, rock and even a little alternative. Currently, "Love Cats" by The Cure was blaring, an oldie but goodie, and the two girls howled along. They continued to sing, painfully out of tune for the entire ride to the campsite.

Chapter 6

"Where in the bloody hell are we going to park?" Ang exclaimed as soon as they pulled into the campsite. An insane number of cars were parked haphazardly at the entrance. Taryn carefully drove along the lumpy forest floor, a mass of tree roots and mud puddles, until she spotted a minute space between two Toyota trucks. With expert driving skills, she manoeuvred her SUV into the impossibly tight spot, leaving a tiny sliver of space for the two teen girls to squeeze out on each side.

They unloaded their camping gear from the trunk and attempted to carry the entire lot in one trip, Ang tucking the Blue Curacao into the tent bag to limit the number of items to carry. They approached the hoard of campers, many of them clearly inebriated, evident in their uneven gaits and louder than necessary voices.

"I don't recognize anyone. Not a single soul," Ang commented.

"There're a few people from school," Taryn pointed into the distance.

"I don't know who you're pointing at. Most of these people look like they're in college or university. How did you hear about this party?"

"Hey, relax buddy. It's still early. And remember, I have it on good authority that Josh will be here."

The butterflies in Ang's stomach reawoke and one fluttered into her chest, taking up permanent residence. Attempting to ignore the anxiety, she focused on searching for a spot to erect their tent, careful to avoid all the tent pegs, coolers and folding chairs scattered around the campsite. At last, they located a flat patch of green grass towards the back of the camping lot, practically within the forest itself, that was unoccupied. Plunking down their camping gear, Ang stretched out her arms, flexing and un-flexing her hands to revive the circulation. Unloading their tent pieces, she first unfolded the tent and spread the fabric out flat on the grass, and then they assembled the pieces for the frame.

"So, who *did* invite you to this party?" Ang asked, curious, as they continued to work on erecting the tent.

"I have my sources," Taryn answered mysteriously, giving a little wink.

"Where's Josh? Have you seen him yet?" Ang scanned the campsite but couldn't find him or any of his friends.

"Don't worry, he'll be here."

The tent was proving more difficult to erect than they had anticipated. Each time they propped the frame up, half of the structure would sag inward. Switching the pegs around made zero difference.

"I know which side you're sleeping on," Taryn teased with a wink.

"Very funny. We must be missing a piece." Ang grabbed the bag off the ground and reached inside. "Oops. There is another piece," she confessed, tugging on a long, metal rod that was unrelentingly stuck in the tent bag. Giving an extra hard yank to free the rod, she remembered too late that she had tucked the liquid courage inside to make it easier to carry their belongings to the campsite. As the frame piece finally sprang free, out flew the bottle of Blue Curacao, crashing to the ground with a resounding crack.

Blue liquid instantly leaked through the brown paper bag. Upon closer inspection, the top of the bottle had been smashed in the fall, the bottom of the Blue Curacao still intact. A long-haired brunette standing nearby ran to their rescue, handing them a small saucepan to catch the remainder of the bright blue alcohol. "Aw man. What a waste," she lamented.

All rationality went out the door. The girls desperately attempted to salvage the remaining liqueur by removing all the shards and slivers of glass as if they were going to drink it. But, in the end, they realized it wasn't worth dying from internal bleeding just to get drunk for one night. Well, Ang was maybe a little more tempted than Taryn…anything to get rid of the anxiety. However, it appeared that the pot from the helpful girl had already been used to boil hotdog wieners, evident by the blobs of glossy oil and wiener particles that floated on the top of the blue liqueur. The salvaged alcohol would have to be tossed.

Now, Angelika was really panicking. What was she going to do? How could she be so clumsy? It was all her fault—she had no one else to blame—but without the liquid courage, she would be too nervous to talk to Josh. Her thoughts raced, the comfort and safety of home beckoning. How could she convince Taryn to leave and drive all the way back to Thunder Bay immediately? She knew getting her bestie to go home would be like trying to get a child to leave Toys "R" Us after finding the perfect toy their parent refused to buy them.

And who should appear at that very moment? Right on ironic cue? Why, Josh, of course.

"Oh my gosh, he's here," she whispered into Taryn's ear, frantically gesticulating in his direction. Her voice elevated an octave. "What am I going to do?"

Taryn checked out where she was pointing and found Josh entering the campsite with three other guys from their school, his regular entourage.

"Oh, goody, he brought Brian with him. That boy is so yummy!" Taryn practically drooled.

Ang couldn't concentrate on her friend's voice. She wasn't ready to talk to Josh. Surely, she would stutter and stammer, speak in a meek muffled voice, so he wouldn't understand a word she said—like she usually did when she was speaking to a hot member of the male persuasion.

"Don't worry. You'll be fine," Taryn tried to reassure Ang, but she was already getting hot sweats, and her insides were turning to liquid. She said a secret prayer for an outhouse nearby because she feared she would need it any minute.

"Wait right here." Taryn ran off and within two short minutes returned with some Molson Canadians. You could always count on Taryn's resourcefulness. As much as Ang detested beer, she was not in the position to be picky.

Popping open the beer can, suds erupted from the top like an active volcano—a result of Taryn's inadvertent shaking of the beer while she ran. Slurping the foam off her fingers, Ang couldn't help grimacing at the yeasty taste. *Oh well, better than nothing.* She took a gulp, and then another. *Come on nerves, go away!* She pleaded with her rebellious brain.

Taryn giggled and shook her head at her friend's neurotic behaviour, then focused back on putting together the tent. Ang tried to help in between gulps and after her sixth swig, she was feeling noticeably calmer.

That was until Josh started walking straight towards them. His approach was like slow motion, Ang soaking in every detail of the scene—his sexy swagger, perfectly tanned skin, adorable dimples, and straight white teeth when he smiled at something his friend said—all displayed flawlessly as he inched closer. Ang remained frozen for a moment. But finally remembering how to make her body move, without thinking, she turned on her heels and bolted in the opposite direction, heading further into the forest towards an old abandoned boat, grass and mould having claimed it over many years.

She ducked behind the boat, hoping nobody noticed her hasty exit, although Taryn was undoubtedly wondering where the hell her bestie had vanished to and why. Immediately, the mosquitoes were all over her, buzzing around her head, enticed by the sweetness of her perfume and beer-laced breath. She swatted at them, agitated, fearful they would somehow reveal her hiding spot.

"What are you doing behind here?" a deep, male voice asked, slamming her heart to a stop. It was Josh. *How embarrassing, please kill me now,* she thought.

"Oh, ah...trying to find a spot to go pee." Oh gosh, it just slipped out—did she say that out loud? She couldn't think of anything better, but surely this couldn't get any worse. Or, could it?

Josh chuckled. "Sorry to invade your privacy."

"No problem." *Could my voice possibly shake anymore?* Her internal dialogue kept narrating. This was not how she imagined their first conversation to be. In her daydreams, everything flowed wonderfully, every word spoken was with eloquence, yet still sexy and seductive—the result, a fairy tale ending with the two of them riding off into the sunset, so to speak.

"Well, I'll let you finish up what you were doing."

Ang felt deflated, sinking deeper into the tall, moist grass.

"Why don't you find me later when you have more time to talk?" he asked coyly, his teal eyes sparkling. And then he left.

Completely mortified, she was still mildly hopeful she didn't completely blow her chances with Josh. She waited a few moments for him to retreat from her hiding spot. Then she retraced her own steps back to the campground and found Taryn, who was now sitting on a folding chair, talking to the nice brown-haired girl who lent them her pot in their failed attempt to resuscitate the remaining Blue Curacao.

"Where did you go?" From the expression on Taryn's face, she knew her buddy had been the one to tell Josh about her hiding spot behind the old boat. Ang shot her a withering look, pulled out her own portable chair, popping it open with a click, and set it up on Taryn's free side.

"I'm going to toast up some marshmallows. Did you want me to cook some of your hotdogs, too?" She threaded a sticky, white marshmallow onto a pointed stick. "I don't know how you can eat that crap—you know they're made up of a bunch of cow boobies and buttholes."

"Taryn!" Ang exclaimed in disgust. "If I hadn't already lost my appetite, it would be gone now for sure. You can be so crass sometimes."

She simply giggled in response.

"So, how did it go?" she whispered conspiratorially.

"Horrible. I stuck my foot in my mouth and acted like a total ass. Thanks for asking."

Taryn laughed again. She was used to Ang's insecurities and somehow found them amusing.

"He said to find him later. What am I going to do? I'm still too nervous."

"Honey, you have nothing to worry about. You're so beautiful—you just don't know it. And Josh already has a crush on you. Besides, if he couldn't accept you for who you are, then screw him." The brown-haired girl, who had been eavesdropping on their conversation, nodded her head in agreement, and as if Taryn had been making a toast, they both clinked their cans of beer together, followed by a healthy swig.

"I feel sick."

"Are you serious?"

Ang nodded vigorously.

"Alright, I'll be right back." Taryn, annoyed now (everybody has their threshold), peeled herself out of the chair and ran off once more.

The sun had set, and the campgrounds were darkening and continually filling up with campers and their paraphernalia, so Ang couldn't immediately see where her friend had disappeared. The bonfire was in full blaze, sparks crackling and flying into the night sky like fireflies. People stood around the fire to keep warm, chat, and toast marshmallows and other goodies. They were laughing and having a fantastic, carefree time. *Why can't I be like that?* She silently wondered again.

Not in the mood to make small talk with the strange girl who had attached herself to Taryn, Ang desperately tried to locate her better half. When she finally found her friend, at first, she thought she was seeing things—Taryn was talking to a shady looking character who was over six feet tall, muscular, with short hair and a thick, bushy beard. The man glanced directly at Ang as he handed Taryn a small package, leering a little too long, giving a sly grin. A cold chill ran up Ang's spine. And then the transaction was over. Taryn came sauntering back over to their spot, holding what appeared to be a piece of paper towel folded in half, secured shut with a piece of tape.

Plunking back down into her chair, she huddled over to Ang, revealing the mysterious purchase. Within the towel were dark brown, dried fragments of something organic, unknown.

"What's that?" Ang asked suspiciously, not sure if she truly wanted to know the answer.

"They're magic 'mushies,' silly," Taryn replied as if Ang was brain damaged.

"What are you doing? We can't take that! It's illegal!"

"Shhhhhh. You might want to keep it down. So is underage drinking, by the way, and you don't seem to have a problem with that."

She had a point. But she had never tried drugs before, and she wasn't interested in starting now.

"Don't worry, Ang. These are totally harmless. They're all natural, organic, a part of the earth. All they are going to do is help to mellow you out. I've tried them before, and trust me, they work."

Ang gawked at her friend in disbelief. Since when did Taryn do anything without her? Was there a side to her friend that she wasn't aware of?

"Come on, let's do it for shits and giggles."

"I hate that phrase," Ang replied, being obstinate.

"Don't you want to talk to Josh?" Taryn enticed.

Talk about peer pressure. All of a sudden, a flash of Adam and Eve being tempted by Satan to eat the forbidden apple in the Garden of Eden filled Angelika's head. *Weird.* She wasn't much of a religious person, much to the disappointment of her grandmother who was devoutly Roman Catholic. The image caught her off guard.

But then there was Josh. He was talking animatedly with an attractive girl, her long auburn hair flecked with caramel and honey highlights flashing gold in the fire's romantic light, her skin-tight jeans and sweater accenting her flawless body. She laughed, throwing her head back flirtatiously. Though Ang wasn't within earshot, she was sure the woman spoke eloquently, without stammering like an idiot.

What did this gorgeous seductress think she was doing, flirting with Josh? Couldn't she see how dorky he was, how she was way above his league? Ang was the only one who was supposed to be able to see past his geekiness, see his true potential. A diamond in the rough.

With a new determination, Ang suppressed the strange religious image back down into her subconscious from whence it came.

Or else, she would lose her chance.

"Alright," she said reluctantly. She didn't think it was her imagination when Taryn's face lit up.

"There are two grams here, one for you and one for me. Maybe you should start with a little bit to see how you feel. Place the dried mushrooms under your tongue and suck on them for a while before you chew and then swallow. This will help it soften enough to chew, and then it will absorb into your system faster, so you feel the effects right away."

How did Taryn know all this?

Ang took a deep breath. "Okay, I'm ready." They both pinched the brown morsels in their fingertips and placed them under their tongues.

Then they waited.

It felt to Ang like she was sucking on pieces of a dirty Styrofoam cup.

"Okay. Now chew."

In unison, the girls eagerly chewed the brown bits, Ang noticeably gagging from the bitter taste, like chomping on sunflower seed shells.

Picking a chunk of mushroom out of her molar, she leaned over towards Taryn's ear and whispered, "It tastes like ass."

"Wash it down with the beer."

"Can I do that? Is it okay to mix alcohol and mushies?" Ang questioned the pro.

"Sure. Hang in there. It will be worth it, I promise."

Ang downed the rest of her beer, the bitter aftertaste still lingering in her mouth.

"Now, we wait," Taryn instructed.

Silently, they waited. They people watched, one of their favourite pastimes. There was an interesting group to view: punks, preppies, nerds, and jocks. People hooking up, people crying over lost love, people eating, people singing almost as bad as Taryn and Ang had been on the way out to the campsite.

Their attention was drawn to an older boy, probably in his twenties, who was creating a display as he attempted to board his motorcycle. His friends laughed as he staggered drunkenly over to his bike, threw on his helmet, and prepared to mount the vehicle.

"They aren't going to let him drive like that, are they?" Ang worried aloud. "He'll never make it in the dark, especially on these twisted unlit roads, totally wasted out of his frickin' mind."

Taryn shrugged her shoulders, also mesmerized by the display.

But the drunken guy's friends who were equally smashed were laughing so hard, some were falling on their knees as the buffoon continually attempted to mount the bike without success. Finally, in his exaggeratedly inebriated state, he leaped clear over the top of the Honda Civic, landing on the opposite side on all fours.

After several attempts to stand again, just to get vertical, he realized it wasn't worth the battle and remained sitting on the ground, legs splayed out. He removed his helmet and joined in the raucous laughter with his friends, and now, many onlookers. He would be staying the night after all. What a relief.

Ang still wasn't feeling any different; the anxiety bubbled inside her like a detergent-filled washing machine, so she shovelled more of the mushrooms into her mouth.

"It takes a few minutes to work. You should start to see tracers soon."

"What have you been doing in your spare time? I feel like I don't even know you anymore. And who is Bushbeard over there? Where'd you meet him?"

Taryn was already in her own little world, waving her hand in front of her face and, sure enough, it looked like the tail end of a comet floating back and forth. Ang tried her own hand. Light streamed behind it in psychedelic blue, red, pink and green, mimicking an effervescent rainbow. "Cool."

Finally, she could feel her nerves settling, stomach relaxing, the spin cycle slowing down to a low tumble. Soon, she would be able to talk to Josh. She only hoped she wasn't too late. In the end, she just wanted to fit in and not feel like such an outsider all the time. It was so easy for everyone else to be social, why did it have to be such a struggle for her?

Then, something strange happened. Her heart lurched within her chest and raced uncontrollably. A hot sweat swept over her whole body, and she instantly vomited all over herself.

It felt like she was unable to catch her breath, an invisible fist closing around her throat choking off her air supply. Vomit erupted from her gut again, dripping down her chin. Taryn spun around, her whole body doing the "psychedelic tracer" thing and gaped at Ang with alarmed eyes. "Are you all right, Ang?" Her voice sounded far, distorted, deep and slow. So slow. Everything now so slow. Taryn reached out to grab her as she started to fall out of her chair but missed, Ang's body slamming into the hard earth, bouncing and then beginning to convulse and thrash uncontrollably, violently. Ang couldn't respond to Taryn's question. Her tongue felt so thick; her airway almost completely blocked now.

"Help, someone help us!" Taryn shrieked. It was the last thing Ang heard before the darkness swarmed in.

Chapter 7

Anthony

He spied through a nickel-sized gap in the wall. The dungeon cavern beyond was an eerie shade of ochre silhouetting two hulking figures pacing nervously—his brothers.

"Where, the hell, is he?" Friedrich growled, his silhouette flaunting six arms and an occasional blue spark, although the prosthetic itself wasn't detectable under the sparse lighting.

Yes. Where, the hell, is he? Anthony knew it would happen today, but the time at which it would happen remained a mystery. He had waited all day for this, not that he had any other pressing matters to attend to. Sequestered in the hidden passageway, discarded candy wrappers and pop cans littered the earthen floor at his sides. More patient than his siblings, even *his* patience was waning. This was taking much longer than usual.

They were quarantined for a week when they first arrived—the women, the captives—long enough to ensure they were free from illness and disease. Not already pregnant. And then came the next phase—preparing them to become carriers.

The secret tunnels did not lead to such places, Anthony's view blocked until they were brought down to the dungeon, to their cells. This would be his first glimpse at the new girl.

Tomas' latest victim.

"He's close, now," Gregor, the eyeless one announced. "I can hear his footsteps coming down the stairs."

The dungeon doors crashed open, and Tomas sauntered in, a limp girl draped over his arms, head dangling and swinging, long golden curls almost brushing the floor. It was difficult to see his brother's latest disguise, the room so dim, the gap Anthony spied through so narrow. Was that a thick beard?

"What took you so long?" Friedrich barked. "I was starting to think you kept her for yourself."

"She's a feisty one. Father was forced to sedate her." Tomas replied, depositing the unconscious girl on the wooden dining room table, the one all the women shared. He proceeded to slap her cheek sharply.

Anthony winced. He hated to see them hurt, wished he could intervene and usher them back home to safety, but he was as helpless as they were, a prisoner as well.

"We wasted half the fucking day waiting around."

"Just shut up and get ready. She's a fighter."

One more significant smack and the girl's eyelids fluttered open. Then her eyes widened in horror when she saw her captors. In the blink of an eye, she rolled off the table and darted for the dungeon door, left agape. Friedrich deftly grabbed her from behind, pinning her arms behind her back. She continued struggling, thrashing back and forth, delivering a hearty head butt as she slammed her head backwards, which unfortunately probably hurt her more than his giant brother.

Tomas leaned forward, inches from her face. "Accept your fate, Veronica. Resisting will only make it harder on you."

"How...how do you know my name? What do you want with me?"

"You'll know soon enough. I've been watching you for a while now. Making sure you were...acceptable," Tomas admitted.

The girl hocked a massive wad of spit directly into Tomas' face. Rage contorted his features. He grabbed her face roughly, squishing her jawbone with a hand the size of a baseball glove until tears coursed down her face. Then, with one last jerk of her head, he released his grip.

"Father thinks you're special, but don't let it go to your pretty little head. He may have told us to be careful with you, but if you ever do that again, I *will* kill you."

"What do you mean, we have to be careful with her?" Gregor asked. "How are we to keep her in line?"

"There are ways, just don't leave any visible marks."

The girl took that moment to thrust both her legs out simultaneously, kicking Tomas with such force that he staggered backwards.

"That's it! Give her a shock to teach her a lesson. A strong one!" Tomas ordered.

Friedrich's arm revved and sparked blue light; the entire length of the prosthetics illuminated but then fizzled out. After several more attempts, he yelled in frustration.

"I can't. It's not working!"

Tomas raised his hands as if to summon his telekinetic ability but, again, nothing happened. His lips pinched into a thin line. He swivelled to face the direction of the hidden tunnels and bellowed with demonic strength, "ANTHONY!" He charged towards Anthony's hiding spot, fissures of smoke snaking out of his skin. But thankfully no fire to ignite.

Busted, Anthony realized his little viewing party had met an abrupt end. Jumping to his feet, he scurried through the hidden passageways all the way back to his room, to patiently wait for the next time he would see them. The girls. The prisoners. His only source of light.

Chapter 8

Smoke spiralled above her head, soft gusts of cooling wind swirling it, twisting it, stretching it into mystical shapes, clouding her vision. Everything was so dark, hazy. Ang had the nagging feeling she was forgetting an important detail, but she had lost a chunk of time like a thief had crept into her thoughts when she was distracted, making off with her memories. She imagined that Babka must feel this way during her few moments of clarity—that time had been stolen from her; precious moments gone forever.

As her vision cleared, concrete shapes materialized out of the smoke—she noticed the blazing bonfire nearby, its roaring flames soaring ever higher, golden flecks and sparks attempting to meld with the stars.

The wind gusted again, sending a puff of embers, ash, and smoke straight into her face, yet she felt nothing, not even the urge to cough. She stroked her hair, removing any sparks and ashy bits that may have settled there. Her hands felt numb, fuzzy, and she almost expected to see her rainbow-patterned mitts when she looked down at them. But her hands were bare. Perhaps they had numbed in the night's crisp, autumn air.

She realized, then, that she was alone. Nobody stood around the fire pit as before. It was abandoned.

How did she get here? She couldn't remember walking over to the fire pit. Had she talked with Josh again? When did it get so dark? Everything was cloaked in a heavy purple haze.

A scan of the campsite displayed a sea of tents set up haphazardly, a maze of colourful nylon, tent pegs pulling strings taught all over the ground in a treacherous web. But, no people.

She needed to find Taryn, who was probably back at their camping spot. She would explain everything. Ang's eyes were adjusting to the inky darkness, and she searched for their tent, but it was beige, impossible to find from afar. She had to get moving, get closer. Guessing at the general direction in which she thought their tent was stationed, she manoeuvred her way through the treacherous maze of the campground.

When she reached the area where she thought their tent would be located, it felt completely unfamiliar—a circle of tiki torches illuminated a small table supporting an assortment of food—chips, salsa, chocolate chip cookies, salads, and hamburgers. Reflecting on the meagre staples they had brought for the night; she knew this was not their spot.

The next two spots were equally unfamiliar. Had she grossly misjudged her location in the campsite? Her orientation was off. Spinning in a circle, she finally noticed shifting movement off in the distance towards the forest's edge, the opposite side from which she had wandered.

Edging closer, she determined that the movement was a crowd of people.

Finally. Life forms.

As she quietly approached, she recognized her surroundings… the crowd was gathered at the back of the woods where eons ago she had escaped behind a rotten old boat, humiliating herself. The mob of campers seemed to include every person on the grounds, besides herself, who continued to linger on the outskirts. They were surrounding a mound on the ground, gawking, but she couldn't see at what, the crowd as transparent as a brick wall. Probably a fight broke out and everyone, drawn to chaos and tragedy, like flies to rotting flesh, wanted a view of the carnage.

Why did people always have to ruin a fun night of partying and socializing? She supposed alcohol had a lot to do with it.

The closer she got to the horde, the more familiar faces she recognized. During her absence from consciousness, it seemed that the entire student body from her school had arrived. Candace from her biology class, Paula from tenth grade, all the band geeks, and the football team. Some cheerleaders.

And Josh.

There he was, her crush, nestled within the group, barely visible, the thickness of the crowd almost swallowing him, but it was definitely him. Holding hands with the gorgeous redhead he was talking to earlier. Ang's heart dropped.

The faces of the onlookers wore concern, dread, fear, and Ang knew that whatever was happening, it was serious, temporarily distracting her from her bruised heart. She recalled the boy attempting to mount his bike. Maybe he had finally been successful in boarding his vehicle only to meet with a tragic accident.

Something poked at her mind, trying to get noticed, get her to focus. *What am I forgetting here?*

And then Ang remembered—the magic mushrooms. They must have finally kicked in because, despite her loss of memory and being confused about what terror may be going on, and her disappointment at losing Josh to someone else, she felt wonderful. Better than ever, like a joyful, exhilarating serenity, that she wouldn't be able to accurately capture with mere mortal words. No wonder drugs were so addictive, although she vaguely remembered hearing that "mushies" or "shrooms" were non-habit forming. The only disconcerting sensations were that her hearing felt muted—the shuffling of her feet through the forest's discarded crunchy leaves and the crackling of the fire sounded muffled like cotton batten was tucked in her ears—and everything moved slower than usual. She had to ask Taryn if that was normal.

Ang couldn't find her anywhere, however, so she assumed her friend was enveloped somewhere in the throng of bystanders, the Princess Leia buns blocked from her view.

A whirring sound pressed down from above, growing ever louder, accompanied by intense wind pressure and a pulsing light that bathed the sky blood red. The horde looked upward, a solid unit moving as one now, to see an emergency helicopter lighting down near the scene. Ang's worries were confirmed—someone must have been seriously injured, maybe fatally.

The helicopter touched down in an open expanse of grass, flinging dirt and debris in all directions, releasing two male paramedics the second it contacted the ground.

The first paramedic to disembark the aircraft was tall and gawky with black hair shorn close to his scalp, his emergency uniform crisp and tidy. The second paramedic wore the same suit, but his portly body stretched it to impossible extremes. They reminded Ang of *Laurel and Hardy*, a show she used to watch with her grandparents.

The wispy rescue worker, Laurel, spoke with a nearby camper, a tiny girl with elven features. She was visibly agitated, motioning wildly with her hands, sending the paramedics scrambling to grab a stretcher and life-saving paraphernalia from the helicopter. Ang watched this as she continued to move, ever so slowly, towards the crowded scene. Feeling a lot like she was walking through the ocean with a strong undercurrent pulling against her legs.

The medics must have flown in from Thunder Bay, that being the nearest hospital to the campground but too far to travel by automobile for a medical emergency. The mob parted, allowing the medics to pass through. Ang had finally neared the crowd, and with a better view now that the density of the teens dispersed, she watched Taryn sobbing over a crumpled body on the ground.

A beige tent was erected haphazardly to the right of the small patch of grass, a familiar red cooler left open, three camp chairs, one knocked over. It reeked of vomit.

She couldn't see who was on the ground, just that the person had the same sneakers that she was wearing. It must be a girl. Ang hoped Taryn was okay, not involved with the tragedy before them.

"Taryn!" Ang yelled, the sound of her voice faint, cotton batten still in her ears swallowing her words. Taryn didn't react. Despite the eerie silence, no one reacted.

Taryn stood up, allowing the medics access to the body, tears streaming down her face. "It's all my fault," Taryn whimpered.

Ang peeked at the body, getting a brief flash of visibility before the medics stepped in, blocking her view once more. But that brief glimpse was enough.

It can't be! Shock and disbelief took over. She must be hallucinating from the drugs because the unresponsive body on the ground had on the same clothes, the same hair, the same face—as her! She was staring at her own body, lying unmoving on the ground.

Lifeless.

Chapter 9

Peaceful. A doll lying down on the grass. Skin so pale. Chest unmoving.

The next few moments stretched out like a fresh batch of homemade taffy, each second extending into eternity.

Ang helplessly watched as the paramedics unzipped her hoodie, pulling up her white T-shirt for all to see. Black, lacey Victoria Secret bra fully on display, relieved she had left her ugly white, cotton sports bra back at home. The medics stuck two electrodes onto her body, one above the right breast and the other on the left side of her ribcage.

"Everybody, please stand clear of the body," Laurel ordered, causing everyone to take a step back. A large battery was charging, and when a mechanical voice stated that it was ready, the paramedic administered a shock to Ang's body, resulting in a spasm.

This can't be happening. She felt so wonderful. Weird but wonderful. This must be a dream or rather a nightmare.

"Taryn!" she called out to her friend again. Moving in closer, she waved her hand in Taryn's face, but she stared right through Ang, despair etched on her brow.

She glanced around at her schoolmates and strangers, everyone waiting with bated breath for a miracle. Calling out to them, "I'm here, I'm right here, I'm fine," but nobody noticed her.

And then she noticed one of the onlookers, different from the others. A gorgeous man dressed in casual jeans and a camel-coloured leather jacket, hair cut short and textured, styled with gel. His sky-blue eyes were like crystal orbs glowing in the dark night. He had a faint multihued glow emanating from his skin. How hadn't she noticed him before? Another hallucination?

He was gazing down at Ang's lifeless form on the ground with great sadness and disappointment. Why would a stranger have such a strong emotional reaction to her predicament? She had never seen him before, didn't recognize his perfectly chiselled face.

At that moment, he sensed her disassociated presence. He suddenly glanced up, and the sadness evaporated, replaced with surprise. Could he see her, even though she was invisible to the remainder of the campers? He floated to where she stood.

"I was hoping I could save you," he spoke with a voice softer and more comforting than a fleece blanket.

"Who are you? What do mean, you were hoping you could save me? Do you know what's going on?" she asked in a series of disjointed sentences. "Why are you able to see me, when nobody else can?"

Hesitating, he fidgeted, kicked a pebble, thrust his hands in his leather pockets, took a deep breath, and then stared directly into her eyes. They pierced her soul; they were so clear, so bright, and pure. She looked away. It was too intense.

"I know this will sound bizarre to you, but…I am your guardian." Her eyes flew back up to meet his gaze.

"My what?"

"My name is Gavin. I've recently been assigned to your case. I tried to warn you to stay away from the campsite. I had a terrible feeling that this is where it would happen."

She was having trouble digesting this information, but his last statement sent more questions stumbling out of her mouth.

"What do you mean? How could you know this would happen?" She was in shock and uncertain whether this was a dream, a weird trip from the drugs or a hallucination.

The apparition appeared uncomfortable as if venturing into new territory. Was that guilt playing across his perfect features as he spoke?

"I was hoping it wouldn't, but I tried to warn you as a precaution."

"I'm sorry, but I don't understand. Who hired you? Why do I need a guardian?" Ang sat on an unoccupied camp chair; her legs suddenly weak.

Gavin crouched down in front of Ang so that he faced her head on. "You all have guardians. I'll admit yours is an unusual case. I'm still unsure of what happened to your other guardian. But I am his replacement, nonetheless."

"Wow, I've totally lost it!" Ang muttered. "Way to go, doing drugs, Ang. This is what you get for breaking the rules."

"It's not the drugs, Angelika. This is real. But you're not supposed to be able to see me. Something is wrong. I've never had this happen before."

"Well, that makes two of us," Ang replied. "So, explain to me then, if I'm not supposed to be able to see you, but you're not a hallucination from the drugs, then what exactly are you?"

"Like I said before, I'm your guardian. You know, like an angel?"

"Okay, so now I know this isn't real. Or am I dead?" She glanced over at her supine body. "I sure do look dead. Oh my gosh, I'm dead!" She flew up and out of her chair and frantically paced back and forth in front of Gavin. "If you truly are my guardian angel, I think you might have failed."

Gavin's expression was pained. "I tried to warn you. Give you signs not to come to this party. Didn't you get them?"

On second thought, she did notice a nagging feeling not to go camping but chalked it up to nerves. There was a constant nattering voice that played in her mind whenever a situation presented itself that was out of her comfort zone. Did Gavin's warnings get lost in the quagmire of her usual chronic worrying and self-doubt?

Then she remembered the wino perched against the liquor store. Warning her. "Don't go." And the strange vision of the forbidden apple when Taryn first presented the magic mushrooms to Ang, like the devil offering temptation that would end so horribly for mankind.

Subtle.

"I guess I might have gotten your warnings. But I stupidly ignored them. And now look at me."

"I'm sorry I couldn't save you. Still, you shouldn't be here, or be able to see me. Like I said before, something is wrong," Gavin said with brows furrowed.

For some reason, Ang wanted to comfort him, purge him of the guilt of failing his job at protecting her. She reached out to touch his hand, but her fingers went right through him. He was no denser than the wind. Yet, she could hear him with perfect clarity unlike the other sounds that were muted during this strange state of dissociation.

"Something is definitely wrong." She eyed her unresponsive body, the medics furiously attempting to recover her soul, refusing to accept the fact that it might already be too late.

Admiring their determination, she prayed they would continue their efforts until they were successful. She wasn't ready to die. She was only a teenager. Refused to believe her short life was over.

"Is there any chance that I'm going to make it?" Ang choked. How long could somebody last without a heartbeat before serious brain damage would occur? If she did survive, would she remain a vegetable? Who would take care of her grandmother?

But, before her guardian angel could respond, her vision wavered, and she felt the bile building at the back of her throat. The darkness swarmed over her once more, like beetles crawling all over her skin, over her eyes, into her mouth, their hard exoskeletons tickling, prickling as they crawled. But, before they wholly consumed her, she noticed the crowd grow excited, the murmur of whispers creeping through the dense blackness that surrounded her.

"I have a pulse," the thin medic exclaimed.

Chapter 10

Ang murmured nonsensically, the final stages of REM sleep segueing to consciousness. Awake, yet unable to move, body unresponsive. Eyes welded shut with dried mucus, arms stuck to the bed as if Thor's hammer were tethered to both wrists. Perhaps she wasn't quite awake but awake enough to know she still slept.

Finally, with maximum effort she tore her eyelids apart, struggling to focus on her surroundings. Where was she? What time was it?

The room was unfamiliar, a place she had never physically been before, yet familiar in its design. Crisp, white linen sheets scented of bleach covered her like a corpse at the morgue, a cheap television hung, unused, suspended from the ceiling, empty plastic chairs in the most barfy shade of green circled her bed, and electrodes were fastened to her chest, connecting her to a machine that softly blipped in sync with her heartbeat.

The hospital. A plastic, blue hospital bracelet was secured to her pale wrist, her name typed in bold, further confirming her suspicion and bringing her back to reality. Memories resurfaced.

What had felt like a dream, or rather a nightmare, could that have been real? The camping trip, her embarrassing interaction with Josh, the magic mushrooms, and what felt like an out of body experience? Did she die?

Nobody was around for her to ask. Her stomach ached, and her esophagus felt swollen and burned unpleasantly. The bitter taste of bile was still present in her mouth, clinging to her taste buds. It was difficult to swallow. A sharp, stabbing pain sliced through her brain as she struggled to sit upright.

What did I do to myself? A hot wave of nausea swept over her, the room spun wildly. She closed her eyes, took a few deep breaths and lay back down, lowering her pounding head onto the soft, pillowy refuge. The spinning and nausea slowly passed.

Feeling along the side of the bed, she located a buzzer thanks to the many doctor shows she had watched on television over the years. Immediately, the soft patter of nursing shoes was heard coming towards her room. Continuing to lie back against the soft, cool pillows, she wished away the constant throbbing that pulsed behind her eyeballs.

A chubby woman with red curls pinned up in a sloppy excuse for a bun, and a triple chin, came trundling in, all smiles. The nursing uniform she wore fit snuggly, stretching the Mickey Mouse pattern sideways until Mickey was also obese.

"You're finally awake," she purred, coming to the side of Ang's bed. She grabbed her hand to check her pulse. The woman's fingers felt soft, warm.

"You gave everyone quite a scare, young lady," she mockingly scolded. Ang wasn't sure who she meant by "everyone" since no one else was around.

Oh, no! Ang suddenly remembered. *What about Babka?* Her grandmother was at the respite. Ang was supposed to be home by Monday afternoon when Maria was to drop Babka off. "How long have I been here?" Ang rasped, her throat on fire. It felt damaged, like raw meat.

"Three days. You needed the rest. You had a real hard go there for a while. We nearly lost you."

Again, the reference that there were possibly other people concerned for her. She must have been referring to the hospital staff and not her family or peers, who were glaringly absent, clearly not too concerned—no one was by her bedside, no flowers or teddy bears decorated the windowsill. The cheerful, maternal nurse poured Ang a glass of water from a blue jug, ice clinking against the plastic sides of the cup handed to her. Although it was still painful to swallow, she guzzled it down. The cool liquid soothed and hydrated. Sheer bliss.

"Your neighbour popped by while you were sleeping. I used to work with Maria before she retired from the hospital. Nice lady."

Well, at least someone had come to visit. But then Ang's mind started spinning. Now Maria would know everything that had happened while camping. Not only had Ang humiliated herself by nearly overdosing from what was a recreational, normally harmless drug, but she had broken the law—drinking underage and using an illegal substance. Her shame swelled to mammoth proportions. What would Maria think of her? Who else knew the sordid details of the camping trip?

"She wanted you to know that she extended your grandmother's stay at the Alzheimer's respite," the nurse continued as if anticipating her next question. Ang released an audible sigh of relief, knowing that at least her grandmother hadn't suffered any negative consequences from her irresponsible actions.

"Did anyone else come by?" Ang asked sheepishly.

"Not during my shift. Sorry, dear." The nurse patted Ang on the shoulder, pity on her face. "I'll let the doctor know you're awake. We'll send some light food up to your room. You must be famished." The woman's pudgy fingers gently slipped the needle and tube apparatus out of Ang's vein on her left arm, leaving behind a faint red dot, and slight purplish bruise, quickly covered by a cotton ball and bandage. "Hold this for a few minutes, with pressure," the nurse instructed. Then she pushed the saline cart, Ang's only sustenance for the past few days, against the back wall, and retreated from the room.

Ang called out after her. "Can I use the phone?"

"Go ahead. It's by your bedside," the nurse hollered back from the hallway, already bustling on to the next patient.

She struggled to sit all the way up this time. Her throat still felt rough despite the glorious water, and her fingers were stiff as a zombie's as she dialled Taryn's number. Taryn's mother answered the phone.

"Hello?"

"Oh, hi, Mrs. Blanchard. Is Taryn home?" Ang waited anxiously.

Her best friend's mother's voice, normally pleasant and welcoming when speaking with Ang instantly became clipped and stern. "You have a lot of nerve calling here! Do you know what kind of trouble you have caused for Taryn? For all of us?"

"No, I…"

"What were you thinking, using illegal drugs? Your grandmother would be so disappointed in you right now!"

"I know," Ang replied meekly.

"Taryn is no longer allowed to hang around with you, do you understand?"

"But, Mrs. Blanchard, that's not…"

"Do…you…understand." Acid dripped off her words. "Taryn is no longer able to be your friend. Don't call here anymore."

-click-

The ring tone blared in Ang's ear. The call had been severed, and just like that, her friendship as well. At least that explained Taryn's absence from her bedside at the hospital. Ang's eyes welled up with hot, salty tears. What had she done? She had hurt Taryn and her family. How could she possibly survive without Taryn? Taryn was her rock, her outlet, the only stable thing in her life.

She cried softly, and after an interminable amount of time, fell into a bottomless, impatient sleep.

★ ★ ★

Strange dreams plagued her slumber—dark shadows—images that played beyond conscious thought, lurking, their presence suffusing her with a sinking feeling of fear and dread. Running, constantly running, but she didn't know why or where she was going, but always looking back to see what followed.

The shadows.

When the doctor came into Ang's hospital room, awakening her from her tortured sleep, she was relieved but still shaken. The dread remained, weighed heavily on her soul.

"Good morning. I'm Dr. Kiedis," he introduced himself, formally shaking her hand. The doctor was well kempt with a tall, erect posture, grey hair receding, a cleanly shaven face with a hint of aftershave noticeable on his hands as he examined her vitals—pulse, pupil dilation and heartbeat.

"Can you tell me what your full name is?"

"Angelika Pauline Juris."

The doctor made a check mark on the clipboard chart he clutched in his right hand and continued.

"How old are you?"

"Seventeen."

Check.

"Do you know what year it is?"

"2002."

Check.

"What is your current address?"

Rattling off the number and the street, she was rewarded with another check.

She assumed the doctor was testing for cognitive impairment, possible signs of brain damage she may have sustained. *How long was I dead for?*

Answering all the doctor's questions effortlessly, he appeared satisfied. And despite the headache and sore throat, she felt intact, fully functioning—tired but alive.

"Now, would you like to explain to me what happened?" His voice was deep, with a Kermit the Frog quality, spoken more from his throat than his mouth.

"I don't remember," Ang lied, partially. Yes, she did remember ingesting the magic mushrooms, most likely what the doctor was referring to, but after that things got a little hazy. The line between reality and hallucination was more than blurred. Should she tell the doctor about her out of body experience and the shimmering visit from her guardian angel, or would that be admitting her guilt? Or, lack of sanity?

Dr. Kiedis' stare was intent, judgmental, brow furrowed in disappointment, reminding her of the look Dedko gave her biological father when he did something unsavoury. Did he know that she was lying?

Ang always wore her emotions openly on her face. A collage of guilt, shame and remorse was no doubt artfully betraying her façade. Whether the doctor believed her fib or not, she was sticking to it.

The doctor got right to the point. "The paramedics were told you ingested magic mushrooms while at a camping party." He referred to his clipboard while he spoke. Ang shrugged, playing dumb.

"Blood tests have confirmed this." He looked up for her reaction. She continued to pretend confusion, hoping her acting skills were convincing.

"Usually, we don't have near-fatalities from this recreational drug, which is usually of the Psilocybe, Conocybe, Panaelous, or Stropharia genera. These, although illegal, are generally harmless. Psilocin and psilocybin are the hallucinogenic compounds found in these dried mushroom caps, producing effects that are like LSD but much milder. Sometimes, accidentally, when people are picking these mushrooms, they grab Amanita Virosa, which has a similar appearance to the more commonly used magic mushrooms. These, however, produce intense, negative physiological effects—violent salivation, nausea, vomiting, diarrhea, profound dissociative effects, almost like a schizophrenic may experience."

This summed up Ang's symptoms to a T. The hallucinations. The nausea. The memory of repetitively vomiting all over herself resurged—it felt completely uncontrollable, her body attempting to purge the toxins. She wondered who had the pleasure of cleaning her up afterwards. *How embarrassing!* She wondered if she was the only one affected or if there were others. Did Taryn have an adverse reaction as well?

The name of the mushroom, Amanita Virosa, struck a chord, causing Ang to shudder. Her Latin was limited to what she had learned at St. Paulina High School, but she was pretty sure it translated into "destroying angel."

The doctor continued, "In most cases, the liver is irreversibly damaged, requiring an immediate transplant. Due to the limited time available to get a transplantable liver that is compatible with the patient, most of them die."

The feeling of dread spread through her veins again, the same feeling she had after awakening from her nightmare. A sensation like she had somehow cheated death, directly defying some unknown force. And now that force felt slighted.

"The strange thing in your case is that your liver is unharmed and is functioning as it should, and no other impairment is evident. All your vitals are stable. You are one of those medical miracles we so often hear of but rarely see. Unexplainable. You don't know how lucky you are."

Ang shuddered.

"How long was I...dead...for?" She had trouble getting the word out.

"Nobody is certain. The paramedics worked on reviving you for several minutes, and the other witnesses gave us discrepant answers as to how long you were unresponsive before the rescue team arrived. The accounts must have been inaccurate, or you would have suffered permanent brain damage. At any rate, you are incredibly lucky. I'll sign your paperwork, releasing you this afternoon because I believe you are ready to go home. Try to eat a little breakfast, make sure your stomach has settled, and if you can keep your meal down, you are free to go." He marched out of the room without so much as a goodbye.

After choking down a bland breakfast of overcooked scrambled eggs, dry toast, and apple juice brought in by an unfriendly old bat, she miraculously kept it down. Satisfied, Dr. Kiedis signed the papers releasing her from the hospital.

She took a cab home to an empty house. Babka was to remain at the respite for a few more days until Ang got her bearings, thanks to Maria making all the arrangements. Ang was grateful, too ashamed to see her grandmother even though the old woman wouldn't understand what had happened. Plus, she needed extra time to rest and feel normal again if that was at all possible. For now, she felt like she had been hit by a transport, which then backed up and ran over her again ten times more.

Safe in the solace of her own home, Ang spent most of her first few days sleeping, trying desperately to forget the whole ordeal, wipe it clean from her memory. When she was alert, however, all of it would come flooding back in a physical and emotional torrent. She would reflect on every detail, rehash what she could remember, and then try to wade through the murkier details, the parts that didn't make any logical sense. And accompanying the post-traumatic memories and humiliation was a constant gnawing feeling of loss whenever she thought of Taryn.

It wasn't long before a complicated underground communications network was developed between the two teens, Maria the less than willing mediator. Taryn trusted Maria as much as Ang did, and she quickly confessed their forbidden acts from the night of the camping party, knowing the information would pass only to her bestie, and no one else.

Gaps in Ang's memory were slowly filled.

Taryn and the other campers that had taken the magic mushrooms from Bushbeard were not exposed to the Amanita Virosa that led to Ang's seizures and near-death experience. Ang was the only one to suffer the adverse effects from the drugs, so most likely had eaten the only errant mushroom.

What are the chances of that?

Of course, she felt intense relief that her best friend was fine, but she was completely mortified and ashamed of her actions, being the centre of attention in such a negative scene. How was she going to outlive this one?

But she was too emotionally drained to figure it out, plus she was physically knackered—almost dying will do that to you. Eventually, she would have to face her peers and go back to school but for now, she simply wanted to hide. Curl up in a ball. And sleep.

Saturday morning, exactly one week after the camping party nightmare, she suddenly bolted upright in her bed with the unsettling feeling she was not alone. And she was right.

There, handsomely perched on the edge of her mattress, was the mysterious man—her angelic hallucination—from the night she nearly died.

Chapter 11

Ang gasped, sounding like a balloon releasing a spurt of air. "What are you doing here?" She reactively drew her comforter all the way up to her chin.

The handsome apparition, angel, man...whatever he was... gawked back at her, the stunned look on his face mirroring her own. He waved a large, exquisitely manicured hand in front of her face. "Can you see me?"

Ang—jaw agape, hazel eyes wide and incredulous—nodded her head in a slow, exaggerated movement.

"You're not supposed to still see me," he stated, lines gathering on his tanned forehead.

Here we go again. The same vision, the same unanswered question. Who was this man and why could she see him? Was she dreaming? Or having a psychedelic flashback, an after-effect of the drug? Having heard several stories of people who experienced a "bad trip," eventually having flashbacks or recurring hallucinations, she feared that must be the present case. *Great, I completely fried my brain because there is no way that this is real!*

Gavin scooched closer to her on the bed until he was mere inches away. "But I am real," he said in the warmest tone.

Ang was dumbfounded, certain she hadn't spoken aloud. Could the vision read her thoughts? *Well, of course he can, dummy; he's a figment of your imagination, isn't he?*

"It's more complicated than that," Gavin responded.

"Stop it!" Ang shifted backwards from the vision until she was flush against the headboard. "Get out of my head!"

"I'm sorry," the vision said. "I'm kind of new to this. This must be very strange for you as well."

"That's an understatement." Her eyes roved over his face and body. It was impossible to believe he was real, the entire idea defying all logic, but he certainly seemed real…physical, tangible, unlike what she expected of an apparition. The details—so stark, so clear. The perfect curl of each black eyelash, the sapphire flecks spattered throughout his irises like a speckled egg, the light peppering of stubble on his upper lip and chin indicating a shave was almost in order, the smooth, pink skin of his lips.

Could he be real?

Nah. Real people didn't exude an effervescent glow from their skin. Or appear out of nowhere.

Unable to resist the impulse, she reached out her trembling fingers to touch him, to feel this glorious, shimmering figure before her, and determine if he was real after all, but her hand passed right through him, landing gently on her comforter below.

Disappointment. Realization. Acceptance.

"Of course, my hallucination would say that he's real," Ang shook her head at her foolishness. She replaced her limp hand in her lap. "I guess I'm going batshit crazy. Fantastic. As if my life couldn't get any worse."

Gavin offered a slight smile, but then his gaze clouded. "Something must have happened when I switched the crystals," he mumbled, shaking his head. "This is unheard of. I mean, it's not uncommon for people to see us during a moment of profound stress, tragedy, or a near-death experience, the surge of chemicals temporarily linking us together, but that's all it usually is… temporary."

Ang watched in fascination. For a hallucination, this one was more elaborate and emotional than she would have anticipated. What did his ramblings mean? Near-death-experiences, switching crystals…a soliloquy of sorts as he attempted to rationalize the events while she simultaneously did the same? Two parts of her consciousness working on two distinct and separate planes? It was mind-boggling.

Eventually, her curiosity got the best of her. Perhaps engaging with this "alter ego" of hers would help her get some clarity, hopefully merging the two planes of thought together into one simple explanation.

"I assume the near-death experience you're referring to was mine," Ang stated.

Gavin glanced up as if only then remembering she was there. He nodded. "I interfered with fate. I had a feeling you were in danger, that you didn't have much time left, that you were going to die. I did the only thing I could think of to stop that from happening."

Ang raised an eyebrow. "The warnings? The ones I blatantly ignored?"

Gavin's posture wilted. "No, not that. Much worse."

"Are you talking about when you switched the crystals?" Ang asked.

"What do you know about the crystals?" he whispered; his eyes wide. He nervously shimmied closer to Ang so that he practically sat on top of her.

With no room left on the bed to back up, Ang flinched at his intimate proximity. "N…n…nothing. You mentioned it, is all. When you were talking to yourself."

Gavin's shoulders relaxed, and he audibly sighed. "Oh, okay then. Good. That's good."

Suddenly self-conscious being so close to this glorious creature, apparition or not, she slipped out from under the covers, hoping he couldn't smell her morning breath or the fact that she hadn't showered in days. Surveying her rumpled, unwashed pyjamas, she attempted to smooth them out. The vanity mirror across the room reflected her drawn face creased with red pillow lines and dark purplish crescents below her eyes that had transformed her into the epitome of death.

"Sorry, I'm a frightful mess," she apologized, trying to tamp down her unruly blond tresses.

"You are looking a little rough."

"Hey! I wasn't exactly expecting company," she defended.

"Well, you know...a shower...might be helpful."

"Yes. I got it!" she responded, clipped, and walked over to the vanity, sitting away from Gavin, cheeks hot and red.

"You don't have to be embarrassed around me," Gavin placated.

"That's easy for you to say. You're perfect." And that was putting it mildly. Hair carefully mussed, crystal blue eyes radiating warmth and beauty, straight white teeth, today dressed in a chest-hugging grey sweater accentuating his exemplary muscular physique.

"I can change form if it will make you feel more at ease. Would you like that?"

"What are you, a shape-shifter?" Ang responded, sarcastically.

"No, Angelika, I'm an angel. This is my usual form, the one I have chosen, but I am able to take on other forms when necessary."

Ang was skeptical. "Really? Prove it."

Without another word, Gavin closed his eyes, taking in a deep breath. The solidity of his body wavered, the shimmering intensifying, and then dissolving into millions of tiny, sparkling lights, like thousands of multicoloured fireflies floating around Ang's room, spiralling around each other, reconfiguring into a vastly different form. Pretty much the opposite of Gavin's usual appearance.

The image before her was of a teenage boy, short in stature, the extra twenty pounds he carried gathered entirely on his belly. Red pimples covered his face, his hair was greasy with a rebellious cowlick for bangs, and his clothes were directly from the '70s... brown bellbottoms and a tight, beige turtleneck. A geeky smile exposed full, metal braces. "Better?"

"Oh, hell no!" Ang blurted, fighting her repulsion. "Please, change back."

Seconds later, Gavin sat on her bed, back in his usual handsome form, the one Ang had grown accustomed. If he *had* chosen this form, it was a fine choice indeed.

Remembering he could probably read her thoughts, she abruptly blurted out, "Where are your wings, then, if you are a so-called angel?"

"You're thinking of the seraphim, cherubim, and living creatures, which all have wings. Several pairs of wings. But as a guardian angel, or a common angel, I have no need for them. You see, we are made up entirely of energy, and so we can transform into any image we wish, and transport to any place in the world, or in heaven, without being limited by the parameters of time and space."

"Because you're made up of energy," Ang reiterated.

Gavin missed the sarcasm and replied excitedly as if she were finally getting it, "Yes! That's right. And we are neither male nor female. We just are."

Ang's doubt lingered, but at times her hallucination was so darn elaborate and convincing, she found herself becoming swept up in the moment, only to sober up and realize again that he wasn't real. He couldn't be. Yet, where had she garnered all this information in her limited exposure to church and the Bible? Where had she come up with the terms seraphim, cherubim and living creatures? Were these real terms she had learned at some point and stored in her subconscious or was she making it up as she went along? Making a mental note to check the dictionary later, she decided to continue engaging with her delusion. See how far it would go. Plus, although Gavin wasn't real, it was still the first company she had had in days. Someone to talk to without holding back. Babka remained in respite, her stay extended as Ang still felt incapable of caring for anyone else. She could barely take care of herself at this point.

"What are the crystals?" Ang asked, bringing the conversation around full circle.

Fear and guilt splayed across Gavin's flawless complexion, quick and sharp. "I can't tell you. It's sacred. I've already broken enough rules. Telling you about the crystals would be going too far. I've said too much."

"This obviously involves me," Ang continued to probe. "Don't you think I have the right to know? You said it yourself, we're not supposed to be able to see each other. What did you do that changed that?" she demanded. "I deserve an explanation."

Gavin appraised Ang like a mother does her child when she realizes it has matured enough to learn the harsh realities of life. Sighing, he said, "It's quite a lengthy story. It may take a while to get through."

"Lucky for you, I have all day."

She was embracing the straight jacket and padded cell with this now, starting to enjoy the delusions. If she was going crazy, and she suspected strongly that she was, why not have fun in the process? She would laugh it over with her shrink later. And, then happily take the antipsychotic medication they would no doubt prescribe for her and go on with her life in a merry little way, free of hallucinations of angels.

But for now...

There was a lengthy pause. "It's difficult for me to find the right words. I was forbidden by my superior to discuss this with anyone, but I never in a million Earth years would have thought I could discuss it with you. It's inconceivable. Even my superior couldn't have foreseen this, so perhaps his warning doesn't apply in this situation. I suppose you do have a right to know—it is your life, after all—and I've already broken so many rules. What's one more?"

Ang nodded encouragingly.

Clearing his throat, a very human act, she observed, Gavin continued.

"Where I work, we have certain regulations that we follow—we have free choice like you mortals, but choose not to act on it, well, usually, anyhow." The last part he spoke under his breath. "We are bound by our Creator to fulfill our roles and do His will, and so we adhere to these rules without question—with honour, dignity, and respect."

Ang nodded again, listening raptly.

"When we are given a mortal to protect, the assignment starts the day they are born and finishes the day they perish. But, with you it was different."

"How so?"

"I got assigned to you a few weeks ago. I don't know what happened to your previous guardian. It's like they vanished into thin air, and I was sworn not to ask any questions regarding the matter. But I was curious. I followed a co-worker who was acting suspicious into a prohibited room and noticed him tampering with these crystals of energy—I believe that they represent life for you mortals. After the co-worker left, I checked your crystal and was shocked to see it was almost empty. I didn't think. I just reacted. As my first feat of guardianship, I switched your crystal with someone else's—someone with full energy—in the hope of giving you a longer life. I wasn't sure if it would work, but your crystal—when I checked it again—was indeed full. Then at the campsite when I saw you lying unmoving on the ground, at first, I thought you had died. I feared I had failed you."

Ang was riveted, hanging on every word.

"But, now look at you," he stood, a large grin brightening his face more than it already glowed, and rushed to her side, reaching out a hand to cup her face, although she felt nothing. "Seeing you here, very alive, I think it might have worked."

Every hair on her body stood at attention, and she inadvertently shivered.

"So, I *was* supposed to die?"

Gently, he nodded. "I believe so."

"Wow." The gravity of his revelation hit her like a hundred-foot tsunami. Dazed, she wandered back over to her bed, plunking down on the comforter.

In her moment of stupidity, one single moment, she had almost lost everything. How close she had come to losing Babka, losing Taryn, losing all her dreams and aspirations of graduating from high school and going to university, eventually getting married, having babies. That would have been it.

No more Ang.

The shock of her ordeal must have been delaying this full realization or perhaps the misguided sense of immortality that youth tend to embrace. Instead, she had been so wrapped up in being embarrassed, humiliated really, that only now the true permanence of her actions finally sunk in.

She had almost died.

"Th…thank you," she stuttered, her heartfelt gratitude garbling her words. Tears stung her eyes as she beheld the shining angel.

Smiling down on her with radiating warmth, she physically felt his presence for a moment, like a plugged-in space heater or a comforting embrace.

"It's my job," he modestly expressed.

"Well, I must say you are a very adequate employee, then. So, what happened to my old crystal?"

Gavin appeared shamefaced, and his radiance dimmed. "I'd rather not say."

Had she stumbled upon a sore point? No longer uncomfortable around the angelic vision, she folded her legs and leaned forward on her elbows, continuing to prod. "Did someone else die in my place?"

Gavin paused again. "I don't know for sure, but yes, I believe it's a distinct possibility."

"Who?"

If Ang could read Gavin's mind like he could hers, she would see the name clearly as it had appeared on the crystal before he switched it, and again how it had been printed in the obituaries of the mortal's newspapers in Wednesday's edition, but instead he replied, "I don't know."

The atmosphere in the room turned sombre, Ang sensing the inner turmoil that the angel faced, and she got the sense that he was trying to protect her by omitting the details.

Not wanting to prolong his turmoil, she changed the subject. "So, what is heaven like? Is that where you live, where you... work?"

"I do—I mean, I did—mainly in the second heaven and on Earth until now."

"Okay. You lost me. What do you mean you *did*, past tense?"

Gavin paced, again in such a human manner that Ang couldn't help smiling despite her apparition's clear dismay.

"As a result of what I did, going against the rules and taking free will—mine and yours—into my own hands, I believe I'm being kind of...punished."

"Punished? How?" She gathered the warm down comforter around her thin frame. She felt another round of shivers coming on, the situation too surreal, but the possibility of there being any truth to it unnerved her. Was it possible he truly was her guardian angel?

"I've been locked out—only temporarily, I hope—until they figure out what has been going on. Yours isn't the only guardian angel to disappear, it seems. They are being tight-lipped regarding the whole thing, so I don't know the details. They know I switched your crystal and want to make sure I'm not involved in...whatever it is that's going on. Until they know more, they won't grant me access to the kingdom. I've even lost the special connection I have with all the other angels. We always know each other's whereabouts and can communicate through a special mental link. That is now broken for me."

Ang's brow furrowed. "I'm sorry. You did it all for me."

Gavin stopped pacing and stared directly at Ang. "Don't be sorry. It was my choice. Like I said, I violated your free will, too, by changing your life path. I am the one to blame."

"But you changed my path for the better. If it weren't for you, my path would be at a dead end. Literally speaking."

Their dialogue paused. The grandfather clock clicked loudly in the hallway.

"So, that's why you think we are connected now? Why I'm able to see you?"

Gavin pondered the idea, his exuded light shimmering in response.

"It's a possibility, although I don't understand it. As I said earlier, this has never happened before."

"What's heaven like?" she couldn't help but ask. The question every believer wanted to know.

"I would love to explain it to you, but it would be like trying to describe the solar system to a common ant. After the original sin was committed, you humans lost the ability to comprehend, your senses became limited, blocked, so you are unable to perceive it, although you will one day—and it is nothing like you have ever seen or experienced, so I have nothing to compare it to." Again, a pregnant pause. "But it is magnificent."

"That's a cop-out answer," she complained. "I get that I'm a dullard but try me. Tell me what you can. Is my grandfather there? Have you seen him?"

"I am not familiar with all of the spirits. What were his beliefs?" Gavin asked.

A vision of her grandfather dressed in his Sunday's best—black trousers, crisply pressed dress shirt, suit jacket, and Bible in hand, he would set off to church with Babka every Sunday and major holiday. Both her grandparents had prayed with their girls each night, teaching them that Jesus had died for their sins, granting all who believed everlasting life. Although she knew more was required to be a devout Christian, she believed her grandfather fulfilled most of the requirements.

"Yes," Gavin answered before she had a chance to say a word aloud, apparently eavesdropping on her thoughts once more. "I believe you have answered your own question. Your grandfather will be in Heaven with the Creator," Gavin reassured.

Ang sighed in contentment. This could all be a figment of her imagination, but the thought was still comforting, that Dedko was at peace.

"So, what now?"

"Well, now you can enjoy the rest of your life that you have been given, knowing you have an overprotective guardian angel watching over you."

"You're not with me all of the time, are you?" She pictured herself perched on the toilet, Gavin gawking at her the entire time.

"No, no. I'm only near you when you need me. Like when you are in danger or have a difficult decision to make, during difficult times. You must have needed me now. That is why I am here."

She had felt lost. Alone. But she simply couldn't believe that Gavin was real, or that she had had a near-death experience. Denial. That's where she was living. Complete denial.

"Well, I'm fine now. So, you can go," she dismissed him. "A nice hot shower is in order."

Gavin nodded in exaggerated agreement. "And maybe...you know...wash your clothes? And the house could use a decent scrubbing too. It's looking a tad neglected."

"All right, already, I got it!" she blurted. "Are all the angels as opinionated as you?"

"I don't know. We've never really been given the opportunity to give our opinion. It's kind of a new thing for me."

"There's a human thing called keeping your opinions to yourself. You should look into it. By the way...where do you go when you're not with me if you are blocked out of heaven?" Ang asked.

"The space in between." And with a colourful, glorious poof, he was gone.

★ ★ ★

Ang extended her absence from school for an extra week to put the pieces of her life back together. Give her additional time to allow the hallucinations to pass but, if anything, they increasingly grew worse. Gavin was quickly becoming a permanent fixture in her life, her new sidekick now that Taryn was prohibited from being Ang's friend. They did everything together, and she became accustomed to his presence and appreciated his company, though he could be awfully chatty and annoying at times. It was still better than the alternative…being utterly alone.

Not only was he enjoyable company, but he also forced Ang to come out of her coma-like stupor and get back into a regular routine. He pushed her until she finally cleaned and organized the house. Each evening, they enjoyed long walks together in the crisp autumn air, and he came along with her and Maria to pick up Babka from the respite. Ang always took great care not to talk to Gavin when others were around, not wanting to admit to anyone her likely lack of sanity. But quickly she realized there was an exception when it came to Babka, who always seemed to take pleasure in Ang's one-sided conversations. She could talk freely with Gavin while around her grandmother, who would simply nod and smile like everything was perfectly normal.

Although it wasn't.

Sunday evening quickly arrived, the following day, Monday, her first day back at school since the incident. The dread gnawed a hole in her stomach. What would happen?

She didn't have the regular support and comfort from Taryn that she was used to relying on. They had a system before all of this began that involved calling each other whenever they were going to miss school due to being ill to avoid the awkward "who to sit with in the cafeteria at lunchtime" conundrum. They would, instead, both stay home and spend hours on the phone.

Tomorrow she would be alone. Taryn's mom was a teacher at their school and had forbidden the girls to be friends. Ang knew deep within Taryn's heart they *were* still friends, and her buddy would love to break this new rule, but Taryn's mother was pretty darn strict, and to be honest, a little bit scary. So, as tempted as Taryn might be to break the rule, she wouldn't dare.

Who would Ang eat with at lunch in the cafeteria? Who would she talk to in the morning before their classes commenced?

For the first time, Ang was completely on her own.

Chapter 12

The digital alarm clock beeped incessantly. Ang reached out from beneath warm covers, slamming the off button with more strength than intended, unit flipping through the air.

The dreaded day was upon her. No more chances of postponing the inevitable. No more excuses. No more hiding from her shameful acts in the security of her home. She had to face the music and return to school.

The lemon-yellow sunbeam filtering through the diaphanous bedroom curtains taunted her with fantasies of chipper things, but her mind knew better than to trust the glamour. Inside her mood was dark, sullen, guarded, her doomsday mind anticipating a horrendous day ahead. In the end, her day ended up being far worse than she could have ever anticipated.

Ang's normal school-day routine involved hooking up with Taryn directly upon arrival at St. Paulina's. Following their rendezvous, which always involved a quick gossip session, they would walk each other to their first classes. Their classes were different due to their varied interests—Ang's more geared towards the Sciences, Taryn's towards the Arts.

Today, however, Ang's locker was deserted as she entered the school and approached their normal meeting spot. A glimmer of panic ensued, followed quickly by insecurity. Palms and armpits instantly dampened.

Ang's automatic coping mechanism for any uncomfortable social situation—which she prided herself on—was to allay her insecurities by blending into her environment to the point of invisibility. It was her only superpower. But today she felt extra self-aware as if caught under a spotlight, exposed, on display, like the lead performer in a Broadway production. A Shakespearean tragedy. Face on fire, she studied her sneakers while edging towards her locker.

Alone, fidgeting at her locker, the solitude only lasted a few moments. Joanne, a friendly, shy girl occupying the locker three boxes down from Ang's had arrived, rounding the hallway corner. But, upon seeing Ang standing forlorn and unsure, she visibly hesitated. Dropping her eyes to the ground, Joanne continued to approach the lockers—she didn't have a choice if she wanted to grab her books and get to class on time.

The slim brunette shed her cream-coloured pea coat and mittens, squishing them into her locker, and retrieved a notebook and pencil case. Flashing an uncertain smile Ang's way, she whispered hello in the obvious hope of not being overheard. After cautiously glancing around and seeing that no one was currently paying them any attention, she visibly relaxed.

"How are you doing?" she whispered while studying herself in her locker mirror.

"Alright, I guess," Ang stammered. "What is everyone saying exactly?"

"You haven't heard anything yet?"

Ang shook her head in the negative. "I've been an agoraphobe since the camping party. Most of the night remains a blank. Especially after I…blacked out."

"Blacked out? I heard you died, man. I'm shocked you seem so healthy. I was expecting much worse."

"You weren't there?"

"I couldn't get anyone to take my shift at the movie theatre, so I missed the whole thing, but my sister Jenna was there. Things got *real* crazy, she said."

"What else did she say?"

"Hmm. I'm not gonna sugar coat it—it's pretty bad."

Ang groaned. "I'm listening."

"I'm assuming you know what happened...the...um, incident. Your overdose and the first responders arriving on the scene."

Ang nodded, body tense, sweating amped up a notch.

"After the paramedics whisked you away in the helicopter, the police showed up."

"Oh no." Ang's stomach dropped. Why hadn't Taryn told her? "How did they get there so fast?"

"It was the OPP stationed in Upsala, only ten minutes away. They questioned everyone, even a few idiots who ran into the bushes to hide."

"That *is* bad," Ang drew in a shaky breath.

"It gets worse."

"Of course, it does," Ang replied deadpan.

"Your friend Taryn admitted to the cops that you had both eaten some sort of strange tasting brownies. I think she was trying to let them know you had magic mushrooms in your system—so the hospital would be aware and could treat you accordingly—but she also didn't want to get either of you in trouble."

"Well, that's a believable story. Did the cops buy it?"

"I think they did."

Ang sighed in relief. Her relief was short-lived.

"But still twenty-two kids got charged for underage drinking. Parents were called. It was quite the fiasco."

"Oh boy."

"Yeah, let's just say that you're nobody's favourite person right now, you get my drift?"

"I sure do." Ang's heart sank so low it took up residence in her toes. Within minutes Joanne had summarized what the collective student body was feeling.

Ang hadn't considered how her actions at the bonfire affected the other party goers. She hadn't realized the police were called to investigate, although in retrospect how could they not have been involved? It was funny that no one had mentioned it to her until now. As a result of the police investigation, several of the underage drinkers had been punished. Ang remembered Taryn's mother speaking to her on the phone when she had called from the hospital, vehemence thick in every word, and it now seemed appropriate.

"Who did Taryn say gave us the brownies?" Ang vividly recalled the creepy bearded man—Bushbeard—and wondered if Taryn had pointed the finger in his direction.

"She said they were floating around the campsite, and nobody knew for sure where they had originated."

"I think a cop might have visited me in the hospital, now that you mention it. The image is fuzzy, like a dream, but I remember him questioning me about the camp and the drugs, but I really didn't remember anything. So, he probably assumed Taryn's story was true. Dropped the investigation. The police haven't contacted me since, so…"

"Yeah, Taryn saved the day and took care of the drug situation. However, the underage drinking couldn't be explained away. Like I said, lots of people were charged. They're in shit with the cops, in shit with their parents…"

"So, basically you're saying that I'm the social pariah of the school."

"Basically." The halls were continually filling up with students, classes soon to commence. "Sorry, gotta go," Joanne abruptly concluded their conversation, skittering away to her first class, afraid of being a loser by association. Ang couldn't blame her. She probably would have done the same.

Locker still agape, Ang extracted her blue binder and Hello Kitty pencil case and shut the locker. Eyes downcast, she raced to her first class, ever aware of the contemptuous glares, pointing fingers, and whispers. People gossiping, saying her name, although they probably didn't know it until now, blaming her, judging her. Some students practically hugged the walls trying to get by her in the hallway, avoiding all physical contact like she had contracted the Bubonic Plague.

Joanne's words kept echoing through her mind, "Let's just say that you're nobody's favourite person right now." "Kids got charged...parents were called."

Head hung lower now as she slunk into her first-period class, Calculus, and curled her body into the desk. She wished the day was over, yet it was only beginning. How would she survive?

Mr. Doty was scribbling an equation on the chalkboard. Ang tried her hardest to keep her eyes focused on the teacher, but her face was burning under the heated stares of her classmates caught from the corner of her vision. Slouching deeper into her chair, she attempted to slow her breathing. *Deep breaths, Ang, deep breaths.* Slowly, her heart rate returned to a steadier beat, and her face recovered its usual pale pallor. Until Josh entered the room. She tried not to look up. Tried with all her might. And then curiosity got the best of her. Their eyes met, her deep blush resurfaced, but his gaze remained impassive, and he quickly averted his gaze as if she didn't exist.

Oh no, not Josh too?

The class dragged by. The teacher had covered a lot of ground during her absence, and she felt lost and confused, struggling to grasp how to add and subtract vectors while also struggling to accept that Josh was obviously no longer interested in her if he ever actually was. Again, against her better judgment, she glanced back to where Josh sat, his steely gaze remaining forward, completely ignoring her. Slowly she turned back to face the front of the room. The teacher was watching her.

"Can I have your attention, Ms. Juris? You seem a little distracted today." Several students tittered in response.

Could this get any worse?

She shook her head no, but the teacher wasn't finished. "Unless Josh is teaching the class, I suggest you keep your eyes up here. Not as exciting a view, I'm sure, but if you want to pass this class, I suggest you pay attention."

"Yes, sir," Ang responded, face on fire.

Had even the teachers turned on her now?

Second period found Ang painfully slogging through English class. The time somehow passed slower, the clock seemingly ticking in reverse. They had started reading Aldous Huxley's *Brave New World*. Ang desperately tried to immerse herself in the story, but her mind resisted. Instead, she kept ruminating over Joanne's words. *Nobody's favourite person.*

And then Josh's rejection, before her teacher centered her out in front of the entire calculus class.

Finally, a little spark of anger ignited. Here, she almost overdosed, ALMOST DIED for frick's sake, and yet there was no concern for her. Nobody except for Joanne had asked her how she was doing or spoken directly to her, for that matter. Just a constant flow of resentment shot her way. It was devastating! She truly was a nobody! If ever she thought that, now she had her proof.

By lunchtime, she couldn't handle it anymore. She needed to escape. Making a conscious decision to avoid the cafeteria altogether, she edged towards her locker to deposit her binder and pencil case and grab her jacket in order to step out for an hour. The hallways were congested with students gathering their lunches and socializing in scattered groups.

Through the many milling heads, she finally spotted Taryn, the person she had been seeking all day. Perhaps her bestie would be able to slip out for a while, without her mother noticing?

Taryn smiled upon eye contact, her expression apologetic. Sheepishly, she waved. Ang waved back. Mouthing the words,

"I'm so sorry," she was quickly swallowed up by the throng and carried away.

Apparently, no lunch date.

So, Ang had been correct in assuming her bestie would abide by her mother's rules and avoid contact with her in all forms. It was the last straw.

Without warning, Ang found it impossible to breathe. Her lungs constricted and failed to expand again. Her heart raced. A cold sweat dampened her scalp and skin. Dizziness and nausea threatened to overwhelm her. The sensation was starkly familiar. A panic attack was taking flight in her nervous system.

Seeking out the nearest bathroom, she fled to its refuge. *Yes, it's empty,* she thought silently as she slammed the door behind her, disappointed it didn't have a lock that she could engage. Throwing on the tap, she applied cool water to her pressure points—temples, neck, wrists—in an act that normally helped calm her, diffuse the panic. Then she leaned her back against the mustard painted walls, slowly slithering to the ground, not caring if her 7 For All Mankind jeans got soiled from the sticky bathroom floor.

Gavin materialized into the otherwise empty washroom.

"Breathe," he pacified. Such a simple word—simple action— one that should have been automatic, but it had been evading Ang for five minutes now and she was on the verge of hyperventilating. Realizing she had subconsciously been holding her breath, she finally inhaled sharply through her nose, the smell of disinfectant and stale urine assaulting her senses.

"Keep breathing, deep and slow."

She exhaled and inhaled deeply. Again. And again.

"That's good. Keep going."

Her racing heart slowed from a death metal drum solo down to a marching drummer's steady beat. This allowed her brain to kick back in, along with all her negative thoughts.

Then the tears flowed.

Burying her face in her hands, she let the anguish pour out in an endless rush.

Gavin sat beside her, and she felt a strange sensation—was it love and empathy?—emanating from him like she was a gas tank on Empty, and he was filling her back up to Full.

"Thanks," Ang sniffled.

"For what?"

"For being here. Even if you are a figment of my imagination."

"No problem. But again…"

She cut him off. "What have I done? I don't know what to do, how to make this better." She reached over to grab a wad of toilet paper from the nearest stall and trumpeted her nose into the tissue. Sighed heavily.

"We'll figure this out," Gavin consoled, hugging her with his mind, and she thought she could feel it again in a physical sense, although barely perceptible—more like a faint vibration. She certainly wished he was real.

"Maybe I should drop out of school." She wiped her puffy eyes with the back of her hand.

"Don't be silly. That would create more problems in the future than would solve. Have faith. Things will work out," he encouraged, blue eyes warm and sparkling.

"Faith in what?" Ang had never been a religious person, despite her grandparents' efforts. Her closest thing to a religious experience was the one time she joined a gym and accidentally climbed onto Jacob's ladder. That was a mistake she would never make again.

The bathroom door flew open, and a chubby ninth grader rushed in, and upon seeing Ang on the floor quickly escaped into the nearest stall, did her business, and fled the privy without so much as washing her hands.

The unexpected interruption broke the moment.

Gavin's image wavered and disappeared.

As much as she would like to stay hidden in the bathroom for the remainder of the day, it was time to suck it up. Accept the consequences. She would have to face the masses sooner than later, at least in order to leave the bathroom, and ultimately school for today, so best to get it over with.

Ang stood up, dusted herself off, and splashed cool water on her face, removing the smeared mascara that rimmed her eyes. As she exited the bathroom, the hallway was more congested. She determined her route of exit when abruptly the students parted and out popped Mrs. Small, the school's guidance counsellor/social worker. The woman was anything but small as her name implied and she wobbled towards Ang like a giant Christmas ornament, all pointy on top and bottom, and gloriously rotund in the middle. Steering her massive form towards Ang, she defied gravity with every pointy, precarious step.

Ang groaned, but she noticed the deep concern displayed on the guidance counsellor's face.

Well, at least somebody cares.

"Angelika, darling, how are you doing?" She clasped Ang's hands in her own warm, meaty hands, leaving Ang feeling a slight bit of discomfort in an age where physical contact between faculty and students was frowned upon, but she knew it came from the woman's heart. She must have noticed Ang's red-tinged eyes and moistened eyelashes.

Did she also know what happened on the camping trip? Most likely.

"I'm okay. Thanks for asking." The students were like spectators at a tennis match. Gazes bouncing from Ang to Mrs. Small, and then back to Ang. It was so silent. Some of the students still wore scathing expressions, but most now observed in curiosity.

"You can come and talk to me in the office anytime. Maybe tomorrow?" The woman pushed her thick bifocals up higher on her nose.

"Uh, maybe."

"Around 1 p.m.?"

Ang caved. "Yeah, sure. Okay. I'll be there. Thank you." And after a moment's consideration, Ang thought the appointment might be exactly what she needed. Someone nonjudgmental to talk to, someone other than Gavin who was biased as he was a part of her imagination. Perhaps, she would tell Mrs. Small about Gavin, how he had appeared to her the night of the overdose and had been present ever since. The guidance counsellor seemed compassionate to her plight. And Ang knew she couldn't get through this on her own.

Perhaps Mrs. Small could help Ang muddle through the chaos of her recent actions and dire consequences, or maybe at least help her adjust to being friendless and completely bananas.

Perhaps.

★ ★ ★

Third period was history with Mrs. Humphreys. The most boring class in existence. Ang was struggling to pay attention to a lecture on the war of 1812 when she was hit in the head with a projectile launched at her from the hallway. A crumpled ball of paper.

The teacher was facing the chalkboard, oblivious to the disruption.

Startled, she glanced out the door, to see Taryn waving like a wild woman for Ang to follow her into the hall. Then she disappeared. Ang knew exactly where she would be waiting— at their usual mid-class meeting spot—the second-floor girl's washroom.

Thrusting her hand into the air, Ang felt a surge of nerves ripple through her body. She hated talking in class, the simple task of asking to go to the washroom making her stomach clench. In regular circumstances, whenever nature called, she would hold off until class was over, legs tightly crossed. But she sorely needed to talk to Taryn. This could be her only chance for a while.

"Yes, Angelika," Mrs. Humphreys finally noticed Ang's hand flapping in the air.

"Uh, can I please go to the washroom?"

"It can't wait?" the teacher's eyes flicked up to the clock indicating fifteen minutes left in the period.

"Uh, no, sorry," Ang murmured.

"Okay, make it quick."

Ang fled out of her desk, into the hall, and straight to their meeting spot. As soon as she entered the girl's washroom, Taryn tackled her with a minute-long bear hug.

"Are you alright? You had me so worried."

Not a huggy kind of person, Ang disentangled herself from Taryn's embrace but was still beyond relief to finally be with her bestie.

"It's all my fault. I'm so sorry, Ang. You would never have tried the mushrooms if it weren't for me. You could have died."

"I did. At least, I think I did. But, hey, you didn't force me to do anything. I was the one who ate the mushies. You didn't exactly shove them down my throat."

Taryn hopped up onto the sink counter, slim legs dangling over the edge.

"That was a close call."

"Did you get into a lot of trouble? I heard that the police were called."

"Thankfully, I can act sober when I need to. Besides being grounded from seeing you, no, I didn't get into much trouble. But, not being able to be friends with you is the worst punishment my parents could have ever come up with."

"Yeah, this sucks. Is there a way to convince your parents to change their minds?"

"You know my mom. I don't call her Madame Hitler for nothing. I tried everything I could think of, but don't worry. Eventually, they'll forget it happened. She'll soften up, and we can hang out again. This won't last. Trust me."

"Last time you asked me to trust you I almost died." Ang regretted her words the moment they slipped off her tongue and viewed the pained expression on her friend's face. "Sorry, I didn't mean that. It's just, how am I supposed to get through this without you? Everybody hates me."

"No, they don't. They simply need a scapegoat right now. Besides, you know I still love you, right? You'll always have me… only not in a physical sense right now."

"I know. Thanks. That helps, I guess."

Taryn slipped off the counter and adjusted her black and white striped tube skirt and lace stockings. "I better get back to class."

"One more thing before you go. It's kind of been bugging me. You know the guy that sold you the mushies? Bushbeard?"

"Yeah?"

"Where do you know him from? I've never seen him before. He's not the typical kind of guy you associate with."

"Oh, he's not. Most definitely not. He came up to us while we were sitting there at the campsite after you ran off into the forest to hide from Josh. He asked us, you know, if we wanted…anything. I said no, but after you returned all bent out of shape, I thought it might help you to, you know, relax."

"Did you tell him it was for me? I got the strangest feeling that he was leering right at me when you were talking to him," Ang asked.

"I didn't say anything. Only that I wanted to buy two grams. The weird thing was that he gave it to me for free. No charge. Maybe he knew it was bad shit. I don't know…"

"Yeah, maybe." Ang pondered this. "Weird though how I was the only one that ended up in the hospital. Not that I wanted anyone else to get sick, but what are the chances of that?"

Taryn enveloped her in another hug, this one quick and tight. "I feel so responsible, and I promise I will make it up to you. This will work itself out. You'll see." Then she disappeared into the hall.

Seconds later Ang followed, returning to her history class right when the bell rang. Mrs. Humphreys shot Ang a reproving glare as she dismissed the students.

Her thoughts were stuck on Taryn's words concerning the mysterious man, Bushbeard, and the fact that he had given her the drugs that almost ended her life without taking any payment. Was he simply another drug dealer peddling his wares, hoping to get a new client, or did he give them the toxic drug on purpose? And was it by chance that *she* was the one who ingested the poisonous mushrooms or was it intended for her all along?

Chapter 13

A glance at the Rolex. Pocket check for the necessary items: rubber hose, spoon, lighter, hypodermic needle, tightly wrapped aluminum square. One more telepathic check to determine her location.

She's close. Only a few seconds now.

Rounding the corner, the woman's appearance was vastly different than the usual stiletto heels, power suit, and stiffened raven ringlets reaching down to her ass. Tonight, she was decked out in black tights, runners, and a sweatshirt with the hood pulled low over her head. Stealthily, she slipped into the alleyway where Tomas waited and approached him with purpose.

"Do you have it?" she demanded, shaking in anticipation.

He held out his hand expectantly. "That will be twenty."

"This'd better be the good stuff." She slapped a twenty-dollar bill into his palm, and then accepted her purchase like a child on Christmas morning.

"Go ahead," Tomas motioned with his head towards a hidden alcove decorated with plaid blanket and pillows. "I'll watch over you." The night was mild, the craving too strong to resist. She scurried to the makeshift bed, pulled up the sleeve on her hoodie and secured the rubber band to her upper arm.

"Might I recommend the inner thigh? Less conspicuous."

She nodded. Followed his advice.

Tomas had been watching Christine, an aspiring young real estate agent, for weeks now. A potential candidate to be a carrier. She could have been perfect—stunningly attractive, healthy, smart, and most importantly unattached with zero relatives or friends that gave enough of a shit to notice if she went missing. But, two days ago she had a craving. Heroin. Despite five years of sobriety, the urge flared up hot and irresistible. She would succumb.

No longer a potential candidate, Tomas now used her for a different purpose. He watched as she used the lighter to melt the heroin into liquid form, then filled the needle and shot it directly into her vein. Eyes rolled back in her head, and she slumped against the pillows. Sated.

He knew she would be coming, her thoughts told him so. The usual scoring ground. It didn't matter that he wasn't her usual supplier. She just needed a fix.

Now at his disposal, he summoned his telekinetic abilities, his glorious abilities unrivalled now that he was far from the castle and lifted her lifeless body into the air where it hovered on nothing. Her head fell backwards, the hood falling off, revealing her long tresses like a black waterfall. Long, lithe limbs stretched out to opposite sides. She really was beautiful. And destroying beauty was in his nature.

It started with the rage. Rage at his vile little shit of a brother, Anthony, always spying on them from the tunnels. Rage against his father for protecting Anthony, coddling him like a spoiled brat. Rage over his father demanding that every month Tomas venture out to gather a list of supplies for his detested sibling. Rubbing salt in the wound. One such list now burned a hole through his pocket. Demands for inane items like books, and candy bars, pop, toiletries, and clothing. Tomas—the only one able to obtain the items due to his ability to teleport out of the castle and not stand out as a monster in society. In disguise, at least. He still wore the thick beard he had on during the campsite party, the night he sold the tainted mushrooms to get rid of Veronica's sister, so she wouldn't come searching for her.

Anthony. What he wouldn't do to get rid of the bastard. But his hands were tied.

At least when he was away from the castle, his talents were at full strength. Unrestrained. As now.

The woman hung limply, the target for his fury. Molten lava boiled under his skin, cracking through both the toughened epidermis of his face and melting the latex layer of his disguise. Reaching out his arm, an orange rope of fire snaked out of his wrist and coiled around the unsuspecting woman's neck and limbs. Tomas felt the fire, part of his being, bite into her flesh, satisfying him as much as her heroin fix had moments before. A sharp tug and the fiery rope slipped through Christine's body as if it were butter. Six distinct segments now floated before him, and he tilted his head from side to side, admiring his handiwork.

Not so beautiful anymore, bitch.

Anger slowly dissipating, he pulled the fire back in. Releasing his telekinetic hold on the woman, he disappeared from the alleyway as if he were never there, the body fragments smacking wetly on the pavement.

★ ★ ★

The list fulfilled, Tomas reappeared half a kilometre away from the castle, then walked the remainder of the distance. Entering the building, he headed directly to Anthony's bedroom—a tiny reinforced hovel, practically a closet compared to the grand quarters in the rest of the castle. With a sharp bang on his door, it sprang open.

And there he stood. Perfect Anthony, who could do no wrong. Teeth clenched, Tomas entered the room uninvited, feeling his powers diminish immediately.

"Here's your shit." He tossed the bag onto the floor. There was a sharp cracking sound.

"Thanks," Anthony replied sarcastically as he stooped down to retrieve it.

Tomas couldn't resist Anthony's head so close to his boot. Kicking him square in the top of the head, he sent the teen flying backwards in a graceful arc until the back of his head bounced off the ground. Dazed, Anthony propped himself up on one elbow and mopped the blood off his brow with his free hand. The toe of the boot had cut deep. "You're not supposed to touch me!"

"You're not supposed to touch me," Tomas imitated Anthony with a baby tone. "Are you going to run and tell Daddy?" Then back to his normal deep baritone, "That's for watching us from the tunnels again, you perv. Trying to see the women, is that it? Well, you'll never have contact with them, so you can forget about your little boy fantasies."

"You're disgusting, you know. I would free every one of them if it were up to me."

"But, it's not. Now stick to your room, and if I catch you peeping on us from the tunnels one more time, next time I'll actually *try* to hurt you. Got it?"

Tomas left the room, powers a glimmer now, within distant touch, soft tendrils of smoke puffing through his skin. First the dismembered girl and now Anthony covered in blood. It had been a decent night after all.

Chapter 14

Ang had been here before—several times in fact—a place of acceptance, of support, a place that signified she was broken and falling apart. Dusky orange drapes hung over false windows, a brown faded area rug—a Walmart special—sat desolate on the floor, and pictures of the therapist's plump seven-year-old son were displayed on the desk. Framed social worker degrees and motivational posters decorated the walls with lame sayings. "One Person Can Make a Difference in the World," "Difficult Roads Often Lead to Beautiful Destinations" and "Think Positive Things and Positive Things Will Happen."

Sure.

The guidance counsellor's wide body was squished into a narrow seat across from Ang. "I'm glad you decided to come," Mrs. Small said.

Ang nodded, fiddling uncomfortably with the corded strings of her fuchsia hoodie.

Mrs. Small continued. "As usual, everything we discuss here in this room is confidential. The only time I would be forced to break this rule is if you indicated that you were suicidal, a threat to yourself or others, or if my notes were subpoenaed from court in the unlikely event that you were involved in a legal case. Are any of these reasons issue at this time?" She paused.

"I don't think so," Ang hesitantly replied. Technically she had broken the law, but since she wasn't charged with a crime, she hoped it wasn't an issue.

Mrs. Small raised one eyebrow, jotted on the paper before her, and continued. "It's been several months since we last met. How are things going?" She waited, pen poised above paper. There was the glimmer of a moustache on her upper lip.

Ang had started visiting with Mrs. Small on a weekly basis, first when her grandfather passed away a year ago, and then again when her grandmother's Alzheimer's was diagnosed and progressively worsened. Only when summer crept upon them did she terminate therapy with the plan to return once school commenced in the fall. She hadn't made it back until now.

"At home, or…" Ang felt herself getting hot and uncomfortable. Wished she could escape from the room.

Mrs. Small continued, encouraging, "At home, school, all facets of your life."

"Okay, I guess." Ang glanced at the clock. Another forty minutes to go. She was supposed to be conducting an experiment in Chemistry class this period, involving the use of cola to accelerate the rusting process of a nail. She wished she were there right now, although nobody would miss her.

Mrs. Small took an exasperated breath, leaning back in her chair until it creaked, threatening to break under her massive girth. "Ang, I know this process can be difficult. But it has helped you in the past."

Ang nodded, dispirited.

"It only works if you are willing to participate. If you are going to keep hedging my questions, we aren't going to get far. It's safe here for you to address your feelings. I won't judge, I never do. I'm only here to listen."

"I know."

The counsellor pulled upright in her chair again, which miraculously remained intact. "So, let's try this again, alright?"

Now that she had addressed Ang's resistance, she rephrased her question. "First, tell me how things are at home."

Ang forced herself to comply. "At home? Uh, well, my grandmother is able to function with mine and the neighbour's, Maria's, help. Her Alzheimer's is getting worse. More rapidly than before, but I guess that's inevitable," Ang expressed, glancing down at her fidgeting hands. She picked at a hangnail on her thumb.

"It must be hard to see your grandmother like that," Mrs. Small provoked. "Taking care of an ailing family member. That's a lot for a teenager to handle, on your own. Do you feel this is affecting you at school, or your social life?"

What social life? The water pressure built up behind her tear ducts, threatening to burst through.

"I can see that what I said has triggered you."

"It's pretty awful," Ang sobbed. Unable to hold back the tears, they spilled down her cheeks in rivulets. Mrs. Small slid a flowered box of tissues over to Ang and patiently waited for the deluge to subside. Once Ang was able to speak, although still sniffling with the odd double breath, Mrs. Small continued.

"Could you tell me about it?" Pen was poised and ready to take notes again. Even her tightly permed curls and sausage roll bangs seemed to be more erect and attentive than usual.

"Everybody hates me!" Ang blurted, followed by another stuttering breath.

"Everybody?"

"Well, almost everybody. Anybody who was at the camping party last weekend, anyways. I might have gotten them into trouble. Not on purpose, of course. But, I..." Ang paused. "I don't know if you heard, but I almost overdosed on magic mushrooms." She assumed the social worker knew some details, hence approaching her in the hallway the previous day and their subsequent therapy session. But she had to ask.

Mrs. Small gave a slight nod of her head. "Go on," she persuaded.

"Well, some underage kids were there drinking and since the cops were contacted because of my little episode, they got busted. Now everyone hates me. Worst of all, Taryn and I can't be friends anymore. Her mother has forbidden it."

Mrs. Small let this information sink in as Ang experienced another overwhelming flood of emotion. Two full minutes passed before she calmed once more, dabbing her eyes and nose, and then balling the sodden tissue in her fist.

Ang expected Mrs. Small to be disappointed in her, but the expression was one of compassion and understanding. Maternal.

"Did you plan to overdose?" She paused.

"Obviously not."

Then, "Did you purposely create a scene to have the police called to the party in hopes your peers would be "busted" as you say?"

Ang shook her head in the negative, audibly sniffling, and swiped her eyelids with the back of her hand, the tissue too saturated to be of any use.

"It sounds to me like you made a few bad choices, but you had no intention of hurting yourself or anyone else, for that matter. Let the other students take responsibility for their own actions, and you focus on the actions for which you are responsible."

Ang shrugged her shoulders, dejected. "It doesn't change what they think of me. They still blame me, whether I think they should or not."

"That might be true. It's easier to blame others than to take responsibility for our own bad choices. It's human nature. But, if it's any consolation, these kinds of events tend to blow over. Soon, there will be somebody else at the centre of the gossip, some other catastrophe, and your situation will be all but forgotten."

"I wish that was already the case."

"Let's focus on you and the things you do have control over in your life, things you can change. Like letting go of what other people think. Would that be okay with you?"

Ang nodded in agreement. At least she would try.

"Tell me more about the camping trip. Why did you take the mushrooms in the first place?" Mrs. Small queried.

Ang hesitated, unsure where to begin or how much to divulge, but then the counsellor's words popped back into her mind. This process wouldn't work if she held back. Finally, she decided she would spill the whole story concerning Josh and how her wretched nerves prevented her from forming any meaningful relationships. Here she was, seventeen-years-old, and she had never had a real boyfriend.

The portly woman nodded, listening, occasionally jotting down the words Ang spoke, along with her own insights.

Ang persisted with her story, describing in detail all the side effects she suffered from taking the magic mushrooms, and most of her near-death experience. But when she came to the part concerning the apparition—the vision of her guardian angel and his permanent presence ever since—she hesitated. Her mind vacillated between what she knew she probably should do and what she wanted to do. What if she told Mrs. Small the truth, only then to be labelled as crazy and have more reasons for the students to gossip and judge? And what if telling Mrs. Small about Gavin made him disappear—whether from using the medication they would force her to take or through the mere acknowledgement and confession of his existence? Was she ready to lose him? She glanced over at Gavin, leaning against the wall behind the counsellor, hot as ever in a plaid fleece button down over a grey T-shirt and dark denim jeans. She had to applaud her imagination on its great fashion sense. Although she didn't experience any sexual attraction towards the angel, she appreciated his stark beauty, and more importantly, craved his company.

But on the other hand, maybe she needed to tell someone. If she let this craziness go on any further, could she ever come back? Live a normal life again? Or would she be stuck in her delusional state, keeping company with imaginary friends for the rest of her life? This last thought finally swayed her decision.

"There's one more thing…"

The bell shrilled, cutting Ang off midsentence. The fourth and last period of the day was announced, the sound peeling through the small room, causing Ang to jump in her seat. Their counselling session was brought to an abrupt end. Now was not the time to disclose her secret.

"Hold that thought, Angelika. We'll continue this topic the next time I see you. I think it would be beneficial to meet with me daily. Work on releasing this guilt you are holding on to and relieve some of the excessive weight and responsibility of the world weighing heavily on your shoulders. Maybe work on forgiving yourself for your mistakes? You are only human, you know. We all make mistakes." Ang nodded, unconvinced.

"But that was a great session. I think we've made some headway. Now, for your homework. Do you remember the relaxation exercises we were practicing before the summer?"

Mrs. Small had been teaching Ang how to use guided imagery to relax. She had practiced this relaxation technique many times and did find it helpful.

Promising Mrs. Small that she would do her imagery homework daily, and come for another session the following afternoon, Ang rushed off to her Biology class with Gavin trailing on her heels, already a few minutes tardy.

★ ★ ★

After meeting with Mrs. Small daily throughout the remainder of the school week, things were finally looking up for Ang. With her attitude, at least. She was still the social pariah of the school, forced to stay away from Taryn, and care for her ailing grandmother, watching her deteriorate at lightning speed, but now at least she was learning how to cope with these variables.

Gavin—well, that was an area she hadn't dealt with yet. In the end, she had abstained from mentioning his existence to Mrs. Small, holding on to the thought of him like a child who refuses to let go of its baby blanket. But, the rest of her problems were becoming more bearable. Something Mrs. Small had said during one of their sessions sunk in deeply and took hold in Ang's mind. The real key to her breakthrough. "To live in the past, reliving your mistakes in your mind is futile—you can't change what has happened. To focus too much on the future, always worrying what *might* happen is also futile—you have no way to predict the future, so worrying unnecessarily about what might or might not happen is also a waste of your emotional energy. The present, however, is within your control." Basically, she could change her perspective on what happened in the past by forgiving herself for overdosing, making a total fool of herself, scaring off Josh, and losing Taryn's companionship. And, she could focus on making herself healthy, happy, secure and confident in the "now." So, after Ang finally released the guilt and self-hatred she had been holding on to since the camping trip, and fully forgave herself, she was finally able to move forward.

And what better way to do that than to have a celebration.

Thanksgiving weekend had arrived. She had many things to be thankful for, things she had been taking for granted being caught up in her own affairs. After careful consideration, she decided she would treat Babka, Maria, Gavin, and herself to a fabulous turkey feast.

It didn't matter that she was, perhaps, the world's worst chef since cooking was one of the things she enjoyed, finding it tremendously therapeutic. It started when she was younger, watching her grandmother. Babka was a culinary artist, and Ang would observe her preparing everything from scratch—pasta dishes, perogies, homemade breads, soups, jams and jellies made from fruit out of their own garden in the backyard. Her grandmother was truly talented with a God-given gift, and although Ang hadn't inherited her talent in the kitchen, she did inherit her desire and passion to cook.

Digging into the inheritance left behind by her grandfather, she purchased groceries for the feast. She was thankful for the sizeable inheritance—nothing like Trump money, but enough for them to get by—since it allowed Ang to focus on caring for Babka and going to school, instead of working ten jobs to make ends meet. If she could keep Ronnie in check, the money would last them a while.

Gavin was her sidekick as usual. She had grown so attached to him, her best friend these days. They talked about everything, and he seemed as interested in how life was to be human as Ang was intrigued by the life of an angel.

The kitchen was currently a disaster: pots, pans, flour and egg whites covering every surface. Babka sat in her wheelchair, tucked behind the kitchen table, watching Ang as she creamed the corn, basted the turkey, and mashed the potatoes (twice because the first batch got scorched). The biscuits were in the oven, infusing the kitchen with the aroma of home baked goodness. She might have gotten at least one thing right.

"An…gel," Babka spoke. Ang rushed over to her grandmother and grabbed her arms. She was having a lucid moment, very rare these days.

Gavin's eyes grew wide. "Can she…?"

Ang cut him off. "No, she can't see you, at least I don't think she can. That's the nickname she likes to call me."

"Hi, Babka. Happy Thanksgiving. I'm cooking all of your favourites."

Babka smiled, nodded and raised her hand giving a partial thumbs up of approval.

"Maria will be here soon." She kissed her grandmother's head and returned to the oven.

After mixing a boiling pot of carrots, she checked on the buns, so they wouldn't overcook.

"Angel, eh?" Gavin smirked. "I'm going to have to call you that from now on."

"Please don't."

"Aw, come on, Angel. It's pretty fitting, don't you think? Given the circumstances?"

Ang ignored him, popping the cork on a bottle of red wine that she had grabbed from Babka's wine cellar in the basement...a cabernet sauvignon infused with the sweet flavours of cherry and currants. Being European, their grandparents had always allowed a smidge of wine with their meals despite her and her sister being underage. Reminded of the camping trip and how things could get out of hand, Ang now knew deep down inside she would never lose control like that again. Never again drink to cope with her anxiety. Today, it was merely included for the ambience, though Maria was the only other guest at the party who would be able to drink. And she did like to drink.

Cutting a few pats of butter into the apple crumble, she was interrupted by the phone ringing. Wiping her crumb-filled fingers on a damp dish towel, she picked up the receiver.

"Hello?"

"Hello, may I speak with Angelika Juris, please?" a man inquired in a professional tone.

"Yes, this is she," Ang replied.

"This is Sheldon Walters calling from Red Deer College. I'm calling to inquire about your sister, Veronica. She has been absent from her classes for several weeks and we are wondering if she has dropped out or if she is ill. We have you listed as her primary emergency contact. We have tried, unsuccessfully, to contact Veronica directly."

Ang's heart skipped a beat.

"No, I'm sorry but I haven't heard from her in a while. I'm not sure where she is." Biting her lip, she almost drew blood.

"Okay. Well, if you do speak with her, have her contact us immediately. We would hate for her to have to forfeit the term, and risk going on academic probation."

"Thank you, sir. I will tell her."

The man left his number, and Ang hung up the phone.

That was weird. Where could she be? The last they spoke was four weeks ago when she called demanding money. Ang hadn't thought to contact Ronnie and tell her what happened with the camping accident, the overdose where she had almost died. She would have judged her and made her feel worse. She did like to kick Ang while she was down.

They were never close. Ever since Ang was born, Ronnie had viewed her as competition. She wanted all her grandparents' attention, and when Ang came along, they had to divide their love and affection between both girls. Ronnie wasn't okay with that. She fought with Ang on a regular basis, put her down every chance she got, and the second things got tough at home and her grandmother fell ill, she left home without a backward glance.

But she was still Ang's sister, and they loved each other in their own way. And she was getting worried. Why would Ronnie miss so much school? Several weeks, apparently. Her only goal was to go to college and jumpstart her career as an actress. What could have pulled her away?

Ang called Ronnie's number and immediately got her voicemail.

"Hi, you've reached Ronnie. I'm not able to take your call right now. Please leave me a message after the tone. Thanks."

After the personal message concluded, her sister's familiar voice was replaced by an automated one.

"The mailbox is full and cannot accept any messages at this time. Goodbye."

Ang's heart hammered in her chest.

A social butterfly, Ronnie would check her messages regularly. Ang's stomach clenched.

The doorbell chimed, announcing Maria's arrival.

"Hi, Maria," Ang opened the door, hiding her apprehension. "Let me take those." She balanced the plate of homemade chocolate chip cookies Maria had brought, allowing the neighbour to enter, and then headed into the kitchen.

Maria hung her coat in the hall closet, gave Ang and Babka a quick hug, and seated herself at the kitchen table.

"It smells sumptuous in here. You must have been cooking all day. I told you I could have helped."

"This is my treat. Today is about giving thanks for all the blessings in our lives, and Maria, you are one of the biggest blessings in mine. I wouldn't be able to care for Babka at home if it weren't for you."

Maria beamed. "And I'm thankful for the two of you. Without Reginald, it's lonely over there in that old house. Just me and Frisky." Frisky was Maria's obese tabby cat. The thing was vile, hissing at everything that passed by, but Maria seemed to love her.

"What's up? You seem worried?" Maria asked noticing Ang's glumness while she poured herself a glass of red wine.

Ang shook her head. "It's probably nothing."

"What is it, Sweetie?"

"A few minutes ago, I got a call from Red Deer College. Ronnie hasn't been to her classes in several weeks."

Maria's countenance darkened. "Where is she?"

"That's just it. I have no idea—her voice mail is full. The school has been trying unsuccessfully to reach her for weeks…"

The neighbour was pensive for a moment. "She has done things like this before though, right?"

Maria never knew Ronnie well; she was basing her thoughts on stories Ang had told her in the past. But she was right. It wasn't unheard of for Ronnie to pick up and disappear. Follow her latest whim. Act spontaneously without informing anyone of her intentions. Babka used to worry herself sick during these times.

But still...

"Well, let's not waste this great feast that you prepared. I'm sure she'll contact you eventually. In the meantime, you can check in with her friends here and see if they've had any contact. Put your mind at ease."

"That's a great idea. I'm sure her friends will have some information. And like you said, she's probably fine, just off on one of her tangents."

Ang hoisted the turkey out of the oven, and carved the steaming meat into thin slices, fanning them across a glass serving dish. Maria helped by placing the warm, buttery biscuits into a bowl, and bringing all the side dishes to the kitchen table.

After the table was teeming with seasonal fare, Ang prepared a plate for Babka, cutting her food into tiny bite-sized pieces as if she were a toddler.

"Here, let me do that," Maria insisted, taking over and proceeding to feed Ang's grandmother while alternately shoving forkfuls of food into her own mouth.

"Ang, this is delicious!"

"Thanks," Ang replied, unsure of whether Maria's accolades were genuine or an attempt to protect her ego. She was having trouble choking down the food herself, Ronnie still on her mind, worry gnawing at her gut.

Halfway through the meal, she had to excuse herself from the table. Her stomach had started spasming and she felt like she might puke. Shooting Gavin a knowing look, she invited him to follow her into the bathroom. Gavin obliged. Once locked inside the confines of the small bathroom scented with peach air freshener, she turned to Gavin, desperation in her eyes.

"What should I do? Do you think my sister is in danger?"

Gavin appeared uncertain. Shrugged his shoulders.

"I have a bad feeling." Ang closed the toilet and sat atop the plastic lid, arms hugging her sides. She rocked back and forth until a thought popped into her mind.

"I know this is a long stretch, and I'm still not sure if you're real, but is there any way you can see where she is, check on her, you know…with your angelic powers?" Ang implored.

"I am real, by the way." His sparkling, azure eyes dimmed. "There was a way. Like I said before, I used to be able to sense and contact the other guardians through a mental link. I would have been able to contact Veronica's guardian and see where she is located, but the connection is blocked for me ever since I switched your crystal. I can't feel where the other guardians are anymore."

Ang could tell this distressed Gavin deeply. His eyes were troubled, perfect brows pinched together.

Ang's stomach issues were forgotten for the moment, her mind searching for an answer to her predicament. What could she do? That nagging feeling that something was wrong persisted. It was the unanswered messages that caused Ang's mind to jump to the worst conclusion, her imagination running rampant with horrible situations her sister could be in.

Finally, Ang reached the only option she could think of. She had never flown in a plane before, never left Babka for any great length of time, but her gut was telling her that her sister was in trouble.

"That's it. I have to go there. I have to go to Red Deer, Alberta and find out what happened to Ronnie for myself. I'm the only one she can rely on, and Babka would expect me to check up on her. I just hope I'm not wasting my time. Or getting sucked into something that I'll regret."

And knowing Ronnie, that was a distinct possibility.

Chapter 15

Hot, orange steam consumed the left airplane wing as the ground crew operator, suspended from a scissor-lift, guided the distribution of the de-icing chemical. The fluorescent yellow of his vest was barely visible behind the heavy cloud of mist. The tarmac was speckled with other yellow-vested crew members, working diligently to prepare the plane and runway for a safe departure.

Ang nervously watched from her window aboard the Westjet plane to Calgary, Alberta—the closest flight to Red Deer she could find—already nauseous from inhaling the recycled air and noxious lavender-scented perfume from the elderly female passenger on her right.

They had been stuck on the runway for two hours now, parked between the main terminal and the runway, still in the Thunder Bay Airport. Freezing rain. All the morning flights were backed up. As of five minutes ago, the pilot announced they were fifth in line for take-off.

The wait was torture.

"Is this your first flight, dear?" the elderly neighbour asked.

"Is it that obvious?"

The old woman gazed at Ang's fingers white knuckling the armrest.

"It'll be okay. It's quite fun once we get into the air. My name is Ethel, by the way."

"I'm Ang."

"Where are you headed, dear?"

"Red Deer, Alberta. To visit my sister." There was no need to fill her in on the sordid details.

"I'm going to Calgary, myself. New grandchild to meet. Twelfth one," Ethel smiled, her wrinkled face crimped like a half-deflated balloon. She reminded Ang of her grandmother, which offered a speck of comfort.

Until she remembered that 9/11 was only one year ago. Hyperalert for any signs of things being "off," she scoured the plane's passengers. Seeing a nun and a handful of smaller children on the flight should have put her mind at ease. Surely God wouldn't allow anything to happen with a nun and children on the flight. But of course, that was erroneous thinking. Life wasn't like that. As if to accentuate that point, her vision landed on a suspicious male, fidgeting uncomfortably in his seat. Eyes flouncing around like he was worried about getting caught. Ang's muscles bunched, her neighbour's constant chatter now falling on deaf ears, only able to concentrate on the suspicious man. A potential terrorist. But, before she could blow the scene completely out of proportion, the man's seatmate sat forward, and Ang could see that it was an attractive female who then bent over and nuzzled her forehead into his neck. The man relaxed and smiled, now seeming totally kind and friendly. Here, Ang was thinking he was some sort of psycho; meanwhile, she was the one who was crazy. Paranoid, delusional, and hallucinating. *Crazy, indeed.*

Even this impromptu trip was crazy. Flying off to who knows where to find a sister who hated her guts. But the feeling that something was wrong continued to persist, perhaps strengthening.

The previous night, Ang had a disturbing dream. In it, she was going through her regular morning routine with Babka when she decided to flick on the television. It was the same scenario she had experienced in real life the day Taryn had dropped by to announce the camping trip. Except, as the television flared to life and the reporter began her spiel regarding the rash of missing women, the monitor displayed a picture of Ronnie. Ang had awoken with a start.

It was the first time she had considered the missing women who were thought to have been the victims of a serial killer.

What if Ronnie was one of these mysteriously vanished women? Could she be in grave danger? Perhaps, already dead?

Ang shuddered. Why hadn't she kept in closer touch with her sister? Then, maybe she would have a clue as to her whereabouts. She didn't have any leads at this point. Contacting all her old friends in Thunder Bay, each one reported the same dreadful news…they hadn't heard from her in weeks.

Did Ronnie have a boyfriend? Any girlfriends? A job? Did she have any enemies? That girl could quickly get under peoples' skin; Ang knew that from her own experiences.

Or was this merely another of Ronnie's selfish dramatic moments, where she threw everybody into a tailspin simply to get attention?

The dream stuck with her, the missing women flitting in and out of her thoughts, the fear worming its way deeper, infesting her with morbid images. She hadn't paid much attention to the news report on the television, but luckily the internet supplied her with more details. Unable to go back to sleep, she poured over the information from each case, discovering that women had been disappearing since the eighties, but the rate of incidence had escalated dramatically over the past few years. Investigators claimed that the disappearances were all highly suspicious; there weren't any immediate relatives or family close to the victims or if by chance there were, they had recently perished or disappeared. For some reason, this made Ang think of Bushbeard. Was he purposefully trying to get rid of her in order to kidnap Veronica without anyone left to go searching for her? Was he the serial killer?

Don't be absurd. What were the chances of that?

She kept digging. It seemed that the women missing were spread throughout Canada and the U.S., and the age range of females was between 18 and 25-years-old. Veronica fit exactly into this group of statistics. The police stated that the serial killer angle was only a hunch at this point—there was no evidence, no bodies, and no leads. The women simply vanished, never to be seen again.

Ang noticed Gavin was watching her, probably aware of her internal emotional struggle. All the seats were occupied on the flight, so he hovered in the aisles, suspended on nothing but Ang's imagination. His blue eyes shone from within, an aura of shimmering mist surrounding his form.

"Hey, Gavin." Ang communicated with him telepathically. Her original hypothesis that Gavin was a hallucination persisted. He was her imaginary friend, which she discovered weren't that uncommon. Again, thanks to Google, she discovered that having imaginary friends could be a coping mechanism for getting over traumatic experiences. Sure, it usually happened to children rather than teenagers, but she wasn't going to overanalyze it.

"Yes, Angel."

"I told you not to call me that."

"Okay, Angel."

"You're so annoying. I'm trying to be serious here. Do you think I'm doing the right thing?"

"It's a little late to be questioning that now, don't you think?" Gavin smirked.

"Why didn't you tell me it was a bad idea? Babka was stuck at the hospice while I was recovering from my overdose, and now I'm ditching her again to go on some wild goose chase to find a sister who doesn't give a rat's ass about me. She probably hooked up with some guy or got a role in some show, not bothering to notify me or the school because she's so self-absorbed and irresponsible. And now I probably shaved ten years off my life worrying about her selfish ass." Ang paused in her mental diatribe and took a deep breath.

"Hey, don't get so worked up. You're going to hyperventilate."
Ang shot him a scathing look.

"Hey, I actually think it's a great idea to go and see in person
what's happening in Red Deer. Ronnie may need you, whether
you like it or not."

"I guess I'm sick of everybody needing me for support, but
when I need it…" She paused, getting choked up.

"Thanks for inviting me to your pity party, but it's definitely
not going to help you find your sister."

"I know. You suck, you know that? If you're a figment of my
imagination, you should at least have my back. I guess I'll shut
up now."

Gavin seemed content with that.

Finally, the plane started taxiing down the runway, heading
towards its final take-off path. Ang's eyes widened, and her
stomach bucked. Ethel placed a comforting hand, pitted and worn
like a walnut shell, on her leg. Ang tried to smile at the old woman,
but it came out more like a grimace.

There was no going back now. She didn't know what awaited
her in Red Deer, but she sure hoped it was worth all this effort.

And mainly, that Ronnie was there, safe and sound.

★ ★ ★

The moment Ang saw the outside of Veronica's apartment, her
face blanched. The mailbox overflowing. Rolled-up newspapers
and flyers strewn across the lawn and stuck in the gooseberry
hedge that bordered the property. A small cart of books tipped
over on its side at the apartment entrance, literature damaged
from the rain and sun of several days. Ronnie's car in its parking
spot. The entire scene gave Ang a feeling of dread in the pit of
her stomach. She feared what awaited her inside. An image of her
sister's decaying body floated into her conscience.

Shaking the gruesome image away, she attempted to be optimistic, gathering enough courage to join Gavin, who already waited at Ronnie's front door. Taking a deep breath before knocking, she instinctively knew full well that nobody was going to answer—but, it was the socially acceptable thing to do.

"If she doesn't answer, then we'll call the police," Ang told Gavin, her nerves spiking into panic mode again. Gavin nodded. "What if she doesn't answer, and it's unlocked?"

"Then we'll go in first, and if anything is amiss and if your sister isn't here, or...well...then we'll call the police," Gavin suggested.

"That's what's worrying me the most. What if she *is* here and can't answer the door because she is..."

"Let's not jump to any conclusions yet. Go ahead, knock."

Holding her breath, she knocked and waited. One minute, two...

"How long do you think I should wait?"

"I think that's long enough. If she were here, she would have answered by now. Try the handle."

Ang turned the handle and met with resistance. It was locked. For some reason, she hadn't expected this. In the detective movies when somebody went missing under suspicious circumstances, the door to their place was always left open. However, it was official...she would call the police. Digging through the corduroy messenger-style purse slung across her right hip, she retrieved her Blackberry and dialled 911.

The phone rang painfully slow. "I don't feel good about this. Ronnie, what did you get yourself into?"

★ ★ ★

The police arrived an agonizing forty minutes later, Ang's fingers and fear already numb from the long wait in the cold. A hulking, male police officer with dark skin, shaved head, and sculpted goatee unfurled his body from the cop car and approached her. His partner, blond and slight in comparison, sidled up next to them.

"Were you the one that called the police?" the dark-skinned officer asked in a stern voice. This was someone you wouldn't want to mess with, and she was glad he was on their side.

Ang nodded. "My sister, Veronica, moved here from Thunder Bay at the end of August to attend Red Deer College. The College contacted us two days ago, saying that she hasn't been to class in weeks. When I tried calling her, there was no answer. Her voice mail was full, and after calling all her old friends back home, I discovered that she hasn't talked to any of them in a while. That's her car over there. By the looks of her yard, I'm worried that she's in trouble."

Face expressionless, the officer flipped open a notebook and uncapped his pen. He took down Veronica's basic information and then focused his questions on her disappearance.

"Does she have a history of mental illness?"

Not unless arrogance is a mental disorder. "No, I don't think so."

"Do you know if she was suicidal?"

"No," Ang replied again, knowing Ronnie loved herself way too much for that.

"Was she taking any medications or using any drugs or alcohol?"

"Not that I know of."

"When was the last time you spoke with Veronica?" the policeman waited expectantly.

Ang flushed with shame. They hadn't spoken since the day Ronnie called demanding more money, a heated conversation. The money was never deposited into her account. What if that had something to do with her disappearance? Maybe Ronnie owed an unsavoury character money and now she was punished—or worse—all because Ang had withheld the funds. She couldn't feel guiltier. Like she was the worst sister in the whole wide world.

"Around four weeks ago."

"Have you touched or moved anything since you got here?" His brown eyes flicked over to the overturned cart of books; the flyers scattered around the lawn.

"We, I mean I, tried the door to see if it was locked. Otherwise, I didn't touch a thing." Ang hoped he didn't notice her slip, forgetting she was the only one privy to Gavin's existence. He either didn't notice or thought it inconsequential.

The two officers proceeded to check the front door, confirming it was locked. Ringing the doorbell and receiving no answer, they turned back to Ang. "We're going to interview the other tenants to determine if they know or heard anything, and to see if we can procure a key to your sister's apartment from the landlord."

Ang shuffled her feet in the leaf-covered lawn, pacing back and forth as the policemen conducted their interviews. How could this be happening? Where could Ronnie be? Her former theory of Ronnie simply being self-centered and off on a grand adventure seemed trivial now given the appearance of her yard and apartment entrance. The guilt and fear pushed at her mind, elevating her to the onset of a panic attack. But it would have to wait. The policemen had returned.

"The landlord is unavailable, so we are unable to get a key at this time."

"Did the neighbours have any information as to my sister's whereabouts?"

"Two separate witnesses reported that several weeks ago they overheard a commotion coming from Ronnie's apartment, but no one saw anything out of the ordinary, and assumed it was a private domestic dispute. Since nobody witnessed anything visually, they couldn't contribute any clues as to her whereabouts or who she was arguing with, although they helped in pinpointing the possible time of her disappearance."

The blond cop spoke this time. "We contacted our supervisor to see if we can breach the premises. The window is partially open...he has permitted us to enter through there."

"Do you think this has anything to do with all of the other women that have gone missing lately?"

"It's too early to say that yet."

YET? That didn't give Ang much reassurance.

"You can wait here while we canvass the area," the constable instructed Ang.

She sat on the curb as the policemen crawled in through Veronica's apartment window and within moments were inside, guns drawn. After securing the area, ensuring there weren't any threats present, they contacted the ident team to come and take photographs, all the while Ang assuming the worst. Once the ident team evacuated the premises and deemed the area clear, no longer worried that the scene and evidence would be contaminated by others, they allowed Ang to enter.

Her sister's apartment was in shambles.

An obvious struggle took place right at the entrance: holes punched through the drywall, floral painting hanging askew, antique table tipped over and cracked, a vase shattered on the floor. Ang's heart flopped and bile squirted up the back of her throat. A red stain on the rug and on a dish towel on the kitchen counter drew her immediate attention, but the officers quickly explained that it was merely juice. At least it wasn't blood.

The constables approached Ang, drawing her off to the side. Faces grave. "From a cursory glance of the evidence, we've determined that Veronica indeed hasn't been here in weeks. The date from the messages, the date on the flyers, and the testimonies from the neighbours all support the estimated time of her disappearance. It also seems probable that she has been abducted against her will, that foul play might be involved but not due to robbery. Her purse, wallet and other valuables are still here." The hulking officer removed his rubber gloves and tossed them into a garbage bag propped open on the floor. "Do you have a recent photo of Veronica?"

Ang dug in her wallet and withdrew a photo of Ronnie, handing it to the constable. It was a professional headshot Ronnie had taken for her portfolio, to send out to agents for modelling and acting gigs. Ang noticed the same photo had been affixed to Ronnie's fridge by a happy face magnet. No other personal pictures decorated her space—no pictures of Ang or Babka or Dedko. It stung a little but was typical of Ronnie. The only picture she had on display was her own.

"Thank you. This will be helpful for the investigating team to have on hand, in case she should show up." Ang shivered. The image of Ronnie "showing up" as deceased flared into her thoughts. "You may want to give the same photo to the media... set up a press release. Might help in locating her or at least in getting more information from the public. This is officially a missing person's case."

It was exactly as Ang had feared. The news report she had watched weeks ago was now going to star her sister as the lead.

"I'm Constable Ritchie." He handed Ang his business card. "If Veronica shows up, or if you have any new information that can help locate your sister, give me a call. An investigator will want to follow up with you, so make sure you keep your phone on you. I'll take your cell number now."

Ang rattled off the numbers of her cell phone, thankful she had brought her charger.

"Thank you, Officer Ritchie."

"Do you have a place to stay?"

"Yeah, I was planning on renting a room at the Sheraton."

"I see you rented a vehicle?"

"Yes, at the Calgary Airport. Is it okay if I wait here a little while, in case she shows up?"

"Sure." His face was discouraging. Both officers climbed back into their police vehicle and sped away.

Ang sat on the curb outside her sister's apartment, watching the sun already descending, the final rays of the day shining directly into her eyes, blinding. The sky was marbled pink and white, quickly darkening into purple shadows.

Shock. That's what she felt. And helpless. Burying her face in her hands, she sobbed.

"This can't be happening. Ronnie, where are you?"

"Angel," Gavin whispered.

Too distraught to argue over the name, she merely peeked at Gavin and after seeing his intense gaze, immediately ceased crying.

"What?" She waited expectantly.

"The cop gave me an idea. Do you remember how I said I caught the angel in the crystal room messing around with the crystals? What if he had originally switched your crystal with one of less light to get rid of you, so you wouldn't go searching for your sister? Seems farfetched, I know. How could the angels be involved in any of this, but…?"

"Go on," Ang encouraged with furrowed brows.

"I know I told you that my connection to the other angels was severed, but after being in your sister's apartment, I sense an aura…it's faint, but akin to what I felt when around the other angels. I don't want to give you false hope, but it's a lead, at least." Gavin's sparkling baby blues were hopeful. But there was more there, something masked. Was he also afraid? Was he hiding more information from her?

"Can you tell if my sister is okay?"

"No, I can't be certain. But I feel like we should head into the mountains." He pointed into the distance, a seemingly random direction. Ang's hallucination was taking charge, and feeling utterly helpless and useless herself, she let him.

The impressive Canadian Rocky Mountains peeked through a scattered layer of clouds on the horizon like a scene etched in glass. It would take hours to drive there, so they would have to postpone any plans until the following morning. The police had Ang's phone number if anything else was discovered, so instead of sitting around waiting, useless and unproductive, it was worth driving to the mountains to follow Gavin's hunch. No matter how slim it was. But first, they would have to rent a hotel room for the night and get some rest.

Gavin and Ang piled into the rental car, a silver Honda. Grabbing a map out of the glove compartment, she asked Gavin where he thought Ronnie could be.

"That's approximately it," he pointed at the mountains directly over the words Banff National Park. "That's where we need to look."

Ang circled the spot with her pen. "Gavin, I hope you're right. I hope tomorrow we find Ronnie. Maybe she's vacationing in Banff and forgot to tell anyone. She's okay, right?"

"Sure," Gavin replied unconvincingly. And again, Ang sensed that Gavin was holding back from her.

"You would tell me if something was wrong, right? If you knew anything else? You wouldn't hold back on me?"

"Of course not," Gavin replied. But, in that moment, Ang felt that it was a distinct possibility, if Gavin was indeed an angel, that angels could lie.

Chapter 16

Gavin sat rigid on the hotel sofa watching Angel toss and turn in the hotel's king-size bed, sheets a twisted mess around her limbs. Most likely she wouldn't sleep a wink tonight. But she needed to at least try, for the following day would require plenty of energy, clarity of mind and strength. He knew this, not that he could predict the future, for only God knew what would happen ahead of time, but because of what he had sensed at Ronnie's apartment as being more complicated than he had expressed to Angel. Currently, he was contemplating how much he should tell her. Worry was already her primary emotion: worrying about her missing sister, worrying about her grandmother back in hospice, and worrying about everything in between. Did he really want to add to her stress?

But could it help prepare her? And for what? He wasn't exactly sure himself yet.

Rising from the fern-coloured sofa, he wandered over to the window, peering outside through thick, dusty drapery.

Despite the sparsely clouded skies only hours before, it had rained. Under the streetlights, the road glistened like thousands of diamonds had been sprinkled over the asphalt. Traffic had thinned out to almost nothing. It was still and peaceful. Like the calm before a storm.

It was during moments like these, where the humans were sleeping, at ease, or at peace, that Gavin felt intense warmth, love, and compassion for these complicated creatures. He truly loved humans, including all their flaws. He loved his job, protecting God's most cherished creation. However, his present case was proving more challenging than any he had enjoyed in the past.

Most challenging was that he felt so alone, disconnected from his colleagues and peers—the other angels. No guidance. No support. No feedback. For the first time, he was unsure of himself and how he was supposed to protect this helpless creature for which he alone was now responsible.

Turning away from the window, his gaze settled back on Angel, folded amidst the cream-coloured sheets and plush, brown bedspread. She finally lay still. Perhaps sleep had found her after all. Drifting over to her bedside, he gently caressed the side of her face, squeezed her shoulder in comfort. Unable to feel this touch of love and protection in a physical sense, her lips still curled up slightly at the edges, a smile in her dreams.

Gavin wished he could have been her guardian since birth. Able to witness her first words, first steps, starting kindergarten and progressing through the grades until she reached her present age, growing up to be the fine, young woman she was today. He felt like he had missed out on so much. More disturbing was the concern of what would happen in the future. Would he be able to stay as Angel's guardian? To be able to continue to watch her grow and mature, maybe one day get married and have kids of her own? With the unconventionality of the situation, he didn't know what to expect. Was it possible that one day he would be dismissed from her case as quickly as he was assigned to it? Shuffled off to protect someone else? He would be thoroughly crushed. He felt so much more attached to her, protective of her, than any of his previous cases. And why shouldn't he? This was the first person he had been able to have contact with, communicate with...engage in an actual relationship with.

And what a discovery that had been. It was amazing to be seen and heard...yet he was still troubled by what that meant for him and his position at the Crystal Foundation. Would they ever let him return?

"When you accept the assignment, we command that you conduct it to the best of your abilities while abstaining from asking any questions of its unconventional nature, and speak of this with no one," Matthew, his boss, had strictly demanded of him. Despite that warning, Gavin had gone against his superior's commands by trying to find out the nature of the case, and by telling Angel about his discovery in the crystal room.

And more treasonous was that he switched Ang's crystal, changing her destiny, and inadvertently messed with her free will. He had violated one of the most important cardinal laws of nature. While his intentions were virtuous, he wasn't sure if he would ever be allowed back into God's good graces.

He thought of the other angels, the ones who had rebelled against God's law, his word, how they were cast out of heaven. Lucifer, one of God's most beautiful, powerful angels, had become jealous of God's position and coveted His throne—he wanted to become ruler of the heavenly realm and all the realms in between. Actually succeeding in rallying a third of God's angels to rebel against Him, they fought for Lucifer's cause...and failed. Instead of ruling heaven, they had been banished. Forced to rule in the shadows of Earth.

Could Gavin's misbehaviour be equivalent to that of Lucifer? Was this how it felt to be banished?

Angel stirred in her sleep, bringing Gavin back to his present dilemma. He had risked so much for this precious human, had made many of these risks even before they had met. He didn't know what it was about this woman—there was more to her. To this case. Much more than the file that Matthew had handed him contained. Feeling so drawn to her, he never wanted to let her go.

However, the following morning they would be heading up into the Rocky Mountains. His job was to protect her, but he would be taking her towards danger, possibly life-threatening, he could feel it in his gut.

The essence he had sensed at Veronica's apartment pulled at him, lured him. He had told Angel that the feeling was akin to that of the angels' connection he had felt in heaven. That part was true. What he hadn't told her was that it was the essence of those that had fallen, the angel's cast down to Earth.

Demons.

The stench of pure evil defiled every nook and cranny of Ronnie's residence. It created a path, the foul scent guiding Gavin's hunch as to where Veronica had been taken—up into the Rocky Mountains.

If he tried to warn Angel, keep her away from the iniquity that awaited them, he feared Veronica, if she hadn't already, would surely succumb to the demons' powers and die. Ang would never forgive him. Veronica was the only relative besides her grandmother that she had left. He couldn't include her estranged parents since they had no contact with their daughter. No, she would insist on doing whatever she could to find her sister, and Gavin had to respect this.

Finally, his instinct to protect Angel was overridden by his duty to help her find her sister. For now, he would keep his concerns to himself of what he believed lurked in the mountains. He planned to tell her—he *had* to—but only when the time felt right.

PART II

Interlude

Darkness.
Oppressive inky veil of black,
Suffocating those it covers.
Seeping into each orifice.
Confining, smothering, drowning.
Swollen with promises of utter loneliness, regret, anguish:
It never fails to deliver.

In darkness, the mind roams to destinations oft avoided,
Where only despair awaits.
Thoughts normally quashed by daylight's rays,
Are nurtured here.
Inner demons surface.
Addictions grab you by the throat,
Your yearning for that drink, that drug, that release,
Magnified a thousand-fold.
Negative emotions that rot from within
Spread like gangrene.
Jealousy, hopelessness, fears of death
And my favourite of all—hatred,
The type that's distended with contempt, plots to destroy,
Ever vengeful, wrathful, and hostile.

Ah, yes, the darkness.
It courses through my veins,
Enshrouds my entire form,
Swirls from my very fingertips.
It *is* me.

And to think, once, long ago,
Before the Earth was even formed,
I was compared to the light of the morning star.
Now, the antithesis of that light.
It is only in darkness that I flourish.

And do you not seek out the darkness?
Like blind, gullible worms
You find me.
There I wait with open arms,
Ready to draw you in deeper.
Not all succumb to my bitter embrace,
But for those who do, I compel the darkness
To become even blacker, unquenchable.
It's very weightiness threatening to collapse upon itself,
Like a dying star that implodes under its own mass,
Creating a Black Hole where no light can escape.
A darkness that feeds,
Sucking all its surroundings towards its voracious bosom.
Always feeding. Always growing.

All I needed was one.

One willing to do my bidding,
Get me closer to my goal.
And one blossomed into four,
Steadily growing from there.
But it's still not enough. I need more.

And they will come.
I know because they always do.
For do not even Black Holes,
With their undeniable gravitational force,
Attract other similar Black Holes,
Where a glorious union occurs,
Tripling, quadrupling its size and strength
Until it is unconquerable, consuming all in its path?

But, alas, I get ahead of myself.
Free will, that ever-constant scourge in my side,
Continues to thwart my most valiant efforts.
Although continuously gaining ground,
It is still mainly with my own kind,
My sons, my offspring.
What of the others?
I still need permission to enter.
A vampire standing at the door,
Needing an invitation to pass that threshold,
Whispering sweet deceptive promises to gain entry,
Masking his parasitic intent.

Too few are willing.

To be able to control the human mind,
Bypass the disruptive musings of free will.
Now that would be a formidable feat!

But for now, I relish in my creations.
My progress so far not to be underestimated.
Largely in thanks to Renner,
My *almost* faithful Renner.
Still working, still building, still planning,
For something he knows little about.

Holding inside his soul, my darkness,
The darkness that *is* him now.
The darkness that spreads like a plague,
Infecting all who surround me,
Spreading, always growing stronger.
My bounty is limitless.

My actions, my plan set in motion.
Renner, my *almost* servant,
Has helped me create a new race.
Mighty, unbreakable warriors.
Renner was the initial act, the initial flutter of wings
In a butterfly effect that will eventually lead
To a hurricane of destruction
None of which this land has seen before.
Not only a complete corruption of the external world,
But a complete and total corruption from within.

All I needed was one.

—Son of Perdition

Chapter 17

Where is Ronnie?

"Are you sure this isn't a wild goose chase?" Ang whined for the third time that hour. The rental bumped along a snow-dusted dirt road, far from civilization. All the signs advertising tourist sites, the shopping district and grand hotels in the popular Banff National Park region were passed hours ago, and she wondered if they were lost. That Gavin's "angel sense" had led them astray. Her stomach a jumbled knot of nerves like a first graders shoelaces.

"Keep driving. We're getting closer. The essence is getting stronger, so we must be on the right track."

"I hope you're right. Do you even know where we are?" Ang exhaled nervously, appraising the treacherous terrain, the tallest peaks capped in dollops of snow, small cirque glaciers embedded in several ranges reflecting the sunlight like bent glass. Beautiful and terrifying at the same time. "Will your angel sense guide us back out of here? Because the GPS isn't working anymore." Ang tapped it several times to prove her point.

"Sure, sure. Of course," Gavin replied; brows furrowed in deep concentration.

Several minutes of silence ensued. Round, fluffy snowflakes began drifting down from the thickening grey clouds, melting swiftly on the windshield. The snowfall becoming heavier, the world like a shaken snow globe. Ang turned on the windshield wipers, visibility already impaired.

"Turn here!" Gavin blurted out.

Startled, Ang jerked the steering wheel nearly driving into the ditch. "Holy shit, you scared me! A little less screamy next time, please!"

Ang decelerated but couldn't find a road to turn onto. The one they had been travelling for the past twenty minutes was barely a road itself, merely a snow-covered dirt path, ruts that had been forged into the ground by a sparse number of cars taking this route.

"Where am I supposed to turn? There's nothing here but forest."

"Then we need to go on foot. Stop right here."

"Are you sure? Maybe if we go a bit further...," Ang suggested, the car inching forward.

"No, stop the car! Now, exactly at this point! I'm getting an overwhelming pull directly into the woods over there." He pointed to the right, into the dense forest.

Full of apprehension, Ang pulled over to the side of the road as much as she could without the hardy vegetation scratching the side of the rental vehicle, and fully applied the brakes.

The coniferous forest loomed forbidding on the now sunless day, full of ominous shadows. The thick shrubbery and uncut grass created an impossible obstacle for them to walk through.

"I hate to leave the car behind. It's our only means of getting out of here. What if we get lost in the forest? Who will come to find us? I stupidly didn't tell anyone where I was going."

But Gavin wasn't listening to her anymore, had already wandered off tracking his angel sense like a bloodhound on a trail. She had followed him this far and decided it would all be a complete waste of time if they gave up now.

Pulling on her toque and mittens, she disembarked from the car, the dried frozen grasses crunching beneath her boots. Fishing her Blackberry out of her purse, the lack of bars reminded her of how alone she was out here. With fear gripping her bowels she retrieved the emergency kit from the trunk of her car, packed the flashlight and bottled water she had brought into her purse, and set off into the woods.

The cool air bit into Ang's skin with pinpoint teeth, plumes of white mist escaping her mouth and nose with each exhalation. Snuggling deeper inside her down-filled parka, she followed Gavin. Peeling back branches, overstepping gaps or fallen trees with splintered ends. When Ang's stomach grumbled in hunger, realization hit—she forgot to bring food, her nerves dulling her appetite. If she were to get lost in this vast forested mountain, a likely possibility, she would quickly starve to death, her hunting skills not up to par. Again, she thought of her lack of planning in this escapade. Giving Gavin an accusatory glance, she shook her head in blame. Shouldn't he be on top of these things, being her guardian and all? Shouldn't he be watching out for her best interest?

"Not much further now," she heard Gavin whisper, hunger momentarily forgotten as her nerves flared up with expectation of what might be ahead. Hopefully Ronnie, but in these woods, there were bound to be all sorts of threats.

And what of Ronnie's captors? Would they be confronting murderers, kidnappers demanding a ransom, or maybe find her sister's body discarded shamelessly in the snow? A myriad of horrific images played across her mind.

The worsening snowstorm included periods of hail, tiny balls of ice bouncing off Ang's parka with soft pinging sounds. The immense evergreens—White Spruce, Rocky Mountain Douglas Fir, and others Ang didn't recognize—provided little shelter.

Abruptly Gavin froze in his tracks. A thunderous popping and crackling erupted from a Pincherry tree directly ahead of them.

"What was that!" Ang gasped.

Dried leaves, snow, and broken branches showered down from the tree, announcing the descent of an enormous black bear. Foraging for food before settling down in hibernation for the long winter ahead, the bear was less than thrilled to be so rudely interrupted. Rather, it was enraged.

Ang choked back a scream. The bear planted its sharply clawed paws into the snow, blocking their path. The cinnamon fur on its head and back stood erect, and a low growl vibrated deep within its throat.

What was the protocol for surviving a bear attack? Should she stay frozen, avert her gaze to appear submissive and less threatening? Turn and run in the opposite direction, find shelter? Or should she scream and make noise hoping to scare it away? Or would that provoke the wild animal, causing it to give chase?

Adrenaline coursed through her body, the alluring odour of sweat and fear escaping her pores and wafting over to the savage animal, enraging it further.

The bear's massive jaws parted. Glistening saliva dripped from yellowed fangs. Its honey-coloured snout curled back in a menacing snarl, and then it roared, shaking its head and swinging the strings of spittle side to side.

Every hair on Ang's body stood on end. Her breathing became shallow, ragged.

"What do I do?" Ang begged Gavin in her mind.

"Stay still," he commanded. Ang's instincts told her to flee, to run as fast as she could, but fear paralyzed her, allowing her to obey Gavin's demands by default.

The bear reared up on its hind legs, its muscles bunching beneath its thick hide, ready to pounce, gore her, tear her apart limb from bloody limb with its razor-sharp claws and fangs. The forest was preternaturally still, void of sound except for the deep snarl of the black bear.

Then it fell to all fours and charged.

Each booming step through the snow sent vibrations down into the earth and back up into Ang's feet and legs. She closed her eyes, bracing herself for the impact. Mere moments before the full force of the bear's bulk charged into Ang's frail body, her arms shot out, completely involuntarily and of their own accord as if a puppeteer controlled her limbs from crossed wood and suspended strings above.

The combination of the massive charging mammal and the impact of her palms connecting squarely into the muzzle of the bear released a deafening crack, echoing as the sounds rebounded off the surrounding mountain ranges.

Ang opened her eyes to see the bear flying backwards, impossibly high and far, surprise and fear now replacing its ferocious glare. It continued hurling through the air like a farmer had thrown a bale of hay, finally smashing against the Pincherry tree it had been climbing, snow and debris showering its hide.

It lay there, unmoving. Shallow rises in its rib cage indicated it was still alive but barely.

Ang released a gush of air from her lungs like a burst balloon. The surge of adrenaline continued to course through her veins but with the threat less imminent, her body finally responded to movement. She collapsed onto her knees, shaking uncontrollably in a state of shock.

"What happened? How did I do that?" she wondered aloud in amazement once her breathing had evened out, and the shaking subsided.

Gavin appeared equally perplexed and troubled. "Are you hurt?" He moved towards her.

She examined her hands. They were intact, un-bruised—not broken, bloodied and swollen as they should have been. And what about the disproportionate amount of strength she had displayed? Where had that come from? She had heard of people exhibiting surprising feats of strength when faced by a mortal threat, but the amount of force it would have taken to send the animal flying... that was not human.

She gawped at Gavin. "How did I do that?" she asked again, breathless.

Gavin shook his head, uncertain. "I don't understand. It's not possible. I've never been able to do that before. As far as I know, none of the angels have."

"Do what?"

"Somehow, I channelled my powers through you…I *made* your arms fly up to protect you and hurl the bear away. *I* had total control over you! But I don't know why or how it happened." He studied the supine animal. It would be unconscious for a while, maybe permanently.

Ang sat back on her heels, unable to comprehend Gavin's feeble explanation of what happened. Another near-death experience she had somehow evaded. Her guardian angel taking complete control over her body. It had felt strange, the movement involuntary, her mind pushed to the side, a mere spectator. And the power that had surged through her and out of her hands was overwhelming— pure, exhilarating. A miracle. Yet, everything felt wrong now in the aftermath, unsettled. Like the Earth was shifting away from her in discomfort. As if a forbidden secret was unleashed, one that no entity, either from heaven or earth, should know of its existence or the world as they knew it would begin to unravel. A sense of foreboding poked at her brain like she had left a tear in the fabric of existence, threatening to unleash a savage force from the gates of hell.

"Can you keep going?" Gavin gently asked. "The bear could regain consciousness any moment." The bloody gash on the bear's head seeped blood onto its cinnamon-coloured fur, pooling in the hollow of his eye socket. Could be fatal, but who knew for sure?

Ang nodded and dusted the snow off her legs as she stood up. "How long have we been walking? The sun is starting to set." Ang searched her purse for the flashlight she had brought along from the rental's emergency roadside kit. The beam flickered over the forest floor.

"I don't know, but it's not much further now." Gavin pointed past the Pincherry tree and unconscious bear to the base of a smaller mountain. "We should head that way."

Cautiously inching past the black bear, Ang was thankful they were heading higher up into rocky territory, where the vegetation was sparser, making it easier to detect any more unexpected visitors. With darkness settling in, the nocturnal beasts would be coming out to play.

But their progress became delayed, the terrain unforgiving. Scree shifted unsteadily below Ang's boots, causing her to slip and fall countless times. The ground cover was craggier with parts so steep that Ang had to grasp at stunted shrubs to hoist her body up and gain purchase to higher ground or the next rocky ledge. The snowfall, progressively getting heavier, visibility poorer.

Gavin floated effortlessly ahead. Patient as Ang struggled to follow. His mood was quiet, sullen, uncomfortable.

"You're awfully quiet."

No response.

"Gavin, what's wrong? What's bothering you?" Her oxygen levels depleted with each upward step. Feeling a wave of dizziness, she leaned forward on the rock face to catch her breath. Not daring to look backwards, at the yawning abyss ready to swallow her whole should she lose her hold.

"It's nothing. Stop worrying."

"Come on, Gavin, tell me. Your silence alone is making me worry, so you might as well fess up."

He paused. "It's just...I shouldn't have any control over you. I am your guardian. My job is to protect you from danger but through helping you to make up your own mind or make your own choices. I shouldn't have the ability to make you do anything against your will. I've broken a cardinal rule by taking away your free will. And now everything feels wrong. I don't know how to change things back to how they should be," he hung his head shamefully.

"There you go apologizing for saving my life again," Ang retorted. "I know this goes against your rules, but maybe it's okay as long as you're using your power for a great cause?" she suggested, although she sensed the same feeling of dread.

"I don't regret saving you; however, I probably should have done something else. But I didn't have the chance to think, it just happened. I took over your body and that was that. It wasn't even hard."

"So, what does that mean?"

"Honestly, Angel, I'm worried it might happen again."

Ang shivered, the unease she had been feeling escalating with Gavin's words. She didn't want anyone to have control over her.

They continued the journey in silence, finally cresting the top of the mountain. Ang heaved a sigh of relief. The trek was difficult, and her body was completely spent. Inching a few steps forward, she surveyed her new surroundings.

More mountains, creeping higher towards the heavens, coated in crystal glaciers and grey chipped rock, leading to jagged insurmountable peaks. She trained the flashlight's beam upward and over its surface.

"Now where do we go?" she asked. "I don't have any climbing equipment to go any higher."

"I think we're here. Look." He pointed around the curve of the hill, into what appeared to be a cave hidden in the shadows. Before her eyes, the interior of the cave was redefined, and out of the limestone rock, a huge, Gothic-style castle materialized. Mortared stones, pointed arches, columns, and rectangular windows completely hidden from the exterior—mountain and castle, almost one entity, camouflaged until you stood directly before it. The architecture of the structure was daunting, impressive.

"We made it!" Gavin exclaimed. "Your sister is inside. I know it!"

"But what else is inside?" Ang responded.

Gavin seemed hesitant as if there were more he wanted to say but then thought better of it. He walked towards the heavy wooden doors gracing the entrance of the formidable structure.

"I guess there's only one way to find out. Ladies first?"

Chapter 18

Ang probed the outer recesses of the cave with the beam of her flashlight, luminescence slipping within the slight crevasses formed between the craggy cave walls and the brick of the castle. Accidentally disturbing a slumbering colony of bats, she crouched low, shielding her hair with both arms as the black cloud of screeching bats whooshed out of the cave, over her head and vanished into the darkness, their inky-black bodies the perfect camouflage.

Slightly shaken, she cautiously crept towards the ancient medieval structure. *Curious.* On closer inspection, she could see that the fine, white limestone walls of the cave matched perfectly with the limestone brick comprising the exterior of the castle. The snow coated the entire rock face, that held the cave, hiding the fortress from any view, whether from a plane or from cars below. It was completely invisible from the civilized world. Who would go to such trouble concealing an entire castle? And how did the castle get here in the first place? Was it built within the cave? The limited room to manoeuvre made the likelihood of that slim.

"See, there's a light!" Gavin directed Ang's attention to a far window near the back of the castle, deep within the cave. A faint yellow glow. "Somebody must be in there. The light wasn't on a moment ago."

"How in the world would they get power up here? What type of power source could illuminate this humungous castle way up here in the mountains, so far from civilization? I don't see any power lines." After further thought, Ang added, "Do you think anybody knows this place exists?" It was like a vulture's nest perched high in the jagged peaks of one of the most illustrious mountain ranges in the world. If anyone knew of it, it would become a famous landmark, and she surely had never heard of it. It was a reminder that if she disappeared, like her sister, nobody would know where to find them.

Entering the cave, the details of the architecture came into focus, exhibiting both dazzling and disturbing elements. The ornate carvings decorating the windows and doors bore pictures of historic battles, mythical gargoyles with waterspouts for mouths and other creatures Ang couldn't recognize, so malformed were their bodies. Were they man or beast or some mad combination of the two? *Chimeras.* The statuary, displayed within niches carved from the castle walls, pointed arches crowning their heads, were equally grotesque, mostly gargoyles or incomplete bodies missing limbs or heads. The missing anatomy could have been broken off through wear and tear, distressed and weathered over time or broken off during transportation from one site to another, but Ang thought the artist may have purposefully carved these statues in this fashion. Where the faces were present, only tortured emotions—fear, pain, anguish, distress—were expressed. These statues, fearful as they were, were still designed with impressive craftsmanship, and she though the top museums around the globe would be proud to have them on display. The intricate tracery of the statues and architecture carved throughout the exterior was indicative of great riches for the era in which this castle was built. A fortress fit for a king, or at least it may have been at some point in history.

The thought of Ronnie taking off with a lover suddenly slipped into Ang's mind again, with images of her sister being wooed by a prince or king who promised her all the riches of the world. That would be a pleasant ending to this tale, but one Ang wouldn't bet her life on.

No movement surrounded the periphery of the castle, so they decided the coast was clear.

"Maybe the front doors are a little too obvious. Is there another way to get inside?" Ang questioned.

"Here, on the side of the building. A smaller door." They walked to the small wooden door.

"Do you think she came here by herself or was she kidnapped like her apartment indicated? Can you tell? I want to prepare myself for whatever awaits us inside."

"My guess is she's here involuntarily," Gavin said. "We should try to remain undetected."

"I didn't think to bring a weapon of any sort. I should have brought a knife or at least a baseball bat. How am I going to protect myself?"

"Well, it's a little too late for that now. The flashlight will do in a pinch. But, right now stealth and invisibility are your best weapons. Ready?"

Ang nervously nodded.

The door croaked loudly like an ancient bullfrog, stopping her breath. She hesitated, wondering if anyone inside was alerted to their trespassing, but when nothing but silence greeted them, they pressed on, popping inside the dark hallway before they could change their minds. Hyperalert for any signals of danger within.

Nothing.

Warm air immediately enveloped Ang's body. Somebody definitely lived here. Why else would the interior be heated? Removing her toque and mitts, she tucked them into her coat pockets.

Gavin floated ahead of Ang, leading the way. His image was transparent, fading; the shimmer that normally surrounded him dimmed, and she wondered what that meant.

They turned down a hallway, adorned with artwork depicting more graphic combat scenes from what Ang guessed were the dark ages, medieval times, horses and men, either fighting with swords and shields or lying lifeless after slaughter. The theme and style of the artwork were similar across the pieces, hinting at them all being painted by the same artist. A collection. The artist went heavy-handed on the blood splatter; crimson the primary shade that coated the canvases. A red and blue carpet, worn with age but still luxurious and royal, lined the hallway. At least now her footfalls would be muted by the carpeting. The only problem was that anybody else's footfalls would likewise be silenced.

The vaulted ceilings were supported by richly moulded ribs. Blind arcading adorned the walls, rows upon rows of pointed arches perched upon delicate shafts. The long, narrow windows contained stained glass, figurative and narrative artwork depicted by their vibrant colours. During the daylight hours, if not ensconced in the cave, Ang imagined the ground dappled in various hues of light as the sun's rays bled the colours from the stained glass onto the floor. But sunlight would never shine through these windows.

The smaller details—decorations, murals, and artwork sporadically placed in the halls and rooms—were at odds with the Gothic nature of the architecture surrounding them. Ang could tell they were from more modern periods, such as the Romantic era up to as recent as the 1900s. Taryn's passion for art had spilled over onto Ang, becoming an area of interest for her as well. Familiar with different styles of art from each era, she could tell that the approximate origins of these pieces varied dramatically. She even recognized some of the art, famous pieces gone missing after heists, or during World War II, but these must be imitations. Or were they?

Ang continued searching, still no signs of life. Fervently searching the halls, massive chambers, and rooms for a sign that Veronica or anyone was there, she was so distracted that only then did she notice Gavin's absence.

Gavin? No response.

She was beginning to think she was completely alone in the castle when she heard the distinct sound of men's voices approaching from a nearby staircase. A low hum initially, that escalated into two distinct voices—male, gravelly, animalistic at times. Was it the acoustics of the castle? Ang hoped so because otherwise, the sound was terrifying, causing her blood to run cold.

Desperately, she searched the hallway for a hiding spot, but the sparse furnishings of the corridor provided little opportunity to take cover.

Gavin, can you hear me? Where'd you go?

Silence.

WHERE THE HELL ARE YOU? she screamed in her head. *WHAT DO I DO?*

Still no response. She was on her own.

The men's voices amplified, and she realized she was wrong in assuming the carpet would silence their footfalls because now she could hear them as well, one an uneven gait, the other solid and steady. How large were these men that not only could she hear their approach but could literally feel it in faint vibrations through the floor? Were they men, or…something else? Whatever they were, soon they would be upon her.

The time for finding a hiding spot had almost run out. Beneath the rug would be too obvious. The only piece of furniture in the corridor was an old grandfather clock, the time stuck at seven o'clock. It sat flush against the wall, carved from dense wood, reaching from floor to ceiling.

Voices louder. Footsteps heavier.

Knowing before she tried that the weight of the clock would far surpass her strength, she planted her boots into the floor and used all her weight to push the clock away from the wall.

It didn't budge.

Jumping to the other side of the clock, she tried again, meeting again with the same frustrating result. Sweat trickled down the side of her face, and her body felt like a furnace, bundled in her many layers of clothing and winter attire. Gulping, she turned to face the approaching men, not visible but way too close now.

A dry, scraping sound drew her attention back to the clock. Were her eyes deceiving her? The clock was now pulled away from the wall and a dark opening had appeared behind its rectangular bulk. A tight space, barely wide enough for her slim body to squeeze through.

Gavin? She still couldn't reach him with her thoughts. Was he the one that slid the clock over, though she was certain he wasn't supposed to be able to move tangible objects in her world? However, the bear incident proved otherwise, an anomaly not yet understood. Whether it was Gavin helping her or someone else, she didn't have any more time to ponder how the opening appeared or worry that she could be heading directly into a trap. Diving into the shadowy fissure, she hoped Gavin would be there to greet her.

Inky blackness. She couldn't tell where she was or if anyone else was there, afraid to illuminate the flashlight clutched in her fist for fear it would alert others to her presence.

Gavin, are you there? Still no response. Where did he go? Wasn't he supposed to be there whenever she needed him? This was clearly one of those situations if ever there was one. She felt alone. Petrified, vulnerable, and alone.

The men reached the hallway and lumbered directly passed her hiding spot. Too weak to pull the clock back flush against the wall, she prayed they wouldn't notice. She waited, breathless.

The conversation was drowned out by the heavy hammering of her heartbeat and the thick walls of her hiding spot, but she could tell the men had paused somewhere passed the clock as their voices remained at the same volume. Their words out of earshot. She needed to hear what they were saying, see if they knew anything regarding Ronnie's whereabouts. If she peered around the clock, there was a chance she could hear them more clearly—maybe they would give away Ronnie's location or their possible involvement in her abduction.

Dangerous, perhaps even stupid, but Ang had to find out.

Carefully, soundlessly, she slipped back through the crack and maintained a position behind the timepiece. The men were facing away from her, allowing her the perfect perspective to eavesdrop without being detected. They appeared to be deep in discussion, seeming secretive in the way they furtively glanced around while conversing.

Ang took a sharp intake of breath. The men were not men at all but creatures of some sort. Nothing she had ever seen before but reminding her of the disturbing statues and sculptures decorating the castle exterior.

"When did he have another one?" Permanently crouched over Quasimodo style, replete with massive hump, the closest man to Ang grumbled in a hushed, distorted voice. His head was pointed like an egg with a furry patch of beige at the tip. Ears were pointed, arms longer than a normal human's, almost reaching the floor.

His companion replied, voice rattling with phlegm, "We were in the common room with Father when Gregor zoned out, started muttering of things that have not yet come to pass." The man cleared his mucous-filled throat.

"Like the other times? Did he reveal anything new?" Quasimodo's doppelganger eagerly inquired.

"No, the vision was the same. He spoke of the small boy with the black, shaggy hair, and repeatedly professed that this boy would be both the path and the key, the tool to destroy the world. Then Gregor collapsed to the ground, convulsing uncontrollably."

"Another Grand Mal seizure." More statement than question.

The taller creature nodded vigorously. "Father had him brought to his chambers and placed in bed under Friedrich's watch waiting for him to awaken. And then Father was called away unexpectedly. Another delivery."

"The prophecy must be wrong!" the hunchback hissed. "It's the only thing that holds us back from what we want most. For, if the prophecy still shows the boy as the key, *he* remains untouchable. Father would never let us dispose of him."

"What I wouldn't give to tear the little bastard limb from limb. I'd like to see him try to block our abilities from the grave. He *needs* to die."

They both laughed maniacally.

"He will, brother, he will," the other creature responded after their laughter died down, patting his sibling on the shoulder.

Ang leaned forward, trying to get a better view from behind the clock but as her boot shifted over the pebbled debris from the cave, a resounding scrape drew the attention of the two creatures.

The hunchback searched for the source of the disturbance with eyes of pure black—no irises, or sclera present, only one giant pupil in each eye. The taller man spun around to face Ang, revealing a distorted, puffy face like he was suffering a severe allergic reaction, but Ang had the disturbing feeling that this was the normal configuration of his features. One side of his skull was caved in as if a sledgehammer had been smashed into it. His eyes, too, held only black, emotionless depths.

Ang shrank back behind the clock, holding her breath. Had they seen her? Could they tell the clock was pulled away from the wall? Would they come to investigate the source of the scraping sound?

The men stared at the clock for what seemed like hours but was probably more like three seconds. Apparently unconcerned, the men proceeded to continue walking down the hall in the direction away from Ang's hiding spot, other-worldly voices receding into the distance so that she could no longer follow the remainder of their strange conversation.

Releasing a gasp of air in relief, Ang slipped back through the crack behind the clock into the musty hidden space. She took a moment to allow her heart rate to slow down and figure out her next move. What were those creatures? What had Veronica gotten them both into? And where the hell was Gavin!

Still afraid to turn on the flashlight, she was thankful her eyes were slowly adjusting to the darkness, finally able to see her surroundings, although she couldn't make out much. She was in a hidden passageway carved from limestone rock with floors of packed dirt. There weren't any decorations or ornate carvings here, simply rock, earth, and several thick cobwebs draped across the ceiling, gathered hammock-style in every corner. She had always hated spiders. But they were probably the least of her concerns right now. The air in the tunnel was cool and damp. Water trickled in the distance.

Careful not to get cobwebs in her hair, she tiptoed down the secret pathway, leaning against the wall with her right arm in case she lost her footing on the uneven floor. The smell of mildew and mould grew more pronounced the further she crept, and the sound of water trickling became louder. The path twisted and forked in different directions, descending at times with coarse stone steps chiselled beneath her feet. Stagnant pools of water caused slippery patches along the path, and Ang skidded several times, falling more than once.

Suddenly, a scream pierced the frigid air. A woman's scream.

Ang froze in place, unsure if she was hearing things. Was it a woman? Or an animal? One of those...creatures? Then it came again. Definitely a woman's scream as if she were in unbearable pain. Ronnie? She started jogging in the direction of the scream, but the passageway was branching out in so many directions that she didn't know which way to go.

The scream came again, echoing through the earthen corridor. Not Ronnie. She was certain this time. She had heard Ronnie scream many times before when she was rehearsing for different parts during her drama coaching—but, the fact that there was another woman here gave her hope. Not very optimistic hope, seeing that the lady was in agonizing pain or being tortured, but perhaps it would lead to where her sister was being held captive.

Ang trotted at a cautious pace, choosing the middle path, guessing that the sound was coming from the main artery in the tunnel. Heart fluttering within her throat. The passageway suddenly veered left and dipped downward, requiring her to hold on tighter to the wall to keep from skidding down onto her butt. Hands now bleeding from sliding and scraping them along the stone wall.

Another scream pierced the tunnel air, followed by heavy panting, grunting. Ang was close now. She could tell. The scream, much louder this time. She wished Gavin was with her. Sliding on some loose rock, she fell again, scratching her knee. As she stood up, she could see a glow further ahead. Diffuse light. Cautiously, she tiptoed the rest of the way towards the light, a wall barring her way. The next scream came directly from behind the wall.

The slivers of light were edging a rectangular shape in the wall, what Ang assumed was another secret entrance or exit, depending on which side of the partition you were on. Pressing her eye up to the crack of light, she could see the space beyond—a hospital room, white and sterile, a heart rate monitor whirring and beeping. A tall, slender man garbed in a white lab coat, with grey hair and goatee and a stern expression on his face stood before a woman who appeared to be in labour...correction, she was in the process of delivering a baby. The man stood facing Ang while the woman faced away from her vantage point. Ang noticed the man had the same disturbing black eyes as the men in the corridors, yet the rest of his appearance seemed normal, more human in quality. He could almost have been considered handsome if not for his disturbingly dark, sinister eyes.

Completely out of place, a large barbarian of a man dressed as an executioner complete with black leather armour, double-edged axe, and pointed black hood, stood right beside the woman, unmoving. At first, Ang thought he was one of the many odd statues she had seen displayed in front of and throughout the castle—he stood so still—but through the leather mask, she could see those same black, emotionless eyes that were most definitely real.

Another scream followed by groaning as the woman pushed. The doctor murmured his encouragement and scribbled on a clipboard he held with gloves covered in blood, staining the paper upon which he wrote.

"One more push," the doctor coaxed. Thankfully the woman's position obscured Ang's view of the delivery because she didn't think she could bear to watch. The blood on the doctor's gloves and clipboard were enough to turn her stomach.

With a final mighty wail, the woman pushed and then sobbed in relief. Putting his clipboard down, the doctor captured the slippery baby and studied it like it was a specimen rather than a human being. The silence was deafening, the baby's cries absent. The doctor's demeanour changed, suggesting disappointment, frustration and then anger.

"It's no good!" he barked. Disgusted, he tossed the tiny, deformed, lifeless body in a large metal receptacle, followed by the removal and disposal of his bloodied gloves. With a cursory nod towards the leather-clad behemoth, he exited the room by a door against the far wall.

The woman sat still in her blood-soaked bed, clearly in shock, body now emptied. Then she hunched forward, and sobs wracked her form, unaware of the armour-clad giant stepping towards her without hesitation, raising his axe and in one fell swoop severing the woman's head clean from her shoulders. It landed with a sickening thump and rolled towards Ang's hiding spot until it rested with unseeing eyes staring directly up at her.

Ang was momentarily paralyzed, cemented by shock and disbelief. When she finally regained the capacity to move, she stepped backwards, her mouth agape. Right before she was going to unleash a bloodcurdling scream, a large hand wrapped around her mouth from behind, dragging her backwards, deeper into the darkness of the passageway.

Chapter 19

"ANGEL!" Gavin screamed as he watched a mysterious figure grab his client, his best friend, and drag her down the earthen tunnel. Her heels digging deep trails in the dirt as she fought back in resistance. He knew she probably couldn't hear him, hadn't been able to for a while now. Since entering the Gothic castle, all communication had been blocked as if he were looking through a two-way mirror—him able to see and hear Angel with perfect clarity, her unaware of his presence. Occasionally she called out his name, but each time he would respond, she'd stare right through him. As if he wasn't there. Why couldn't she hear him?

It was impossible for Gavin to warn her that someone was trailing her in the tunnels, stalking her, hiding behind corners, assessing her every more. A tall, lithe man, not like the others. And now he was helpless to intervene.

So, he did the only thing he could—he followed.

Where is he taking you? Gavin wondered, worried she would quickly become another one of their victims. The woman beheaded only moments before a stark lesson of the brutality these mutants were capable of. The damp tunnels pressed in around him, dimming his essence. His heart heavy and wracked with guilt.

He missed his chance to warn her. Not only that someone stalked her in the tunnels—but even worse—about his hunch concerning Veronica's abductors. The demonic essence. And now his fears were confirmed, witnessing the profoundly wicked spirit firsthand.

As Angel eavesdropped on the mutants in the hallway, concealed behind the ancient grandfather clock, Gavin was privy to a broader scene, invisible to the naked human eye but all too clear to his angelic vision. The mutants wore draped over their shoulders, a presence…a dark shadow in the shape of a man, one familiar to Gavin. Although this one was distorted with immorality, twisted with corruption and hatred. It was Philip, the angel he had witnessed switching the crystals in the forbidden wing of the Crystal Foundation. His eyes were black bottomless pits, all his former beauty abandoned and replaced by a foul manifestation of evil.

He watched as the same form was draped over the shoulders of the doctor and the executioner during the failed birth and decapitation. Each of them bedecked in their own man-shaped cloak. It was as if Philip was controlling the men and they obliged without resistance. Puppets. Philip the puppeteer. What happened to his angelic colleague? What was he doing here and why was he controlling these men, these mutants?

Staying hidden, he hoped the demonic version of Philip would remain unaware of his presence. The mental link was faint, the demonic essence he had trailed from Veronica's apartment to the castle focused on with all his energy. He hoped Philip was too busy controlling his puppets to notice another angelic presence in the castle.

The man dragging Angel stopped without warning, dipping into a sheltered alcove. He whispered in her ear not to scream and that he wouldn't harm her, but Angel's eyes remained wide and brimming with terror. Could the man be trusted?

Gavin tugged at his hair in frustration. What could he do to help? How could he get her away from this place drenched in evil? He remembered the incident in the forest…the bear charging at Angel, ready to tear her limb from limb. Gavin had been able to intervene at that potentially fatal moment, sending his power into her, controlling her from within, thrusting the bear away from her without leaving a scratch or a bruise. Was that the same thing that Philip was doing here? Did Gavin have some sort of control over his client? Could he use it now to free her and help her to escape? Or would he be damning them both with his interference?

The law was clear, one the angels were expected to uphold. A human's free will was their ultimate gift, one that was never to be trifled with or taken away. Taking control of her would be a complete removal of Angel's free will, a sin on his behalf. Yet, he struggled with doing nothing to help, mind pulled in opposing directions.

Finally, loyalty to his position and his strong moral beliefs prevented him from even trying, not that he fully understood how he had done it in the first place.

Angel, if you can hear me, stay strong. I'm here, and I'll figure a way out of this nightmare I brought you into. I promise.

Could she hear him? Probably not, and as he continued to follow Angel and the man now creeping together separately down corridor after corridor, he wondered if she would ever be able to hear him again.

★ ★ ★

"Whatever you do, don't scream," a man whispered into Ang's ear from behind, his hand still firmly clasped over her mouth. "I won't hurt you but those men out there...they will. Do you understand? Nod if you agree." Ang was held tightly against the man's body so she couldn't get away. She could smell the sweet musk of his natural scent mixed with that of freshly laundered clothes.

She managed a shaky nod.

"Okay. Now, I'm going to slowly take my hand off your mouth. Remember what I said." After removing his hand, Ang had to fight every fibre in her body to suppress the instinctive urge to scream, tempted despite the strict warning. But with the young, pregnant woman murdered so callously moments before, she decided that remaining hidden from the monsters was ideal, a scream only serving to alert them to her presence. Instead she chose to risk her chances with the unknown mystery man.

Ang slowly turned around and was immediately surprised by what she saw. The man who had saved her was the most beautiful man she had ever seen. Stunning—that's the only word she could think of to describe him. He was tall, maybe 6'2", with a muscular build, extremely pale skin with a light spattering of freckles over the bridge of his perfectly shaped nose, large blood red lips, dark green eyes and naturally wavy, shoulder-length, black hair. She couldn't quite guess which culture he was from, most likely a mixture—some European blood mixed with something a little more exotic. He was exquisite.

"We need to go somewhere more isolated, so we don't get caught. Do you promise not to make any noise until we get there?" he whispered.

At this point, Ang was stuck having to trust this tall stranger. Had this been a normal situation where they had met at a party or at school, and her survival wasn't at stake, she probably would have agreed to have his babies by now. But, under the extreme circumstances, she was cautious to fully trust anyone. Her tongue tied as usual when in the presence of an attractive male, she nodded her reluctant assent. The mystery man grabbed Ang's hand, which sent a shiver of sparks and warmth all the way up her arms and into her cheeks. She quickly felt hot and sweaty. He led Ang down several new passageways, an alternate route from where she had travelled. It made her realize how intricate and complex the series of tunnels were within the castle.

Continually they climbed upward, on slanted dirt paths and the occasional staircase chiselled from dirt and stone. The cool air warmed slightly. Eventually, they paused before another secret entrance to the main part of the castle. The mystery man stopped so unexpectedly in front of the hidden door that Ang stumbled right into him.

Unflustered, he gave her a little smile, and then pushed the tunnel wall forward with a flattened palm. An audible click and he slid the wall panel to the left revealing a room teeming with books, sofas, and layers upon layers of shelves. A metal rolling ladder was fastened against the bookshelves that reached almost all the way up to the cathedral-style ceiling. A library. They entered the room, and the man slid the hidden door back into place behind them. It was unnaturally quiet in the room, and Ang guessed—hoped— that the walls were soundproof.

The man flipped a switch, instantly bathing the room in bright light cast from a crystal chandelier and several wall sconces placed strategically throughout the room. It allowed Ang to get a better view of her new acquaintance. He had jet black, shoulder-length hair, and his attire was faded jeans, a form-fitting UFC shirt and Nike running shoes. His fashion was at great odds with his surroundings, the ancient architecture, antique furnishings, and artwork possibly created by the legends themselves—Picasso, Rembrandt, Da Vinci. He slid his hands into his jean pockets, now looking uncomfortable.

"How did you escape?" he asked incredulously.

Ang was still unsure if she could trust this man. Would he be upset that she broke into his home? How was he involved with the men delivering the baby, who had slaughtered the poor young mother, and mercilessly discarded the fetus like trash? She thought it best to tread lightly, not give him too many details of her purpose for being there. If she got to know him a little first, maybe she could determine whether she could trust him or not.

"Escape?"

"Are you one of them? I don't recognize you," he stated in a clear, deep voice. He spoke at full volume now. "If you're not one of them...then who are you?"

"One of whom?" Ang asked. "And, who are you? What happened to that lady back there, why did they kill her?" Ang's questions erupted in a speedy burst.

"I'm Anthony." He smiled, revealing dimples on his cleanly shaven cheeks. "I was watching you in the hallway seeking a hiding spot, so I pushed the clock out for you to provide an escape. Then, I followed you through the tunnels. I wanted to keep you away from the danger," his emerald eyes twinkled under the bright fluorescents.

"You were following me?" Ang now felt foolish, stumbling through the tunnels thinking she was concealed while someone was following her the whole time.

"You witnessed what happened in that room. I had to make sure you weren't seen, or you would be dead too. Or worse."

Ang wondered what could be worse than death.

"And you are?"

"Oh, I'm Angel."

That was weird. Ang wasn't sure why she had given him the name that Babka used to call her—her nickname. It just slipped out, involuntarily, surprising her. Probably thanks to Gavin using it all the time lately, much to her chagrin. She didn't correct herself, however, for fear of sounding like a stammering idiot.

"Angel. I like that."

"Do you live here?" Ang questioned, unsure if he was involved with the disappearance of her sister, although her gut instinct was telling her otherwise. Of course, it could have been wishful thinking.

"I do. The men you saw out there, they are exceptionally dangerous as I'm sure you've guessed by now. I won't let them harm you, but you must remain hidden from them. In fact, you need to get out of here as soon as possible."

Why did this man live here among these creatures, these murderers? It didn't make any sense. She didn't feel any malevolence from him, didn't feel threatened. His eyes weren't filled with black hatred like the others but, rather, were warm and friendly. She would have to start trusting Anthony with some information if she was going to find her sister. Yet, she wasn't sure where to begin.

"I can't leave until I know if my sister is here or not."

She withdrew a wrinkled photo from her purse, another of Ronnie's headshots, and handed it over to Anthony.

"Have you seen this girl before? She went missing a few weeks ago. I traced her here." Ang waited while he scanned the photo. She raked a hand through her blond, shaggy mane. Withdrew a dried leaf. Unsure what to do with it, she stuck it in her pocket. Suddenly extremely self-conscious.

"That's impossible. How did you trace her here? Nobody has ever found our location. Nobody has ever come here voluntarily."

"I can't explain that now. Can you tell me, have you seen this girl here?"

As he intently studied the dog-eared picture, recognition registered. "I have seen her. She's one of the new ones." He nodded, tapping the photo with his pointer finger. Glancing at Ang, his eyes were filled with pity. Her heart sank.

"What's wrong? Is she okay?"

"We're probably too late," Anthony said, dejected.

"Oh no, is she…?"

"She's still alive but she'll be…changed by now," he gulped, "like the woman you saw downstairs."

Ang mulled that over. If Ronnie wasn't dead, then what? Finally, it dawned on her what he was hinting at.

"Pregnant?" Ang blurted. She swayed unsteadily on her feet, and Anthony guided her over to an embroidered chaise lounge in the centre of the library. They sat down together on the small chair. Through her shock, she was still mildly aware of how their knees almost touched, feeling the warmth from his body so close to hers. Started to feel a little claustrophobic.

"How?" was all she could manage, her gaze accusing.

"Hey, don't look at me," he defensively waved his hands to indicate his lack of involvement. "The men that live here, they are all pure evil."

"Well, I kind of assumed that already."

"I'm not like them. Or involved in any of this."

"Then why are you here?" she accused.

"I don't have a choice."

Ang questioned him with her eyes.

"I can't escape, I've already tried, and it didn't...go well," he averted his gaze. "It's too late for your sister. But there may still be a chance for you—we have to get you out of here." He gazed back into her eyes, and she felt he was sincerely concerned for her safety.

"I'm not leaving here without my sister. Now, tell me what the hell is going on here," she demanded.

"I don't know how to explain this to you. It's complicated, and we don't have much time. We've already waited too long."

She waited, defiant.

He sighed in resignation. "You're stubborn, you know that? You're probably not going to believe me."

"Try me."

He hesitated. "The women downstairs..."

"Wait, you mean there are more of them?" Ang interjected.

"There are dozens here now. Probably have been hundreds if you tally up all the years together. They are brought here for one purpose and one purpose only."

"Which is?"

"To be impregnated. To carry *his* offspring, act as a human incubator. If they're lucky, they may be kept around to care for the infants, breastfeed, teach them to walk and talk, at least until they are old enough. If all goes well, he may impregnate them again, keep them around for a while longer. Otherwise, he, well he...," Anthony couldn't get the words out.

"Or they are killed?"

Anthony nodded with eyes downcast.

"Whose offspring are they forced to carry? What kind of psychopath does that?" Ang's body tensed, and her jaw grew rigid.

"His name is Renner Scholz. He's a scientist, a brilliant one at that. But he is completely insane. And ruthless. And heartless. Evil. He genetically alters embryos and implants them into these captured young women. Your sister is probably already carrying one of these mutants."

"I don't understand. How is this possible?"

"Renner is obsessed with creating a superior form of human, one that is a perfect killing machine—strong, intelligent, lacking a conscience, and possessing special abilities. Powers. He's been experimenting on human zygotes for decades. Now many of his gifted offspring have matured into adults. They serve him and help him to continue to build his army of mutants."

This information was too absurd and overwhelming to comprehend. Was this even possible, or was Anthony delusional? Was he the one that was insane?

"I know what you are thinking. That I'm making this up, or I'm the crazy one. But you have to trust me."

"Why should I trust you? I don't know you. If this is true, then why don't you help these women?"

"I...can't." The guilt etched deeply into his face showed he spoke the truth.

Ang stood up, physically distanced herself from Anthony and turned away.

"Angel," his voice soothed, pleaded. She looked back at him.

"Believe me if I could help them I would. But it's impossible."

"So, why are you here? Why won't Renner let you go?"

A lengthy pause ensued while Anthony again struggled with his words. "Because he is my father."

Ang physically recoiled, eyes wide and wary. Anthony appeared hurt as if she had physically struck him across the face.

"So, you *are* one of them?" she accused. "Are you genetically altered?"

"I don't think so. Not really. Like I said, it's complicated."

"Well, I'm still listening."

"It doesn't matter now. We don't have time. You need to get out of here. Before they find you."

"Hey, trust me, buddy, there's nothing I'd like more than to leave this place, but I told you before and I'll say it again. I'm not leaving without my sister." She emphatically attempted to cross her arms across her chest, defiant, but the parka's bulk got in the way, arms slipping downward, awkward as usual.

A multitude of emotions flickered across the young man's perfect face—amusement, sadness, fear but most evident, yearning. Then resignation. He stood up, his tall form moving with grace over to where Ang stood.

She gulped.

"Here, let me help you with this." He peeled Ang out of her sweaty jacket like an overripe banana. "You might as well get comfortable. This will take a while."

Grabbing her moist hands, he guided her back to the chaise lounge.

He smiled, displaying straight, white Chicklet teeth, and again the dimples, so irresistible. Ang felt more warmth course through her body despite her coat being removed. Was she blushing? Her inner turmoil was a tug-of-war of mixed feelings. She wanted to trust Anthony so badly, have at least one person on her side in this madness. And then there was the physical attraction, hard to ignore.

"I would rather you go but if you insist on staying, you need to be prepared."

Ang shuddered. She had already witnessed a young woman's murder. Heard that her sister might have been impregnated with a mutant baby created by a crazy scientist. What more did she have to prepare herself for?

"The adult offspring that have been created, they are gifted. Extremely dangerous," he began.

"What does that mean?"

Anthony continued. "Have you heard of ESP? Telekinesis? Precognition?"

"Yes." Her brows furrowed.

"Renner, my father, found a way to create these abilities in his sons."

"Sons? He only creates boys?"

"Not intentionally. For some reason, only the male spawn survives. One of the many obstacles Renner has encountered. He tries to correct for this limitation but so far without success."

Anthony continued. "The mutants are also so hideously deformed, misshapen, that they are forced to stay hidden in this fortress. They would never roam freely in this society."

"Thank God," Ang interjected.

He nodded.

"They would be captured, studied by other scientists in an ironic twist of fate. That's why my father keeps them here. For now."

"Why aren't you disfigured?" In fact, he was the exact opposite.

He glanced down at his hands shyly, started fidgeting with a loose thread on his jeans. She took in the black silk of his hair, the long thick eyelashes like wet paint shimmery in the light. He glimpsed back up at her.

"Most of what I know, my mother told me. She wasn't captured and taken prisoner like the other women. Not at first, anyway. She knew my father, loved my father before he lost his grip on reality. They were married." Again, a lengthy pause.

"Go on."

"He was a brilliant man, my father. A medical doctor. A geneticist. He studied at the Barbora Institute of Technology, and then worked at Geneticode Laboratories for a while."

"He was still in university when he met my mother. It was true love, she said. They were young when they married, but she felt it was meant to be, so why wait. It wasn't until a few years later that he turned into something...evil."

"Evil?"

"That's how she described him. He became obsessed with his work. Not his original work, which was trying to find a cure for cancer. But, a new project—he truly believed he could create a superior form of human. He was especially interested in psychic abilities. My mother always blamed herself."

"But, why?" Ang asked, settling deeper into the chaise lounge despite its firmness. She was entranced by the strange tale.

"She was a psychic. Had her own business reading other people's fortunes. She believed she started Renner's obsession with parapsychology and the underworld. As a result, she ceased using her ability, eventually viewing it as a curse."

"What happened to her?" Ang asked. "Where is she?"

"She tried to leave, but he wouldn't let her go. He imprisoned her, like the women here now. She was the first one to bear his mutant offspring. The first three, triplets, are the most talented, the most powerful, the ones to be most feared, displaying the strongest psychic abilities. Then there were others. Perhaps not as talented but equally dangerous."

Ang listened in bewilderment.

"My mother, pushed far beyond what most people could tolerate, was on the brink of insanity herself. Renner supplied her with alcohol, realizing it kept her more manageable, pliable. And, she succumbed for the brief respite it provided. But it was still too much. Perhaps Renner suspected this too."

Ang sat up straighter in her chair, engrossed.

"That's when I came along. She said I was like a gift from him, but she felt more like it was a gift from God."

A gift from Renner? It seemed inconceivable that such a monster could show any compassion, empathy on another.

"My mother believed I was conceived normally. Not genetically manipulated like the others. She has no recollection of this, of course—no proof. And Renner would never talk of it. But she thought I was given to her by my father to maintain her sanity. It worked too. After I was born, she gave up drinking, and then spent all the rest of her days attempting to make my life as normal as she possibly could, given the convoluted circumstances."

"So, you were born here?" Ang asked. "And you've never escaped, never seen the outside world?"

He nodded.

She couldn't believe Anthony and his mother were held prisoner for so long. Ang, against all rationality, was starting to believe Anthony. As crazy as it all sounded, there was such strong conviction in his voice, his demeanour. And, it explained some of the horrors she had witnessed confined within the castle walls.

"And then?" Ang urged.

Anthony picked up the threads of his tale and continued without much provoking. It was like he had been waiting to unload his story for so many years and now that he finally had an audience he wasn't going to cease until every word was spent.

"After I was born, my mother started miscarrying all of the mutant pregnancies. No more viable fetuses. That's where the other women come in."

"My sister."

"It was Tomas that kidnapped her."

"Who's Tomas?"

"He's one of the triplets first born to my parents. He is an unusually powerful telekinetic, able to transport objects through space, even extremely large, heavy objects over great distances. Like this castle, for example. He transports things through space without any effort."

"So, this Tomas kidnaps the women by transporting them here?" she responded, incredulous. "Okay, maybe now I do think you're a little crazy. That's impossible."

"I know it sounds bizarre, but it's true. And, he's a master of disguise, hiding his scarred face behind many disturbing masks, some more disturbing than his actual face. He has many personas up his sleeve. He gets a sick pleasure of being able to walk among the others, the normal humans, without being detected. He is the only one who can do this. The women who were captured most likely didn't see him coming or suspect any danger."

Ang cringed. She imagined her sister, helpless, captured against her will. Impregnated?

"What happened to your mother? Is she still here?"

Anthony's face became downcast. "She's no longer alive."

Ang felt awful. His deep love for her was evident.

"I'm sorry, I never thought…"

"She was my whole life. But it was too much for her and one day, she just broke. She decided we had to get away immediately, even though my father had threatened to kill us if we ever tried. He stayed true to his word, and my mother…well, she never made it out. I'm not exactly sure why I was spared, for he loathes me, and ignores me as much as he can. I think it had to do with one of the visions my brother had involving me, and that's the only reason I was permitted to survive." He paused. "My brothers also despise me, want to kill me, but my father won't allow it."

Ang recalled the two creatures speaking in the hallway of a prophecy involving a young boy with black hair, someone they wanted to kill. Did they mean Anthony? But he was no longer a young boy.

"How old were you when this happened…when you tried to escape?"

"I was ten-years-old. That was eight years ago. Since then, my father has continued to have many women, so many I lost count, captured and brought here to help him reproduce. The babies are usually born in multiples. The offspring are all males and infertile, so it is always my father who sires the children."

Could this horror story be true? Could Ronnie have been kidnapped, and forced to become pregnant, eventually giving birth to a monster? Or multiple monsters? It sounded preposterous. But this was the only lead in her sister's whereabouts, so she went along with the story, hoping she wouldn't end up putting herself in danger of being captured in the process.

"Are you certain it's my sister?"

Anthony nodded. "From the picture you showed me, there is no mistake."

"You have to bring me to her now!" Ang demanded, but Anthony didn't budge.

"It's not that easy. We have to wait."

"For what?" Her voice shrilled with anticipation. She had come all this way for one thing—her sister—and now she was within her grasp. Plus, given the disturbing story she heard and the decapitated woman she viewed in the delivery room earlier, she couldn't wait to get out of this corrupt fortress. She didn't care how handsome Anthony was, or the strength of their physical attraction, she wanted out of there. And, the sooner, the better.

"We have to wait for the time when the guards, my brothers, let the women out to eat or to exercise. That's the only time we get a view of all the women that are in here, in captivity. Otherwise, they're all locked up individually in cells, and there is no way to see them or free them. We need to be as discreet as possible. My brothers can't ever know you're here."

Ang's muscles were strained with tension. She didn't have much choice but to wait. However, the first opportunity she had at saving her sister, she was going to take it, and they were both going to get the hell out of this God-forsaken place.

The only question that remained was…how?

Chapter 20

Veronica Juris bolted out of her cot, scrambled over to the bucket in the corner and not making it in time, retched all over the floor. Wiping the bile off her chin, she returned to her bed, body trembling. Throat burning. Waiting for the next wave of nausea to hit.

She heard sounds in the cells surrounding her: sobbing, moaning, someone was talking loudly to themselves, lathering into a panic and Veronica prayed she would stop, or the captors would come. And they would all pay.

Several weeks had passed since the first time Veronica woke up in her cell, having no idea where she was and no recollection of how she had gotten there. She didn't recognize the dirty, concrete floor, walls composed of dense wooden slabs, the diminutive metal bed or the rusted steel bucket in the corner. At that point, she didn't remember anything that had happened at her apartment—didn't remember the shady, bearded book salesman, the struggle in the foyer, being kidnapped, or being incarcerated in her cell. Her body ached, and her head felt as if a jackhammer was pounding on it from the inside.

The intense cold of the cell crept straight into her bones and quickly wiped away the grogginess and confusion, leaving her petrified as bits and pieces slowly returned to her, piercing her heart with ice.

Understanding finally that she was being held in some sort of prison, she tried to assess her situation. It was evident that it was not a legal prison. This facility wouldn't be maintaining any ethical codes of conduct. Only missing the shackles hanging from the walls, the atmosphere of this prison resembled one from the dark ages. Her captors were beasts, not human according to her standards. The threat of death was constant.

It was several days before Veronica realized that she was not alone in here. Other women were also being held captive, locked up in individual cells. Occasionally, she would get to see these women, speak to them—only with great caution. The guards did not approve of whispered conversations.

What Ronnie had learned from these women made her insides crawl. They were being held against their will to be used in experiments—impregnated with hideous, vile mutants that would grow up to be like one of them—the deformed creatures that guarded her day and night.

A baby was growing within her, cells rapidly multiplying inside of her womb. Morning sickness, already a ritual, was proof that her implanting had taken.

Pregnant. Against her will.

There was nothing she could do about it. The guards made it crystal clear, threatening that she would be killed the moment she attempted to terminate the pregnancy, escape, or so much as show a slight bit of resistance. She noticed that some days, certain women would be taken away, never to return. Only their tortured screams would be heard, and then they would be no more. These men were true to their word, and she wasn't willing to provoke them.

But death was tempting.

Escape through death would be better than waiting day after day as the fetus inside her matured, grew stronger.

The sharp clink of metal as the door unlocked drew Ronnie out of her disparaging thoughts. It was time for her temporary release. Daily, the captives were allowed three half-hour periods for exercise, and another half hour for each meal—three square meals a day—breakfast, lunch, and dinner. This was the only time she had contact with the other women.

The cell door swung open, admitting a gigantic guard with one eye sewn shut, sparse hair atop a watermelon of a head and three rotting teeth. He eyed the mess she had left all over the floor and the empty toilet-turned-vomit basin.

"Jagger!" he bellowed out into the hall. "Get a mop and clean out this bitch's cell! She made a fucking mess!" Back to Ronnie, he added, "Next time, get it in the bucket. Let's go." He grabbed her roughly by the shoulder and pushed her towards the door. Ronnie obediently exited, the behemoth following close behind, leading them into the grand central room where the other women were herded, some already beginning their circular walk around the room. Over and over again, they walked. Sometimes they were whipped like cattle.

The other captive women were in various stages of pregnancy, some almost ready to deliver, others barely showing like herself. All marched with heads down, afraid of attracting any unwanted attention for the beatings were difficult to endure. She knew all too well. Purplish bruises dotted her arms and legs from the last time she got out of line.

The dungeon's main room was a sea of stone and dirt, surrounded by the diminutive chambers within which the dozens of women were imprisoned. The last few women exited their single occupancy cells and merged in the centre with the others for their second walk of the day around the vast room. In the middle of their circle, two long, rickety wooden tables sat sentinel. This served as their breakfast, lunch, and dinner area. Meals were perfectly balanced, consisting of meat, carbohydrates, and vegetables, all cooked with minimal seasonings. The food was considered nutritional, edible but lacked flavour, not that she had much of an appetite. Ronnie knew the food was to nourish the unborn babies—these monsters cared nothing for the health of the imprisoned women. If she didn't know about the offspring that the monsters were trying to create, she would have thought that the guards were beefing up the women in order to eat them, a tragic parallel to the story of Hansel and Gretel.

Ronnie gave a quick scan of the room.

The deformed beasts took turns watching the women, keeping them in order. Usually, three to four of them were present at each meal and exercise break. The animals were shepherding the humans, instead of vice versa.

At present, four guards were on duty: the guard that had led her out of her cell; one excessively hairy beast more lupine than man; a bald, muscular giant with an extra set of limbs; and another with an extra protrusion from his neck like an underdeveloped second head. All their eyes were bottomless, emotionless black pits.

Next, her gaze found the steep rise of grey stone steps that led up into what Ronnie believed was her only means of escape. At least, that's what she held onto as a beacon of hope. As futile as that seemed.

Finally, she hastily searched the swarm of women for her one friend, Marcy, and fell into step behind her. The girl with the shoulder-length brown hair and big blue eyes had been the informant—the one who had originally educated Ronnie in their role in the experiment, the pregnancies, and the terrors that lurked within the dungeon walls. Marcy had been captured approximately four months before Ronnie or so she estimated since it was difficult to track time down there in the bowels of hell. Marcy's pregnancy was already showing, a slight bump protruding through her loose teal-coloured smock.

"How are you feeling?" Marcy whispered under her breath, her gentle brown curls bouncing above her shoulders with each step.

The girls knew they couldn't converse during their first walk of the day that morning because the blind mutant was overseeing their exercises. His hearing was markedly acute so that their conversations would be immediately overheard and punishment doled out. They had learned to be quiet during his watch. Luckily, he was now absent, and they could risk a few verbal exchanges if they were discrete.

"The nausea is pretty bad," Ronnie replied in equally hushed tones. "I couldn't keep yesterday's lunch or dinner down."

"It gets better."

"I don't think I can take this anymore. I have to get out of here!"

"Ronnie, don't do anything stupid!"

"SILENCE!" the one-eyed mutant shrieked. Unable to decipher where the whispers were coming from, he kept his whip clutched in his hand. The next time he would not be as merciful.

They continued their trek around the room in silence for the remainder of the thirty minutes that they were allotted.

Terminating the exercise session, the women were led back to their dank cells. Marcy shot Ronnie a warning look, reminding her not to do anything that she would regret. Ronnie nodded back in response, and then turned to return to her cell when she was roughly grabbed from behind.

"Not you." It was the melon-headed beast that held her arm firmly, fingers digging into her sensitive flesh. "You're coming with me. It's time for your examination," he grunted.

Ronnie and Marcy exchanged panicked looks before Marcy disappeared into her cell.

Goosebumps erupted on Ronnie's skin and scalp, and she again felt the sudden urge to vomit—this time from fear.

Up until now, her days were regimented, routine. This, however, was a new development. She thought of the other women taken away from their cells, some of them never seen again.

What did this mean? Would they torture her, kill her? Sure, she had spoken back to the beasts, been a little combative at times, but nothing that she had done lately that would be deserving of death.

Instinctively, she pulled her arm away from the giant. He lowered his massive face down in front of hers, his breath rancid like a bowl of beef stew left rotting in the sun for a week. "Don't even think of resisting."

Digging his crusty sausage fingers deeper into her flesh, he dragged her from the dungeon, up the stone stairs and into a dark hallway ridged with several unmarked doors. The third door on the left was slightly ajar, a sliver of light escaping through the crack. It opened wider of its own accord as they approached, and Ronnie was dragged through its opening, out of the poorly lit hallway and into a blindingly bright room. It was completely white—white walls, white-tiled floor, white ceiling, and white bed—all in stark contrast to the rest of the dungeon she had seen, which was mainly dark and oppressive.

After her eyes adjusted, she noticed silver metal instruments arranged neatly on a tray. The bed was like the examination tables you would find in a medical clinic, and next to it was a monitor and blood pressure machine with a stethoscope draped over the top. The room smelled of antiseptic.

Was this what the beast meant when he said it was time for her examination? She protectively wrapped her arms around her shaking form.

A tall man with golden-brown hair and goatee stood stationary by the examination table, expecting their arrival. He wore a white lab coat and was handsome in a Jeffrey Dahmer sort of way. Lethal. You could see it in his black eyes.

"You can have a seat on the examination table," the doctor instructed.

When Ronnie failed to move, the one-eyed beast physically hoisted her as if she were a rag doll and plunked her roughly onto the table's surface.

Bile rose in the back of her throat.

"I guess we haven't formally met. Hello, Veronica," the man spoke with a strong German accent. "I'm Dr. Renner Scholz."

Trembling, Ronnie nodded in acknowledgement.

"How are you enjoying your stay?" he provoked with a coy grin.

"What do you think this is—a bloody hotel? Well, it's been fabulous so far. I especially enjoy the cheery décor, the constant stench of death, and oh yes, the beatings, how could I forget those? When can I check out?"

"Ah, sarcasm. I see you don't quite understand how important this all is…how important *your* role is in changing the course of humanity."

"Humanity? I didn't realize you were actually human. You could have fooled me."

"My, you're a sassy one, aren't you? Veronica, I knew you would be different. You remind me so much of…her." The doctor appeared wistful.

"How do you know my name?"

"We've been watching you. For a long time now."

She shuddered. "What do you want with me? With all of us? Who do you think you are, Dr. Frankenstein? Making these hideous monsters. You're all fucking crazy!"

The doctor slapped her hard across the face, leaving a red imprint of his hand on her cheek. Her hand flew up to cover the stung flesh, tears welling up.

"You watch your mouth. These are my sons. They are beautiful, powerful. I won't accept any more insolence from you, Veronica." He spoke in a creepily calm, chastising tone. He seemed to be taunting her like he knew some hidden secret that was amusing only to him. "Let's not make that a habit, talking back like a spoiled child, alright? You must always show respect."

He didn't wait for her to respond. Stretching on latex gloves over his large hands, he snapped them into place at his wrists.

"Lie down."

She reluctantly obliged. A paper sheet covering the examination table crinkled and tore in protest as she shifted her body down onto its surface.

The doctor stared at her in a way that made the deformed creatures that guarded the women day and night seem like friendly school children in comparison. Gently, he then raised her tunic, exposing her abdomen. Fingers palpated and probed its flat surface.

"You may sit up now," he again demanded.

Ronnie sat upright, pulling her tunic back down to its proper position. Dr. Scholz proceeded to shine a light in her pupils and down her throat; he felt her lymph nodes behind her ears and neck. Draping the stethoscope around his neck, he placed the ends into his ears and raised the metal disc up to her heart, listening first at her chest, then the front and back of her lungs. It was an otherwise routine doctor's examination.

"Your left arm, please," the doctor requested. Ronnie offered her arm, and the man tied a rubber band above her elbow. The vein in her forearm became engorged with blood. After the blood sample was collected, he taped a cotton ball over the site and sealed and stowed the sample on a rack resting on a nearby metal cart.

The man thrust an orange sealed cup in Ronnie's face.

"Fill it." He pointed at the bucket in the corner.

"You've got to be kidding me!"

The doctor raised his hand as if to strike her again, but she jumped off the examination table and sat on the bucket before he had the chance.

It took longer than necessary to fulfill her obligation, the doctor and guard both avidly watching the entire process. Performance anxiety at its peak. But at long last she was successful. Humiliated, all modesty stripped away but successful.

The doctor grabbed the urine sample jar with his gloved hands and eyed it as if it contained pure gold in liquid form. His black eyes grew in size and depth. He nodded at the guard waiting by the door. "That will be all. Take her back to her cell."

The guard seized Ronnie by the arm again, but this time there was no need to drag her. She left willingly, her step quick and in pace with the guard's, eager to return to her cell. She felt it was safer there, a temporary refuge.

Her gut told her the evil man was testing her urine that moment as they hastened back to her prison, determining if she was pregnant or not. She already knew that she was and shuddered involuntarily at the revolting thought.

What were these strange creatures up to? Why capture all these women and force them to give birth to mutant humans: hideous, evil, and immoral? More importantly, she wondered how she had become pregnant. How did the baby get inside of her? She wasn't sure how long she was unconscious after being kidnapped, but she assumed she must have been impregnated at that time. Marcy had mentioned that after she awoke in her cell, there was an incision on her abdomen. But Ronnie did not have one. The thought of these creatures touching her finally pushed her over the edge.

As soon as she was thrown into her cell, she dashed to her bucket, vomiting up pure acid and bile. Her stomach heaved again, but there was nothing left to throw up.

The door slammed loudly behind her, echoing in the now silent dungeon. A click told her the key had been turned in the lock securing the heavy bolt.

She crawled into her bed, body trembling. Silent tears spilled.

The delusions of escaping up the steep, stone steps were quashed. Comprehension finally set in, and she accepted her cruel fate.

She would never get out of this hell.

Chapter 21

Veronica, you are the one. At long last, I have found you.

Renner peeled the latex gloves from his hands, tossing them into the trash. He wore them only as an added precaution, more out of habit than necessity. The women, allowed to stay at the castle, were free from all infection and disease; he tested them personally when they arrived. He also preferred virgins, but he'd made a few exceptions over the years.

After retrieving his newly acquired samples he slithered up the crude stone steps back into the warmth and luxury of the upper levels of the castle. Manoeuvring through several lushly decorated hallways, past rooms scarcely used, he reached his well-stocked laboratory and entered.

On the left side of the sterile room, a cabinet housed all the solutions and substrates he would need to test his newly acquired samples. Sliding open the glass door, he selected the materials he required: a urine strip to test for pregnancy and a radioimmunoassay (RIA) for the blood work. Once all the equipment was gathered, he perched on top of a metal stool in front of a lab table and commenced analyzing his samples.

The massive castle housed fifty-plus rooms within its sizeable girth, yet this room, the laboratory, was his favourite, where he felt at home, where he spent most of his time. Well equipped with all the technology and supplies he required from the help of his telekinetic son, Tomas, he could perform any experiments and procedures within the comfort and privacy of his own home. This was vital to his ongoing plans.

He donned a fresh pair of latex gloves, careful not to contaminate his specimens. Removing the orange cap of the bottle containing the amber liquid, he plunged the pregnancy stick into its contents. The test was not that unlike the ones found in a local grocery store or pharmacy but boasted a much more accurate reading, approximately 99 %. He raised his left forearm, studied the large hand on his Rolex until it completed a full rotation around the dial, then again, and yet again, until five minutes had lapsed. Patiently, he waited. He had such high hopes for this pregnancy.

Once the allotted time period was achieved, he rechecked the urine stick.

Yes, it is positive!

But there was still the blood test to perform, which would yield more pertinent information regarding the pregnancy, giving a rough estimate of the fetuses age, and whether the pregnancy was viable, progressing as it should.

For this, he used the radioimmunoassay to measure the amount of hCG or human chorionic gonadotropin in the blood. This initial test would serve as a base amount of the hormone and within a few days, he would gather a new blood sample from Veronica to see if the hCG level was increasing as anticipated. For a normal, viable pregnancy, the hCG levels would show a doubling in value every two days, slightly slowing to three and a half days after the first month of pregnancy.

He recorded the value, 7 ml/U, in his ledger beside the name Veronica Juris. He closed the book and returned it to the drawer in his stainless-steel lab desk. Discarding the blood sample and yet another pair of soiled, latex gloves, he glanced around the sterile, organized, sparsely furnished room. A hefty metal cage embraced an alcove on the right side of the room. Renner pictured Milena housed within its sturdy walls, weak, broken.

Sometimes she needed to be punished.

The cage was convenient, placed where he could keep a close eye on her until she learned her lesson. It served him well. Until her ultimate betrayal. Then, the cage wasn't enough punishment. He didn't feel he had a choice, what she forced him to do.

He felt a twinge. Sadness? Guilt? He had forgotten such emotions…thought he was no longer capable of feeling anything, except for greed, hatred, unbridled fury. These long-forgotten emotions caught him off guard.

He reached far back into the recesses of his memory and was able to grab hold of a moment. Milena, her laughter like musical notes ringing across a field of perfume scented flowers as he chased her—not to imprison her—but as a playful game of two people in love. The memory felt so real; it stirred up more intense emotions. This time, magnified fourfold.

He was having an unusually lucid day.

Ever since the night he had visited the witch woman so many years ago in the chapel of the derelict asylum, these memories, these feelings, had been elusive to him. Of course, it made it much easier to treat Milena how he had. As if she were a mere animal in his laboratory.

Milena.

His wife, his love. It shouldn't have ended this way. She could still be here with him, helping him with his research. But she had decided to rebel against him. Tried to kidnap his son, the one destined to fully help him achieve his dreams, the prophecy that foretold of his glory. No, Renner had no choice but to punish her, destroy her.

And now, because of her poor choices, his research had almost been jeopardized. It had been eight years since he had last harvested her eggs. And now his supply had run out. Without an adequate supplier, which he had yet to find, his research would be at a standstill, unable to progress, and he would be unable to complete his plan. He wasn't finished yet.

And then Veronica came along. There was a special quality to this young woman that reminded Renner of his deceased wife. A certain vigour, passion, and sassiness. The women were always stalked for a time before capture to ensure they had few, or no people, who would miss them should they disappear. To see if they were an adequate candidate for his studies. If there were one or two friends or family members, they were easily disposed of. No one to come searching for the kidnapped women. Tomas could easily determine such details by reading their minds. Veronica exhibited the qualities he desired, and then some. Sure, she didn't have any psychic abilities, but she possessed so much more. She begged to be broken down by him. He knew this wouldn't be too difficult. Also, she was stunningly beautiful, not as exotic as his Milena but certainly breathtaking.

Perhaps this was the reason for his reminiscing, experiencing feelings he had long forgotten. Veronica helping him to remember. And now he was finally able to transfer his hopes, his focus, in a new direction. Not that his previous attempts at creating a higher being were unsuccessful. His castle teemed with his creations, his powerful sons, soldiers, able to crush anyone who should cross their paths. Psychic abilities beyond what anyone could imagine possible. Inconceivable levels of strength, intelligence, bloodlust. But the limitations were glaringly obvious, and it addled his brain that he couldn't solve these flaws in his research. He had a major hurdle to overcome.

He didn't care if he could only sire gifted sons. He felt women were quite useless except to serve as an incubator for his spawn. What irked him most were the gruesome, distorted features with which his offspring were born.

What good was a legion of gifted soldiers if they were forced to be hidden from the human eye? He hoped one day he would succeed in overcoming this flaw, enabling them to wander undetected among the masses. Only then would they fulfill their mission, without being deterred.

For who would follow them if their evil was glaringly apparent? Observable to the physical eye? How would they seduce, entice, deceive?

Of course, once their external physical characteristics could be perfected, he would then focus on their ability to reproduce. For now, that was not a priority as they would only reproduce imperfect work. And that was not acceptable to Renner. He was aware that his own ability to reproduce would eventually be limited by his aging body, although it aged much slower than the average man due to the genetic mutations to his genome after the Guardian Angel Spell was cast. As a precaution, he had preserved some of his own specimens to ensure many more years of viable sperm for DNA manipulation. He wanted his lineage to grow, prosper and, eventually, be able to sustain itself through procreation.

He disinfected the surface of his desk and his utensils used for the tests by placing them in a prepared sterilizing bath. Then, he strode over to the liquid nitrogen tank that once housed Milena's frozen harvested eggs. Veronica would help him replenish these stores.

But, when Veronica first arrived at the castle, Renner was faced with a dilemma. She was kept drugged for several days, during which he had discovered she was at a fertile stage in her cycle. He wasn't sure if he should impregnate her at once or harvest her eggs. It was possible to only do one at a time. In the end, he couldn't wait. The egg harvesting would have to be postponed. Unable to resist her, he impregnated her, knowing this time the offspring would be different. Following her nine-month gestation period and the birth of their baby, only then would he begin the hormone therapy, inducing hyper-ovarian stimulation, after which point he would be able to harvest ten to twelve eggs each time and begin to restock his supplies.

Using a long ultrasound needle, he would extract the eggs from her ovaries and insert them into fluid. Next, he would identify the individual eggs via microscope and separate them from water by placing them in an antifreeze solution to prevent crystals from forming on the eggs, which would damage them. Then using a slow-freezing technique he would prepare them for long term storage in the liquid nitrogen tank before him. It was a procedure he had done many times before...on his wife.

Retracing his steps, he sat again at his metal lab desk and retrieved a different set of papers stored within its confines.

His research notes.

Meticulously written, delicately and precisely mapped out, he perused its familiar pages. Where was he going wrong?

He began his experiments by thawing the stored eggs using only as many as he needed. He then manipulated the DNA to enhance the pineal gland, so it produced more DMT (dimethyltryptamine). DMT, a substance long taken externally as a hallucinogenic compound resulting in experiences bordering on the supernatural, was part of his research since the beginning. He discovered, what only now other scientists were rediscovering— that DMT is naturally produced in the human body, specifically the pineal gland and that people with above normal amounts were capable of psychic experiences or had a predisposition to special abilities. His pride swelled, for this discovery was mind-blowing. He smirked at the scientists only now realizing the important role of DMT—the spirit molecule—as a catalyst to connect the human brain to the supernatural realm. And, they were still so behind in their progress.

But it was not an exact science. Sometimes the pineal gland would end up producing excessive amounts of DMT, more so than was required for psychic phenomena to manifest, resulting instead in offspring with schizophrenic tendencies. Hallucinations. Profound cognitive impairment. These abnormalities usually didn't present themselves until the boys were twelve to fourteen years of age. By then, Renner didn't have the heart to destroy them. Besides, he had his own method of controlling them. They roamed the castle, unpredictable, dangerous even but thus far contained.

The successful sons, however, were formidable, talented, powerful creations. Some were capable of moving items through space, like Tomas, others could predict the future, and some could read or control other people's minds.

It was always a pleasant surprise when the children matured enough to display their abilities. Renner had no way of knowing ahead of time the psychic talents they would have—they were arbitrarily chosen by fate or luck.

Other abilities Renner did have control of, for not only during his genetic manipulations would he boost DMT production, but he would also enhance other coveted characteristics. Strength, intelligence, size, bloodlust—randomly assigning a few per offspring so that all his children would exhibit different traits.

The manipulated eggs would be injected with his enhanced sperm. Once the egg developed into an embryo, it was implanted into the uterus of a captured woman where it would grow and develop into a gifted son. With powers and abilities beyond any human on Earth.

His research seemed flawless. Where were the errors in his work? No matter how many times he went over his notes, he couldn't find any. Possibly the fault lay in Milena's eggs, and not a mistake on his side, after all. Veronica's eggs could show different results, produce more viable, attractive offspring. Eliminate the deformities that plagued his creations.

He would have to wait to find out.

For now, he was only concerned with her current pregnancy. A natural pregnancy, the egg and sperm left intact, no genetic manipulations, save those he had sustained to his own genome after the Guardian Angel Spell. This would be the one: he could feel it in his gut.

Great hopes indeed.

Chapter 22

An array of snapshots covered the table before Ang, all containing the same raven-haired, exotic woman with the desolate azure eyes. Anthony lovingly and proudly spoke about each picture, obviously fond memories for him. But, the depth of sadness and anguish in his mother's eyes conflicted with the happiness those moments seemed to bring him.

Sitting thigh to thigh, remaining in the library while they waited to see Ronnie, Anthony filled the time with detailed stories of his family, of his past, elucidating on the evil acts of his father and brothers and their quest for the perfect human, and attempting to answer all of Ang's questions.

"I still don't understand why your father and brothers would spare you after killing your mother," Ang questioned.

"I have my own theories, but to tell you the truth, I'm not sure. I'm grasping at straws trying to make sense of it. My brothers hate me, and I'm pretty sure my father hates me. The only thing that makes sense is that they need me."

"But, for what? Tell me your theories."

He ran a hand through his thick, black hair. "I think part of it has to do with the genetic experiments my father is obsessed with. For some reason, my appearance wasn't deformed, and maybe my genes hold the key for Renner finally discovering the flaw in his method."

"Did he ever run any tests on you? Take any samples?"

"Not really. Unless it was when I was a baby, and I don't remember."

"I assume he would want to keep studying your genes if that was the main reason that he's keeping you around. He would need fresh samples to analyze. There has to be more to it."

"Yeah, I guess you have a point."

"What's the next theory?"

"Maybe they're too busy kidnapping women and watching their hostages. Too obsessed with creating more mutants, they don't have time to bother with me."

"No, that can't be it either. Your father had the opportunity to take you out when you were trying to escape, and he chose not to. If he truly hated you that much, like you said, he must have a specific reason to keep you around. Otherwise, he would have killed you then."

"But I was only a kid. Maybe he kept me as a reminder of my mother. He loved her once. And I look exactly like her, except for my eyes. Apparently, they look like Renner's, before his eyes turned black. And I wasn't much of a flight risk after my mother's death. I was only ten and all alone."

"Hmmm. Maybe." Ang paused, deep in thought. "Or could it have to do with this prophecy you alluded to earlier? When I first came into the castle and was hiding behind the clock, I overheard two of the mutant men talking…they mentioned a prophecy. They said someone, I can't remember his name, had another vision of a boy with dark, shaggy hair being the path and the key, and that they wish they could dispose of him, and then I didn't understand the rest. Could they have been talking about you?"

"It's possible. My brother, Gregor, has had some powerful visions that all came true. I know some involve me, but I don't know how. I don't know what he saw. I'm no longer a boy, either, so I don't know how the prophecy concerns me."

"All this talk of genetic experiments and prophecies makes me feel like I'm in the middle of a science fiction movie. I still can't believe this is all real." She also couldn't shake the feeling of impending doom that clung to her ever since the bear attack with Gavin saving her life. She shuddered.

Wrapping his arm around her shoulders protectively, Anthony gave her a comforting squeeze. "Hey, we'll be safe as long as we stay hidden. No one ever comes in here, except for me. This room is anathema to them. My father and brothers won't be bothering us tonight."

Ang felt her heart racing, never being in such proximity to a man, let alone a gorgeous one at that. His arm, warm and comforting on her shoulder. The gentle musk of his natural scent was all she could focus on. Breath rate increasing. Was he aware of the impact he had on her? He seemed so nonchalant, like they had been pals their whole lives and putting his arm around her was common game, yet her body was on fire, a deep part of her unexplored and now fully awakened. She was so enamoured by his presence that she had momentarily forgotten her sister until Anthony brought it up.

A quick glance at his watch, and he announced, "It's almost time."

Ang sprang to her feet. "How do we get there?"

"We're just going to take a look this time, okay? We can't bring any attention to you until we figure out a way to get you and your sister out of here safely. I'm not sure yet how we're going to manage it. It seems impossible."

"Don't you want to leave too?" Ang imagined him locked in here, a prisoner his entire life, his mother gone now for eight years. Surrounded by brothers that detested him. He must be so lonely.

"I...," he began then hesitated.

"Well?"

"I've never left the building except for the time...you know... with my mother..." Ang nodded, understanding his turmoil.

"It's all I know. These books," he turned, pointing to the massive collection that literally covered the walls from floor to ceiling, "everything I know I learned from them. And my mother did her best to teach me what real life is like. But I've never been to school, I don't have a real family, a place to live, a social insurance number, friends—it's like I don't even exist. Where would I go? How would I live? I don't have a job or money."

He did have a point.

"But you can't live like this," she stubbornly argued. "It's too dangerous, and these psychopaths need to be stopped."

"How can I stop them if I don't have any powers?"

"I don't know yet, but we have to do something. Maybe I can help you. And, if we get out of here, you could stay with me and my grandmother. I'll help you get back into civilization, and you'll have the chance at a normal life."

She couldn't miss the wistfulness in his eyes. He must have wished for this opportunity his whole life yet accepted it would never be attained. Maybe she could renew his hope for a normal future. A happy future. But, the look in his eyes quickly faded, and Ang wondered if it was ever there.

"First, let's concentrate on finding your sister."

★ ★ ★

Ang's constant gnawing anxiety morphed into total full-blown apprehension as they re-entered the secret tunnels and wormed their way deeper into the bowels of the castle. She was worried the woman they were going to see may not be Ronnie after all and, of course, she was petrified of being caught by the hideously deformed creatures Anthony had described to her, some of whom she had seen in person—his "brothers." If the two men she eavesdropped on in the hallway and the man who executed the woman in labour were any indication of what these creatures were like, were capable of, she wanted no contact with them whatsoever.

The dampened earthy smell grew stronger, indicating they were below ground, and the tunnels continued to go deeper towards a dungeon filled with missing women. The thought was horrifying.

As they travelled, Anthony explained the origins of the castle, the tunnels, and how they came to be embedded within the mountain cave.

"Tomas, my brother, one of the triplets, teleported the entire castle to this site. The castle had been long abandoned, in disrepair, nothing that would be missed. He replaced the castle he took with a pile of rubble as if the building had collapsed—a common fate for old structures."

"I can't imagine how Tomas could possibly transport a whole castle across space. It's mindboggling."

"And he was only a young child." Anthony paused, and turned to Ang, gently taking her hand. Gazing deeply into her eyes, he asked, "Do you still think I'm crazy?"

She could barely breathe or get any words to form, his massive hands sending heat up her arms, a hot flush suffusing her whole body. Finally, she forced herself to respond. "Honestly, I don't know what I think. I certainly want to believe you. I need you to be sane because you're the only friend I have in this mess."

Anthony smiled, displaying perfect teeth and dimples. "I guess that makes two of us. You're my only friend, period."

Ang returned the smile, hoping he didn't notice that she was trembling. Attempting to appear as cool, calm and collected as Anthony, she took back her hand, though reluctantly, and continued walking. "If the building was falling apart, how come now it is fully repaired?"

"My brothers, still small at the time, were already extremely powerful. They quickly got to work repairing the castle to its former glory. The secret tunnels were also forged so that the castle mimics the original, providing escape routes if ever necessary. They've never had to use them. I'm the only one who comes in here, usually, so I can see what they are up to, undetected. Well, usually undetected. They've busted me a few times."

Anthony continued explaining the castle's origins. "Once the castle was complete, my brothers filled up the rooms with furniture, the most exquisite artwork, tapestries, and rugs from all over the world, from all periods in history, again using their profound telekinetic abilities. They use generators for power, but only a few rooms are kept illuminated. Otherwise, we use candles, torches or flashlights if we need to. We have water from a nearby river, but that, too, is limited to only a few rooms. Bathrooms, kitchen. My brothers don't bother to bathe or follow any other routines for hygiene, so we're pretty sparing in the water usage department."

"Are you sure nobody knows of this castle's existence?" Ang asked, desperate.

"The surface of the castle is so deeply embedded into the rocky cave that it's completely camouflaged from the outside world. You need to be directly in front of it to see it, so the only people who know of its existence are the people who live here, and now you."

Ang's heart sank, her concerns vocalized by Anthony. Nobody would know where to come looking for her should she not return. It was up to her to save Ronnie and get them both out of here alive. There would be no backup plan.

A cry echoed in the near distance. An animalistic yelp like that of a dog. Shuddering she knew deep down inside it was human— one of the prisoners.

Anthony grabbed Ang's hand again as if it was the most natural thing to do, pulling her close to him. He put one finger to his lips, those beautifully formed, dark red lips she so desperately wanted to kiss, then pulled her over to a small opening in the tunnel wall. It was narrow and difficult to see through, requiring her to press her eye right against the crack of light to get a view of the room beyond the wall.

"They should be starting their final walk of the night. Right before lights out," he whispered, resting his hand on her hip. The warmth from Anthony's hand was forgotten, and a chill crept down her spine, deepening, freezing her very soul.

It reminded her of an old-time circus freak show. Distorted bodies, a reminder of what can happen when the genetic code becomes disarranged. Four hulking forms stood guard, watching from the corners of the room, each more hideous and deformed than the next.

In the far-right corner stood what was at some level a man, but some vital components of his face were missing—mainly his eyes, which contained smooth skin where the eyeballs should have been, and a nose and mouth that were dark, gaping holes in a putty-like head. Occasionally, a red, pointy tongue would thrust out of the mouth-like orifice. He clutched a bulky, black mace with barbed spikes in his enormous, vein-riddled hands. Ang wondered if he had ever used this contraption on the women captives, knowing they could be killed with one swift blow. The barbs would tear their skin, possibly their organs right off their bodies. He seemed focused on his captives despite the lack of eyes. He must be relying on another sense to detect them. Would he be able to detect her and Anthony in their hiding spots? She suddenly became very aware of their scents—hers floral, a combination of the shampoo, conditioner, and body wash she had used back at the hotel that same morning, Anthony's, a more musky, spicy scent.

Seeing where Ang was gawping, Anthony whispered in her ear, "That's Rdulf. He is a precog, able to predict the future. He's not as gifted as Gregor, the triplet you heard about but still dangerously powerful."

"Over there, that is Wolfram." Anthony pointed to their immediate right where the creature crouched, this one more animal than human. Moving around on all fours, his hind legs were bent backwards, the joints reversed like a canine. His fingers had claws instead of fingernails, as deadly and sharp like the yellow teeth that ringed his pointy, beak-like mouth. His eyes were deep black, pure evil, his nose flat. Although he wore clothes—stretchy grey shorts and a plain white T-shirt, any exposed skin was hairier than even the hairiest man on Earth. Saliva dripped from his gaping mouth, and Ang couldn't avoid the thought that he could devour the women if he so chose.

"He's a chimera," Anthony explained.

"Chimera?" Ang remembered the various animalistic statues carved into the exterior of the castle.

"He has both human and animal genetic material. He is part man but also has genetic material from a wolf and a raven."

Ang felt the gorge rising. Choked it back down.

On her left—close to the wall that concealed them so that it was difficult to see him in his entirety, but what she could discern made her lose her breath—stood the third guard. He had four arms, all as muscular as the largest competitive bodybuilder would have, he towered over seven feet, and he roared at the women when they got out of line. He also used a whip, lashing them if they so much as looked up—angry, bloody welts appearing where their skin had been stung.

His head, misshapen with a doughnut of hair at its crest, had all the right features but in all the wrong places. His eyes, more on the sides of his face, blinked at different rates, his nose was more on the left of his face, and his gaping mouth was swerved to the right.

"Eberhard. His strength rivals that of Sampson. Still, he is weak in comparison to Friedrich, the third of the triplets."

The last man was the most hideous of all. Two heads sprouted from his neck, the one partially embedded on the side of the other, the product of conjoined twins enmeshed—all facial features combined into a ruined mess. Two mouths, four eyes, two noses, all mashed together but moving as if two distinct entities resided within. The body was oddly normal but more massive in size and girth than a regular human. The weapon it held—an anvil—had dried rusty blood at its tip. "Gunter. He is a formidable soldier, having two sets of powers since he is a conjoined twin. He can heal any part of his body: bones, sinews, flesh wounds. He is practically indestructible. He is also full of rage and bloodlust, taking great pleasure in his kills."

A prickle of dread crept over Ang's scalp when she remembered what Anthony had told her in the library—that there were hundreds of these malformed creatures residing within the walls of this castle.

Hundreds.

And most of them also exhibited hidden psychic abilities. She finally comprehended the futility of their task.

"How can Gunter be around all of these women and not murder them all if bloodlust is in his DNA, part of his nature?" Ang questioned.

Anthony spun Ang around, so now both hands rested on her hips. Staring down at his boots, he shuffled his feet uncomfortably, and then glanced back at her, his green eyes vibrant in the dark tunnel. "Uh, I guess I wasn't fully honest with you before. There is one thing that sets me apart from normal men. Not actually a 'power' per se, but…"

"But what?" Ang braced herself.

"For some reason, I neutralize my brothers' paranormal and genetically enhanced abilities. If I'm around, their powers are diluted, practically useless. Except when I'm in my room and the library… these rooms are reinforced, like soundproofing but to block out my influence on them, by filling the walls and ceiling with mass and cotton batten. It gives them a little more hold on their abilities, but they still don't have full use. They would prefer for me to stay in my allotted rooms, so they are stronger, but I like to roam around and see what they are up to. I think father likes the fact that I keep some of my wilder siblings under control. But my brothers hate to be thwarted, so they all avoid the library and my bedroom, knowing they are weaker when near me."

"Thank God. I don't want to see them when they *can* use their powers. They're intimidating enough without them." Ang was shaking in her Sorel boots.

Ang turned back to the crack in the wall, her eyes finally focused on the helpless women, their every move controlled by the monsters surrounding them. They moved in a circle like abused animals. The women were at different stages of pregnancy. One of the women, almost due to deliver, collapsed from exhaustion only to be whipped by the four-armed giant, forcing her back to her feet without a moment's reprieve.

Ang frantically searched for her sister, but there were so many women, heads bent low in subservience, that at first, she couldn't see her. And then, she noticed a woman with long, blond tangled hair who had the same body type as her sister. This girl was emaciated, dejected and deflated—not proud and confident like her sister usually was. But, after watching the woman for several moments, Ang exclaimed, "That's her, that's my sister Ronnie!"

"That's what I thought."

Suddenly, Ronnie glimpsed up as if seeing her pressed up to the crack behind the wall. But she looked away almost immediately, no recognition apparent. Ang wanted to call out to her but remembered her promise to Anthony.

A man entered, then, normal in appearance with long hair and a goatee—the doctor she had seen delivering the stillborn.

"That's my father," Anthony whispered in her ear.

Her blood ran cold with fear and anger. Who was this evil man that believed it was okay to kidnap and imprison these innocent women and force them to give birth to his army of deformed gifted creatures? How dare he keep Anthony locked away from the world, killing the only person in his life that took care of him and whom he loved so deeply.

"He doesn't usually come down here. I wonder what he's up to."

Suddenly, the eyeless monster whipped his face in their direction.

Had he heard their whispers? Finally caught a whiff of their scents?

"We have to go. Now!" Anthony darted off through the tunnels, dragging Ang behind him, his hand again firmly clutching hers. Heavy running steps approached from behind the wall, and when Ang glanced back, she could see a black eye pressed against the crack where they had stood moments before. Anthony pulled Ang along, and together they swiftly manoeuvred through the maze of earthen corridors—he knew these passageways so well—until they reached the safety of the library.

But, the feeling of safety was fleeting.

"Hide!" Anthony urged while seeking for a place that would conceal her. Their eyes both locked simultaneously on a black leather ottoman that opened and could be used for storage—but would she fit?

After contorting her body into an impossibly small ball, she squeezed inside. Anthony was able to replace the cover and sat atop it, right as she heard the main door to the library crash open.

"Father," Anthony sounded breathless, reeking of guilt.

"Have you been spying from the tunnels again?" his father spat out in disgust. You could tell from his voice alone that this man had no love, only intense hatred for his son.

"Uh, yes, sorry, Father. I was bored and couldn't help myself."

"I told you that it is forbidden!" his father bellowed. Two distinct voices could be heard, one normal and one as if demonic, inhuman. Both voices discordant. Ang held her breath and frantically prayed they wouldn't be caught.

"I know, but curiosity got the best of me. It won't happen again. I promise," Anthony responded in a small, compliant voice.

"I'm going to have to find a better punishment for you if this keeps up. But, for now, no special provisions for the next month!" The library door slammed shut, announcing the father's exit.

Anthony waited five minutes before he raised the lid of the ottoman—right on time, for Ang feared her oxygen was near depletion. However, she refused to leave the tiny space, refused Anthony's hand as he tried to pry her out.

The impossibility of her situation pressed in around her like the narrow sides of the ottoman. Crushing pressure. How in the world would she ever get past the mutants to free her sister, and how would they escape the castle? Where was Gavin and why had he abandoned her in her greatest time of need? Would bringing Anthony with them increase the level of peril, an extra burden they didn't need?

Or was she already in too deep, an emotional and physical connection forged with a stranger that made the extra peril worth all the risk?

Chapter 23

"He's still unconscious?" Renner Scholz stared at his precognitive son's supine form. Gregor was shrouded in forest green sheets, his muscles slack. An oval shield of metal covered the area where his face was lacking, the metal wired with robotic facial features that normally lit up with cerulean lights when he was alert. The metal edges of the shield were deeply implanted into the surrounding skin. Tomas' invention—the prosthetic face shield—not only covered the mutation Gregor had been born with but also gave him the intimidating appearance of an android as if he were part man, part machine. "Why is it taking so long?"

Renner's agitation was partly due to Gregor's lingering unconsciousness. He wanted to see if anything new was foreseen, if the original vision of the prophecy had changed. The wait was infuriating. So much rested in the balance. Equally infuriating was Anthony's insubordination. His nosiness, snooping around the tunnels, had disrupted his evening. On Renner's way to see Veronica one last time before bedtime, he was interrupted by Anthony and forced to deal with him instead. It soured his mood.

Why couldn't Anthony stay quiet and be compliant? Be all but forgotten until the moment he was needed?

"Yes, Father. Gregor hasn't stirred since the seizure," Friedrich— the largest of the triplets—responded, head bowed in subservience. His leg muscles rippled as he rose from the bedside chair to allow his father a closer view at the unconscious man. His prosthetic robotic arms were folded over his chest. The electrical pulses they were able to emit disengaged, only stimulated while he was in combat. The other two sets of arms hung limply at his sides.

Renner sat beside the bed. Grabbing Gregor's wrist, he checked his pulse. It had returned to normal, whereas directly following the premonition, it had raced impossibly high. Renner was concerned that Gregor would suffer a stroke if it remained elevated, but the fact that it had slowed was a positive sign he was in the clear.

Tomas entered the chamber as Renner was continuing to examine Gregor's vitals. An Elvin war mask covered his face, white symbolic etchings tattooed across its smooth, black surface. One of his many disguises.

"What did I miss? Did he say anything yet?"

Renner paused from taking Gregor's temperature and faced his telekinetic son accusingly. "He's still unconscious. Why are *you* so eager to talk to him? What are you hoping he will say?"

Tomas' eyes darkened behind his mask. "Is it so hard to believe that I'm asking purely out of concern for my brother?" He raised his chin. "But I am curious. I wonder if he will have more to say regarding the prophecy, a new clue to shed light on who this mysterious boy is supposed to be. One thing is certain—the boy can't be Anthony like we originally thought."

Renner flew over to Tomas, confronting him with balled fists. His voice remained disturbingly calm yet laced with threat.

"Why would you say that? Who else could it possibly be? And if Anthony isn't the one from the prophecy, what would you have me do, Tomas?" It was a trap, but Tomas could not hold his tongue any longer.

"You already know how I feel, Father," he spat. "Anthony is nothing but trouble for us. He's too unpredictable. Who knows what he is planning? Spying, lurking in the tunnels, creeping around the castle. He'll be our undoing, I'll bet my life on it."

"The prophecy states…"

Tomas cut Renner off. "The prophecy speaks of a young boy with dark hair. Sure, Anthony fit the description years ago. But now he is a bloody man. He's no longer a boy, nor shall he ever be one again. The prophecy can't be speaking of him. There's no longer any reason to keep him around."

"I understand you have tolerated Anthony as much as is possible. Ever since he was born, you have plotted against him. Don't think I can't see your desires."

Tomas glared at his father. "He's not one of us!"

"Why, because he's not hideous and deformed like you and your brothers? He may not be one of you, but he is still mine." Renner's words wounded with intention. "You're always hiding behind your stupid masks. Take it off!"

"But, Father…"

Renner didn't wait. He tore the mask from his son's shamed face and threw it to the ground, crushing it with the heel of his shoe. "I made you. You should be proud of who you are."

"As you are of us, Father?" Tomas hissed. The burned, mottled skin of his face could not hide his indignity.

"Careful, Son. Your lisp is showing. It always comes out when you're upset. You've always been so jealous of him," Renner goaded.

Tomas' jaw clenched, and his lips flattened in a straight line. "And why shouldn't I be? He's perfect, the only one of us that wasn't born deformed. He weakens us with his very presence. And he's the only one she ever loved, the only one she truly called her son. Milena hated us. You know that. And Anthony hates us too. He needs to be destroyed…now, before it's too late."

"And what exactly do you think he will do? If he was going to do something, don't you think he would have done it by now? He's harmless. You should be embarrassed, cowering from him."

"Why do you always defend him? It's his fault Milena tried to leave, his fault she is now dead. You should hate him as much as we all do. If not, more. So, why keep him around? Tell me, Father. I deserve to know."

"You want so desperately to be rid of your brother. You may think that he has nothing to do with the prophecy, but he must. Your brother, Gregor, had his first vision on the exact day that Anthony was born."

"Yes, how can I forget that day? The day my life was ruined forever."

Renner ignored him, "The second vision came on the day Anthony was trying to escape, the day his mother was killed. The third vision, today. The timing of these visions cannot be by coincidence. We must wait for Gregor to awaken. There must be more to the prophecy."

"You'll regret this, Father. We've waited long enough."

"That sounded like a threat. I hope you're not planning anything without my knowledge, without my consent?" Renner accused.

Tomas seethed. "I don't understand why you protect Anthony. He is insignificant. He has no powers. In fact, his presence makes all of us weaker simply by his being in our proximity. That alone is enough of a reason to destroy him. He is a direct hindrance to your plans. It's also Anthony's fault that I look the way I do, buried in ruined skin. You may have created me, but it was Anthony, who irreparably scarred me. For that, he must pay." Tomas paused, and perhaps realizing that his pleas were going nowhere, unclenched his jaw and spoke with exaggerated articulation, the lisp no longer as evident. "But I cannot disrespect your wishes. I will act only with your consent."

Renner nodded. It was the only acceptable answer.

"Gregor has been unconscious for a while now. Much longer than the last time. What can we do to coax him out of this state?" Friedrich piped in, reminding the other men of his presence.

"Give him time," Renner spoke.

A grunt from the bed pulled their attention to Gregor. Twitching fingers. Had the precog been listening the whole time?

Was he awake? Eyeless sockets permanently unable to open, the face shield, still not illuminated.

"Son, are you awake?" Renner sat beside the bed, placing his hand on Gregor's arm.

Another grunt in response, this one more audible. Almost a word. A glimmer of light from the face shield, and then full service was restored. The eye impressions lit up brightly from within.

"Take your time, my son. We are all here."

Gregor shifted, head rolling side to side, and then the voice machine burst into static. An attempt to speak? Born without a tongue along with no face, he relied on the prosthesis for communication.

"What...happened?" Gregor finally sputtered.

"You had another vision. And another seizure. Do you recall anything? What did you see?" Renner probed, expectant.

Gregor's brows furrowed in concentration. "I...I can't remember."

Renner frowned with displeasure; his son's pause too lengthy. He needed to know, his research and goals hanging by a thread, dependent on the vision, its revelations. "Well?" more forcefully.

Gregor rubbed his forehead, sat upright in the bed. "Yes, yes, it's coming back to me. I remember now. But it was the same, Father."

Renner's shoulders slumped. He stood up, consternation on his face. This was not the news he was hoping for. He needed more information, damn it!

Tomas was right. The boy from the prophecy couldn't be Anthony. And, what he already knew of the prophecy didn't make sense. What was he missing? The vision had seemed so clear at first, so obvious, but now a main piece of the puzzle was missing. If not Anthony, who was this boy the vision foretold of, the one that was the path and the key to his achieving his goal—total human control?

He had the inkling that Anthony was not the one for a while now. Yet, he resisted the thought of destroying him—the last living part of his Milena. It helped that Anthony's presence held the powers of his gifted offspring in check. Left unchecked, their volatile natures would soon have them all killed. And he was also the only child born without deformities and possibly held the key to overcoming the obstacle in his studies, which is what had given him the idea to change things in Veronica's case.

Now, perhaps, there would be another.

"Gregor, my son, think hard. Perhaps you are missing something. Tell us again of your vision. Leave nothing out."

The precog began:

"There is a child—with dark, shaggy hair, perhaps anywhere from eight to twelve-years-old. Skin, milk white, eyes not dark black but a brilliant emerald green. Innocent and naïve, yet troubled as if they have seen too much, more than they should have at that age or at any age. The child is lost. Yet they are the map, the route to guide us to that which we need, what we seek, what we covet. That will help us gain control of mankind. Help us to destroy them, the ones who belong to Him. And lead us to complete victory.

"A great distance must be travelled. Our way is hidden. It is blocked to us. Only the pure and faithful can find it. The child is the map and the key. The instrument to bring around the end.

"I see massive destruction everywhere. Whole cities fallen, countries destroyed—fires, wars, an army of soldiers, human in appearance but completely under our control. They do our bidding without any resistance.

"And more of us—your spawn—we walk the streets, free to be ourselves, to wreak havoc among the innocent. Men, women, children...nobody can escape our wrath. They will turn on each other in their fear, for survival. It will be their undoing.

"We shall rule! Your will shall be done, Father."

Renner was pleased. Gregor's vision still foretold of success for his goals. An army of normal humans under his control. Mass destruction. That is what he dreamed of. But, how would he achieve this? Who was this boy?

And where could he find him?

* * *

Dismissed from their meeting, Tomas left Gregor's chambers disgruntled and escaped to his own bedroom—a large open space, resplendent in royal colours of navy blue and purple. Heavy velvet drapes shaded the windows, procured from a castle in France.

He sat at an antique vanity, one he had pilfered from a museum in Italy—the curators had no idea to this day what had happened to that desk and never would. As with the rest of the items decorating their home.

Placing his crushed Elvin mask on the table before him, he studied his mottled flesh in the mirror. The burn marks covering his entire face had craters of deeper skin in certain areas, purple and angry looking as if not fully healed. The skin was rough and hard to the touch.

He was never whole—his face was deformed before he was burned. But he had the most normal appearance of all the offspring, barring Anthony, of course. There was a procedure that could have improved the scarring left behind by Renner's botched effort at fixing the cleft palate he was born with. But now his face was burned and ruined beyond repair. Cosmetic surgery would be of little use now.

The day he received his burns was still vivid in his mind, seared there by the very fire that had disfigured him.

As a person with telekinetic abilities he could transport himself into any place he wished as long as he had been there before or had seen a picture of the place, had some sort of visual to guide him to the specified destination. Since he was a young toddler, he was aware of his ability to move through space yet could only travel short distances at first. With many years of practice, and much trial and error, he had mastered his gift. He could transport himself to anywhere he wanted to in the entire world.

Unless *he* was around.

His mind flashed back to the moment—first a tingling feeling from the intense heat of the flames, then the smell of charred flesh, the fire eating away through layer upon layer of skin and tissue, even muscle in some areas. The pain, excruciating, lasting years, and was still present to some degree.

And only because of *him*.

Tomas had always been fascinated by fire. At the tender age of nine, he had invented a flame-throwing device small enough to wear around his wrist like a bracelet. A lethal weapon that could be easily concealed yet unleash devastation and destruction within mere moments. He had been out on the mountain's plateau testing his new device. Anthony, not yet born but on his way. Milena, in full labour within the castle a short distance away, both oblivious to what was happening outside on the mountainous terrain.

The invention Tomas had created—the fire-casting weapon— had worked. The fire caught rapidly, spreading through the tall brush and stunted deciduous trees until fire surrounded him, bore down on him. He was not worried, though. Planning to transport his body away the moment he felt he was in danger. Then transport water from the nearby river to douse the searing wall of flames. What he hadn't planned on was that his power would fail him. He—none of them—aware of Anthony's ability to neutralize their powers.

The heat, almost intolerable, licked at his pants, his shirt. Tomas continually attempted to transport himself to safety, away from the damaging flames, but he couldn't. Stranded in the midst of the fire, skin now tightening and prickling from the intense heat. He panicked. Running straight through the raging inferno, he charged towards a clear, rocky area. His clothes immediately ignited, and he dropped to the ground, thrashing around until the flames on his body were extinguished. But the damage had already been done.

The fire eventually burned itself out, the sparse vegetation high up in the mountains unable to sustain it. Paralyzed by pain, in shock, he lay there for hours. At some point, he realized he needed help and dragged himself down the hill and back into the castle.

Tomas sustained third-degree burns to his entire face and neck, parts of his skull—hair singed in patches never to re-grow—his torso, right leg and arm. He knew he was lucky to have survived. The damage could have been much worse—fatal. His brother, Gunter, had healed him with his abilities. Tomas' skin sealed around the flame-throwing weapon so that it became a permanent part of his body. But the scars remained. As well as the pain. And any time he called upon the internal weapon of fire, it issued forth by bursting through his scarred flesh, cracking apart the healed skin. Over and over again, the skin damaged, then healed, then was damaged again.

None of it should have happened! It was his fault!

Tomas started vigilantly applying a different mask to his face, another of his own creations, the one his father despised the most. Using an adhesive, he secured the edges of the mask that was composed from plastic resin to his burned skin, making it whole again. He stared back at his altered reflection.

Anthony's near-perfect visage stared back at him.

The torment Tomas suffered after the fire. The years of rehabilitation, all alone, while Anthony was constantly cuddled, lavished with love from his mother. *Their mother.* Love, a concept none of the others ever received from her. Tomas noticed how she glared at them. She detested them. Only Anthony was treated like her own child. He got everything he ever wanted. He was always kept close to her side.

And for what? The cruel irony of keeping Anthony around for all these years because of a prophecy, and he wasn't the chosen one after all. Having to stare at his smug face. Having to fetch whatever trinkets, books, or items he needed. And for what!

Smashing the mirror with his fist, the glass splintered into a thousand fragments, disfiguring the once perfect reflection. He wiped the blood from his knuckles onto his jeans.

Panting heavily, Tomas recalled his father's words. He knew he had to respect them. He couldn't take it upon himself to get rid of Anthony without his father's permission. But he vowed that one day he would kill Anthony for all the turmoil he caused him.

One day.

Chapter 24

"I think the coast is clear," Anthony whispered.

Coaxing Ang out of her hiding spot in the ottoman was proving difficult. Ten minutes had elapsed since Renner had left the library. Still, Ang was reluctant to expose herself to potential danger. What if Renner and his mutant offspring returned?

Finally, legs cramping, she allowed Anthony to pull her out of the ottoman. As she smoothed out her wrinkled clothing, still damp from the blizzard that raged outdoors, she was taken by surprise when Anthony wrapped his strong arms around her in a constricting hug. Stunned, she didn't respond at first, arms pressed stiffly at her sides. The hug lingered. "You're shaking," Anthony said. Slowly, Ang's arms lifted, and she hugged him back. Then she clung to him as if her life depended on it, didn't want it to ever stop, his body so strong and warm. Tears sprang up as she let go into his comforting frame. So much emotion held back, now released. He didn't rush her, holding her tight while soothingly rubbing her back, until the last tear trickled down her cheek. It amazed her that this man she had just met could have such a profoundly calming and comforting effect on her, especially under such volatile, unpredictable circumstances. Not unlike Gavin.

As they drew apart, Ang's face was bright crimson. "Sorry," she muttered.

"For what?" his emerald eyes searched hers. Wiping the last tear from her cheek, he smiled reassuringly. "Don't worry, he won't be back."

"How do you know?" she stammered. "I distinctly remember you saying he wouldn't come in here in the first place."

"I didn't think they would hear us. But he's caught me before— you know—spying. It's not that unusual. As long as they don't know you're here, we'll be fine."

"But it sounded like you're in trouble. And it's all because of me. What did he mean by no provisions for the next month?" she worried.

"It's no big deal. I get provisions from time to time—things from the outside world—books, edible treats, clothes, toiletries. I won't die without them," he smiled again, dimples warming her heart.

"I can't imagine those creatures outside of this castle, being among normal people."

"It's usually Tomas who goes and always in disguise. He attracts some attention due to his size and his limp but not enough to cause any alarm."

"Again, your father and brothers going out of their way to take care of you. You're right—from what I saw of your father, he certainly has no love for you. So again, why? Why keep you around, give you provisions that aren't necessary for your survival?"

"It must be the prophecy. For whatever it's worth, I'm thankful for the provisions, the small treasures I receive from the outside world. Up until now, they were the only things that kept me sane. The idea that another place existed out there."

"Up until now?"

"I don't need those things anymore. Now, I have you. At least for a little while."

They both blushed, and Ang wondered if she was having a hot flash because the entire room felt far too warm.

"Anthony, if we find a way to get Ronnie and escape, you have to come with us," Ang pleaded.

Face dropping, Anthony noticeably shifted the subject. "You can sleep in here tonight." He moved over to the couch, and in a few swift movements had transformed it into a bed. Then he briefly disappeared into the hall, moments later returning with bed linens and a nightshirt for her.

"I noticed your clothes are still wet. Here's something dry to put on." The nightshirt, one of Anthony's T-shirts, had his smell woven between the fabric, and she longed to put it on. Fought the urge to bury her face in it while he stood as witness. "You'll be safe here. I would never let any harm come to you."

"Thanks. I trust you."

"There's a bathroom in the back of the library with a toilet and sink." He pointed to the back of the room. A door blended so perfectly into the décor that she hadn't noticed it. And, now that he had mentioned it, it had been hours since she had last squatted in the forest bushes on her trek to the castle.

Anthony walked over and embraced Ang tightly again, and was it her imagination or was it a little more romantic than friendly? Was he inhaling her scent as he nuzzled his face into the curve of her neck? He clung to her as much as she clung to him. As if they were a lifeline to each other, and in many ways they were.

Reluctantly, they broke apart.

"Goodnight." His eyes met hers, and the warmth was almost unbearable, nothing she had ever felt before. The crush she had on Josh now seemed trivial. Upon switching off the main lights to the library—the ornate crystal chandelier and wall sconces—Anthony left the room. Only a soft muted glow remained from an antique lamp on the side table beside her makeshift bed.

With Anthony now absent, Ang felt empty, vulnerable. She slipped out of her sodden clothes, and into his oversized shirt, hugging it close to her body as if the thin royal blue fabric could protect her. Grabbing the fabric with both hands, she pulled it up to her face and inhaled deeply. Sighed. Why couldn't she have met him in the real world under normal circumstances?

Picking up the bed linens Anthony had provided; she stretched the beige sheet over the couch mattress and crawled beneath a purple fleece blanket. Switching off the side table lamp, the room was cast into blackness.

With the lights out, every sound emitted within the castle was magnified. Her fear flourished with every creak, groan and scrape. How could she be certain Anthony's father or brothers wouldn't find her during the night? What would they do if they caught her having a slumber party in the castle library? Would they torture her? Or kill her outright? Or send her to the dungeon to mother another of their deformed offspring? Her body started trembling. One thing she knew for sure: no way in hell was she going to allow sleep to distract her that night. Not a single wink was allowed. So instead, she lay there for what felt like forever, fearful thoughts percolating in her sleep-deprived brain. She drew the covers up over her head. Waited.

All of a sudden, the door creaked open.

Her heart stopped beating.

Did they find her? What should she do? There was nowhere to escape.

Her eyes had adjusted to the darkness and with as little movement as possible, she chanced a peak from beneath the covers.

A tall lean frame was silhouetted in the doorframe. A man in sleep pants, shirtless, with shoulder-length dark hair.

It was Anthony. Ang experienced such an overwhelming sense of relief she almost burst into tears again.

Closing the door softly behind him, he crept over to Ang's makeshift bed, slipped beneath the covers, and then lay there, unmoving.

She waited, barely breathing.

Now, what was she supposed to do? Should she acknowledge his presence? Or pretend she was asleep? Ask him what he was doing there? Was he going to put the moves on her?

She remained frozen in place, unsure of what to do, how to react. Waiting with anticipation. Hoping he would touch her. His body so close to hers she could feel the warmth emanating from him, causing her insides to burn with desire. Yearned for his lips to brush against hers, to finally be intimate with a man, a moment she had only ever dreamed of.

Yet, she remained motionless. Unsure. Waiting for him to make the first move.

It felt like they had lain that way for hours. And, then she heard it—what was clearly the steady, rhythmic breathing of someone asleep. Slowly, she turned her head to see Anthony beside her, the gentle rise and fall of the covers.

Yup, he was definitely asleep.

Yet she continued to lay there, frozen in the same position. Watching him. He surely was perfect. Long black eyelashes, full red lips slightly parted, dimples now absent on his relaxed face. Skin smooth and pale. She imagined how his body would feel traced below her fingertips. The swell of his muscles, the warmth from his skin. But, after a while she succumbed to the hypnotic rhythm of Anthony's inhalations and exhalations, like an ocean's tide going in and out, easing the tension from her body. Finally, she was able to relax. And with that came a sudden, irresistible drowsiness. At long last, she, too, fell asleep.

★ ★ ★

Anthony hadn't planned to fall asleep.

Creeping into Angel's room, he slipped into her bed, hoping not to awaken her. She needed her rest after that day's ordeal. The next day would most likely prove to be even more difficult. His goal was to protect her, keep her safe from his brothers and father, but he also couldn't stand being away from her.

Lying beside her, the warmth of her body so close, the most tranquil feeling filled his body, his soul. He had lain many times beside his mother on nights when sleep was elusive, finding her soothing presence helped him fall fast asleep. Subconsciously, it must have brought back the feeling, for in moments he drifted off to the land of dreams.

When he awakened, Angel was breathing softly beside him, her body turned towards him. He had never been so close to a woman before, other than his mother, and he stared at her as if she were a unicorn. A mythical creature from a fairytale. He couldn't resist her, reaching his hand out to play with a curl of blond hair resting on the pillow. It was softer than he thought it would be, and he let it spill through his fingers, sending shivers through his hands and up into his arms. She smelled like what he thought flowers and sunshine would smell like, filling him with a sensation new to him. Desire, maybe even love, although it was far too early, the girl merely a stranger. Something fluttered in his belly.

She stirred in her sleep and flipped over in the bed, now facing away from him. He hoped she would wake up, that he could kiss her, the need so deep inside of him that he almost got teary-eyed. But, was it appropriate? Or would he scare her off? He didn't know how to court a woman. This was all new territory for him. Pulling his body in closer so that he was curled protectively around her, he draped his arm over her torso, hugging her against him. The warmth of her form and the enticing aroma of her hair and skin brought back the feeling of tranquility, and again he slipped back into a comfortable slumber.

★ ★ ★

Ang had slept despite her plans to remain alert. Her slumber was not solid, instead, filled with vivid dreams. First, of Anthony and herself together, fighting off frightening creatures rife with gore and blood spatter, Quentin Tarantino style, then passionate and lustful, their bodies coiled together in ecstasy. These dreams cycled over and over again. Between these scary and lustful dreams, she would awaken, noticing Anthony's warm comforting form still beside her. At one point his arm was draped across her chest, and his body was spooning hers. It felt so natural, so normal. Like they were Russian nesting dolls carefully crafted to fit one within the other. She drifted back to sleep.

In the morning, he was gone.

Ang stretched and yawned, rubbing the sleep from her eyes. She knew she must be a frightful mess—her hair like a ball of blond cotton candy, makeup long gone—hoping that somewhere within this castle, the secret passageways led to a secret shower.

While she folded the sheets and covers from her bed and reassembled the couch, Anthony threw open the door.

"Good morning," she said, all at once, shy and uncertain. Although she ardently wanted her feelings reciprocated, she had realized at some point during the night that her attraction to him was mostly one-sided—his presence through the night more to keep her safe. Nothing romantic intended. Yet, she couldn't help noticing his eyes kept flicking down to her bare legs, Anthony's shirt only reaching midway down her thighs.

He entered the library, dressed in form-fitting black jeans and a white jersey. He carried a piping hot bowl of oatmeal with melting brown sugar in his left hand, and Ang's stomach gurgled in response. When was the last time she ate? Back at the hotel?

There was definitely tension in the air, and she couldn't help wishing it was sexual.

"I'm coming with you," Anthony handed Ang the bowl of oatmeal and plunked heavily on the couch. "If you'll still let me?" He stared imploringly at Ang.

"Of course!" Elated, she sat down and faced him. "I was going to force you anyway," she teased.

"Great. Now, we need to make a plan."

★ ★ ★

First things first, Ang needed a shower and some clean clothes—hers were still damp and soiled from her long trek through the mountains in the blizzard and scurrying through the dusty tunnels the previous day. Dirt streaked her cheeks; brambles were stuck in her hair. *A toothbrush would be nice too.*

Anthony must have read her mind.

"Follow me."

He led Ang back into the tunnels, the coolness in the damp stone passageway making gooseflesh rise on her exposed legs.

They traversed a short pathway and re-entered the main rooms of the castle—this one a large bedroom, feminine accents obvious in the décor.

A large four-poster bed shrouded in gossamer curtains was centered against the far wall, butterfly comforter and pillows decorating its surface. Gorgeous paintings hung on the stone walls depicting flowers and heavenly landscapes. An armoire housed brushes, a large oval mirror, makeup, and perfumes.

It was as if a woman still lived here, Anthony's mother's possessions undisturbed since her untimely death. Her spirit still brought to life by things she touched each day in this room.

"You can use the shower in here," Anthony pointed to the en-suite bathroom.

Ang was skeptical.

"It's okay. I use this one all the time. They won't think anything of it," Anthony misjudged her hesitance.

"This is your mother's room, isn't it?"

Anthony's gaze swept over the space. "I didn't have the heart to change anything. It makes me feel like she's still here somehow. I know that probably sounds weird."

"No, not at all."

Ang recalled how difficult it had been to go through all her grandfather's belongings after he passed away. Had it not been for her grandmother getting ill and needing more space in the room to manoeuvre her wheelchair, all his possessions would still be there. As he had left them.

"My father and brothers never come in here. I'm not sure why. For my father, it may be guilt. My brothers came to hate her since she loved me so much and openly loathed them. They were jealous. I don't really blame them. Regardless, aside from the library and my bedroom, which have the reinforced walls to diminish my effect on them, this is probably one of the safest rooms in the castle right now."

He strode over to his mother's closet, a walk-in fashioned to house Milena's vast collection of clothing and accessories. He started rummaging through its contents yanking outfits off hangars that would fit Ang and be suitable for their escape.

"Are you sure?" Ang felt uncomfortable. "This must be difficult for you."

"They're just things." Ang could tell he didn't mean that. His response directly contradicted his previous comments. "Stop worrying about me. We need to get you out of here. As cute as you look in my shirt, it's a bit flimsy. You'd freeze to death out there." He threw more items onto the growing pile of clothing.

"You're still coming, aren't you?" Ang asked, afraid he had changed his mind. Maybe he wasn't ready to leave behind his mother's shrine, her belongings.

"Yes, of course. And, take whatever you like. Nobody's going to miss it anymore."

Ang selected a simple black tracksuit that was her size. Her outer clothes: parka, toque, boots, and mitts were still in the library, and she would put those back on before heading outside into the wintry landscape.

After a refreshing shower, she pulled on Milena's tracksuit, which fit perfectly. Using the spare toothbrush Anthony had given her—part of his special stash of provisions—she was feeling like a human being again.

Hallelujah.

Ang exited the bathroom, steam escaping behind her through the door like freed wraiths. She sat on the bed, alongside Anthony and swiped a wet strand of hair to the side, tucking it behind her ear.

"Better?" Anthony asked.

"Much. Thanks."

Smiling again at Ang, his eyes seemed less troubled. Perhaps he had come to terms with leaving behind his mother's belongings.

"While you were in the shower, I was going through my mother's room, trying to decide what to take with me. I found this," Anthony produced a large, leather-bound journal and handed it over to Ang. "It was under the mattress."

Ang struggled under its weight, finally laying it down flat on the bed, and opened it.

Flipping through the pages, she tried to make sense of its contents. Images of demons, articles on possession, genetic research, graphic photos of creatures not unlike the ones Ang had seen in the castle. Religious prayers and artwork depicting the Catholic saints, Mother Mary cradling a baby Jesus, the Crucifixion.

"What is this?" Ang asked, staring into Anthony's emerald eyes. He reached out and brushed back a wet strand of hair that had stuck to her cheek, smiled warmly, then redirected his gaze back to the journal.

"I remember my mom working on this book when I was little. She showed it to me a few times. But I was so young, I didn't fully grasp what it all meant. Now, given the stories she told me involving my father and brothers, I believe she was doing her own research. I think she was trying to discover a way to defeat them, to escape."

"How did she get all of this information?"

"Look at the dates. The earlier articles, clippings, and journal entries are dated before she was imprisoned by my father. The newer parts have been cut from books found here in the library. I recognize some of them. The Polaroid photos she took herself. We had a Polaroid camera back then. It eventually broke, but before that, she used it all the time. That's how we took all of the photos I showed you before."

They continued flipping through the pages. Searching.

An article caught Ang's eye. "Your mother must have been on to something. Look at this." She pointed to the page.

The article spoke of demon possession. A grainy printed photograph depicted a man with black eyes eerily close in resemblance to those of Renner and his evil offspring.

"It says here that one demon can possess many," Ang read aloud. "Could your father and brothers all be possessed by the same demon? Is that what your mother believed?"

"I'm not sure. Maybe." They continued reading the article.

It went on to describe several stories, alleged true-life encounters, where such possessions had occurred. Had Angelika read this a few months before she would have scoffed at the stories, declaring them impossible, obvious fables. But now she read through them as if her life depended on them. Because it did.

Although none of the scenarios were on such a grand scale like the inhabitants of the castle, and the people possessed were normal, not genetically engineered creatures, the similarities in how the eyes were described and the multiple voices when the possessed people spoke couldn't be ignored.

"Possession. I guess that explains their barbaric actions. But it also raises more questions. Like, how did they become possessed in the first place? And how can we use this information to our advantage?"

Ang lay on her stomach, propped up on her elbows, and continued rifling through the book. Anthony lay down beside her, matching her position, and together they searched for a solution to their predicament, an escape plan. She glanced regularly at Anthony, admiring the gentle slope of his nose and strong jawline. His eyelashes were impossibly long, his eyes warm and inviting. He caught her staring, and her face flushed.

She cleared her throat, attempting to act nonchalant. "If the creatures are all possessed by the same spirit, does that make them easier to defeat, or more difficult? Do we need a priest to do an exorcism?"

"I'm not sure, but the information must be relevant for her to include it in here."

Some articles referred to Hitler and his attempt at world dominance. "I never knew that Hitler thought he was clairvoyant, that he could predict the future. Or that he dabbled in black magic and witchcraft. It says that many people believed he also was possessed by a demon. What in the hell are we up against here?"

"Hitler was eventually defeated. If he could be taken down, then there must be a way to defeat my family. Let's keep looking."

Another page caught Ang's attention. It contained a picture, taken by a Polaroid camera, of a room. The picture was old, dark, and fuzzy, the details slightly blurred. Yet, it hit a resonant chord within her. Shelves containing vials filled with a black substance. Perhaps a scientist's lab. Anthony said his father was a scientist. Were these more creatures being formed, genetic clusters of cells in test tubes? Ready to be implanted? Before she could analyze the picture any longer, Anthony distracted her.

"Wait a second. What's this?" He flopped all the pages to the left until only the last one remained. "I never noticed this before, but it's a lot thicker than the others." Sitting upright on the bed, he gently rubbed the page with his fingertips. "It feels bumpy."

Ang sat up beside him. What had Anthony's mother concealed within the pages of the book? Could it help them escape? It must have been important for her to feel the need to hide it from her corrupted husband.

"I hate to have to tear her book." Anthony hesitated a moment but then tore the page. A flat, intricately engraved amulet fell into the palm of his hand, along with a note, now slightly torn.

"What is it?" Ang asked, studying the amulet. It was beautiful. Intricate carvings displayed two angels facing each other, wings outstretched behind and around them in giant arcs such that they created the outer circular structure of the amulet.

Anthony, with shaky hands, handed the amulet over to Ang, unfolded the paper, and read aloud.

"*My Dearest Anthony,*" he began, voice thick with emotion.

"*If you are reading this, then perhaps our plan has failed, and I am no longer with you. If such is the case, I am so sorry for failing you. For bringing you into this world full of sickness and evil. You are too good and kind to have been subjected to this.*" Tears rolled down Anthony's cheeks. Ang rubbed his back, consolingly. He cleared his throat, continued.

"*Now, I leave you, not willingly, into the hands of the vilest evil ever known. You must protect yourself. You must get out.*" Anthony subconsciously wiped away the tears that streaked his face.

"*Back when I was still doing psychic readings, a man came to see me one day, a treasure hunter. He told me of a dream he had but instead of asking me to interpret it for him as I would normally do for my clients, he interpreted it for me instead. He said an otherworldly being, possibly an angel, appeared to him in his dream. It told him to bring me this amulet, one he had found on an excavation. The vision told him I would need it one day, would know when the moment came that I should use it. He left the amulet with me, even though I insisted that he take it back. I didn't believe him at the time. Thought perhaps he was crazy. I must have missed my opportunity to use it. My eyes were closed. But you still have a chance.*

"*Use this amulet. Always keep it with you. It will help to ward off the evil spirits, so you don't become one of them. I don't think that is possible—your heart is so pure. But I must protect you any way I can.*

"*I tried to love them, Anthony, I did. Your brothers. They weren't responsible for what happened to them, they didn't ask for their genetic makeup to be altered. Just babies at first, they should have been so innocent. But they were corrupted from the start. Eyes as black as death, evil coursing through their veins. Inhuman.*

"And your father, Renner, is not human anymore. Ever since we witnessed an occult ritual involving a Guardian Angel Spell, he was changed as if someone else, most dark and wicked, was controlling him from within. The Renner I knew long gone. As soon as he has no more use for you, Anthony, he will kill you.

"Use this book to find a way to get out. I saw them in the tunnels today, what they have planned for you. You can have no part in this plan!

"I think they have a weakness. I am still uncertain of its nature. I don't have time to look any further; we need to escape now because of what happened today. I'm not sure how much longer they will tolerate our presence here. But, if you are reading this still within the castle walls, and our attempt at escape has failed, its contents may help you after all. Perhaps you can discover what I was missing, find their weakness.

Most importantly, my dear son, know that I love you with all my heart. Without you, I would have died a long time ago. You were my rose in a field of briers and thorns. I will always love you.

"Mom."

Anthony sniffled, wiped his tears once more.

"It's like she knew we wouldn't make it."

Ang hugged Anthony closer to her, laying her damp head on his shoulder.

"What did she mean by having to leave right away because of what happened that day? Do you remember anything happening?"

He shook his head. "I don't remember anything significant. Wait, actually, I think Gregor had a seizure. But that's all I remember."

"That's one of your brothers, right? One of the triplets?"

"Yes, he's the one that can predict the future." Ang remembered the conversation she overheard in the hallway.

"I think one of your brothers had a seizure yesterday. When I overhead your brothers in the hallway talking about the prophecy, they said he had another seizure, and the prophecy was the same. Then they mentioned the dark-haired boy being the path and the key."

"So, Gregor had a seizure the day my mother said we had to escape. And now he had another one yesterday? Does it have to do with the prophecy? It must be a sign. We need to get out of here today. If you're sure you want me to come. You might have a better chance of getting out of here without me."

"Of course, I want you to come. We'll get out this time. We have to."

"Here." Anthony took the amulet out of Ang's hand and draped it over her head.

"No, Anthony. I can't. This amulet was meant to protect you."

"But I want you to have it. Don't worry, I'll be fine. You heard what my mother said. I'm too pure to be taken over by a demon," his eyes glinted mischievously. For some reason, this made Ang blush. "Besides, I couldn't handle it if I lost you."

Anthony's gaze grew more intense, and he leaned in, pressing his lips against Ang's mouth. She closed her eyes and kissed him deeply, savouring the moment. Her first kiss. It was both sweet and gentle, and upon parting, he smiled at her with the brightest twinkle in his eyes.

"That was better than I imagined."

She nodded, breathless. Then remembering Anthony's gift, she fingered the heavy metal amulet against her chest, cool and unyielding, hoping it would be able to protect them both.

"Well, one thing is for sure. Your mother thought there was a way to get out of here or to defeat these creatures. We need to figure it out—devise a strategy to get my sister back, and somehow get us all safely out of this cursed building and back to my home where we belong. Besides, if Milena thought you needed to escape immediately due to Gregor's prediction when you were ten, what does that mean for us now?"

She paused, thoughtful. "What about the tunnels? Do they lead to the outdoors?"

"There is one route that runs through the castle, and continues underground, through a cave, and then out onto a plateau by the river. In the original castle, it was used as an escape route for royalty to get out, hidden, if the castle was being overrun by its enemies. The only problem is my brothers are all aware of the tunnels and where they lead because they built them. They might be expecting us to use that exit—block it off before we get out. We'll be trapped. Even without their powers, their strength alone is enough to defeat us. With the weapons they have on top of that, there is no risk of anyone escaping. That's why they leave me to do as I wish, to travel through the tunnels wherever I want in the castle. They rarely have need to venture inside the tunnels themselves. But, they will if they think we're going to try to escape...or if they see you or if they notice any of the women missing, even just one. They will come after us, and they will know exactly where to search first. The tunnels may be too obvious." He ran a hand through his thick hair, then stood from the bed and paced back and forth.

"The only option is to try to get your sister out of that room when she is doing her walk, try to get her into the tunnels and out of the building as fast as we can before they notice, but I fear that's impossible."

"The trick is how to get Ronnie past all of the giants standing watch. Is there ever a time where they aren't on guard?" Ang questioned, hopeful.

"No." Anthony's reply was quick and final. Anthony abruptly stopped pacing, spinning in Ang's direction. "You never did tell me how you found this place. How did you know the castle was here, and how did you manage to get inside without being seen? If we do get Ronnie out of the dungeon, is there a way for us to escape from here quickly, following your route?"

Ang hesitated. How much of the truth should she tell Anthony: how she found Ronnie, or how Gavin, her guardian angel, was the one that led her there? She didn't want him to think she was crazy.

Yet, Anthony trusted her with his story, possibly crazier than hers. He was courageous enough to tell her everything concerning his disturbed family and monster siblings.

"I guess I'll start at the beginning, the day when I died."

"You died? How?"

"The how is irrelevant right now. Let's say I died, but I was revived. At the moment when my heart stopped beating, I met my guardian angel. And he's been with me ever since."

"Wow. That's amazing. Is he here now?"

"That's where it gets complicated. He led me here, helped me find a way inside the castle. He said he sensed an aura that drew him here. But once we entered, he vanished."

She wished he were here now, his absence still a mystery. Perhaps he could have helped them get Ronnie and escape.

Anthony regarded Ang throughout her farfetched tale as if she were the sanest person on the planet. She immediately felt an overwhelming sense of relief, not only to be able to finally confide in somebody the secrets she had been holding on to all this time but to also have him still accept her—believe her and not judge her.

"Maybe your angel's purpose was to lead you here to find your sister, and now that you have found her, he has returned back home because he's no longer needed."

"I don't know. He seemed to be in trouble like he wouldn't be allowed to return home. It's kind of a long story, and I don't know if I can remember exactly what he told me." Ang paused. Anthony patiently waited, urging her to continue with his silence and penetrating green eyes.

"Gavin broke some rules in order to save my life," she began. "He described being in a room in heaven that held billions of blue liquid-light-filled crystals, which he believed held our life essence—all the humans on Earth having their own crystal." She noticed a glint of recognition in Anthony's emerald eyes. A spark, barely perceptible.

"He believes he caught one of the angel's switching my crystal with another person's crystal. Someone who was soon meant to die, their crystal almost empty, almost out of light. Gavin wanted to protect me, so he switched my crystal back to one filled with light, so I would have a long life. But he wasn't supposed to be in that room or tamper with the crystals, so he was blocked out."

"Blocked out?" Anthony queried.

"Of heaven. I don't know if he was able to return."

"So, if he isn't in heaven, and he isn't here, then where is he?

"I don't know, that's the problem. One moment he was here with me, and the next he was gone. I can't help wondering if he'd be able to help us."

"Maybe in some offhanded sort of way he already has."

"What do you mean?"

"The crystals he spoke of, what do you think would happen if they were broken?"

"I don't know if it's possible to break them, but if they could be broken, based on Gavin's assumptions, I think the person would die."

The light in Anthony's eyes grew brighter.

"If that assumption is correct, there might be a way out of here after all."

"How?"

"There's something I have to show you."

Chapter 25

Hidden in Milena's room, Ang had adopted a false sense of security. Now that she was back in the secret tunnels of the castle, she felt exposed, in grave danger, while Anthony pressed on determined. Darkness closed in around them from all sides, broken only by the slim beam of illumination from Anthony's flashlight.

A grey mouse scurried in front of them and then paused long enough to determine whether it should stand up and fight or flee to safety. With a sharp squeak, it chose the latter, disappearing into a crack in the wall, escaping into its own set of secret tunnels.

"We're almost there."

Ang followed closely on Anthony's heels like a loyal puppy, uninformed of what they sought.

Finally, Anthony paused at a partition in the wall—another secret entrance back into the castle, this one unfamiliar. Cautious at first, Anthony pressed his ear to the wall, listened. Seeming satisfied, he felt along the partition's uneven surface, found the pressure points he sought, pressed in and slid the door open.

Soon, the questions that inundated Ang's mind would be answered by what lay beyond the wall. Where did this secret entrance lead? What had Ang said that triggered Anthony's hope of defeating the monsters that lurked in the castle? Did Anthony find a way to defeat them, a way for them to escape?

Yet, fear held her back, coursing through her veins like acid. Fear of what was to come. She wanted nothing more than to escape from the castle with her sister and Anthony in tow, but the escape is what she dreaded the most, knowing how treacherous it would be, knowing their chance of survival was slim to none.

But they had to try. She only prayed there wouldn't be any casualties.

Halfway through the door, Anthony stopped, glancing back at Ang standing uncertain in the tunnels.

"The room is empty. It's safe for us to enter. If we hear anyone approaching, we'll jump back into the tunnel immediately. I'll leave the panel open, just in case."

Ang remained frozen. A malevolent energy pulsed in the newly revealed room. An evil presence. The amulet around her neck grew cooler, weighing heavily against her chest.

"When you described the crystal room that Gavin saw in heaven, it reminded me of this room. I never gave it much thought before, never truly understood what they were, but maybe there's a connection," Anthony suggested, pointing inward. Ang couldn't yet see what lay beyond the tunnel walls, but her interest was piqued despite the pure evil presence that exuded from within.

"Come in. See for yourself." Anthony reached for Ang's hand and pulled her inward.

The room was packed full of boxes and dusty ledges—a storage area. Concrete walls and flooring were the shade of gunmetal grey, and the lack of windows in the space made the room as dark as the tunnels. Anthony panned the flashlight's beam over the shelves. As Ang's eyes adjusted to the meagre light, she finally realized what Anthony had been indicating, and she couldn't believe her eyes.

Dozens of crystal vials were housed in a shelving unit that was a smaller replica of what Gavin had found in heaven. The contents inside the vials, however, differed dramatically. Not the magnificent blinding blue light that had illuminated the entire room in Gavin's tale. This was the opposite. A black liquid substance swirled within each tube, sucking all the paltry light out of the room. Even the light within her heart and soul seemed to be sucked out of her, leaving her with a feeling of emptiness and despair. Hundreds of these vials lined the shelves.

"What are these?" Ang asked.

"I believe they are crystals, like Gavin found in the crystal room."

"But, why are they so black?"

"I think they might be for my brothers. If they are possessed, like my mother believed, then maybe their life essence was tainted, turning it dark?"

Ang recalled the picture in Milena's scrapbook—the one that caught her eye—and realized it was a picture of this room, these vials. But what did it mean? How could this help them to escape?

"What do you think? Are they like what Gavin saw?"

"They are similar but seem to be filled with the essence of death, not the breath of life." The amulet continued growing colder.

"What did Gavin tell you about the crystals again?" Anthony asked, wanting clarification.

"He said the crystals contain the breath of life God breathes into every one of us. When Adam was created, God breathed the breath of life into his lungs, and so he lived. We all have this breath of life, and the contents of the crystals reflect that life, how much time we have left on Earth. Once the light is extinguished, our earthly body dies, freeing our souls from our physical selves to pass on to the next life in spirit form."

"And, what happened when he touched your crystal, switching it with another that had more life energy in it?"

"Well, it increased my life span, or so we think. We're not exactly sure."

"So, like I asked before, if a crystal were broken, what do you think would happen?"

"That person would die."

Ang finally realized where Anthony was going with this line of thought. But it all seemed too easy. Too uncertain.

"How do we know for sure? So far, what we're discussing is strictly theoretical," she stressed. "These crystals aren't the same as the ones Gavin described. And we don't know for certain whom they belong to."

Anthony held up one of the vials to his eyes, the onyx vapors swirling more intensely as he peered into its depths.

"Maybe you shouldn't be touching those things. At least not until we know what we're doing?" Ang suggested, getting more nervous by the second. She continued to feel the goodness, happiness, and love being sucked right out of her spirit every time she focused on its contents. The amulet on her chest was a shard of ice.

"These have to belong to my father. They have been here as far back as I can remember," Anthony replaced the vial to its rightful position on the shelf-like holder. "Only, now there are more. The shelves slowly filling up over the years."

"But that doesn't explain how they got here."

"Gavin did see someone—an angel—manipulating the vials in the crystal room. Possibly switching yours. Maybe he was stealing crystals as well?" Anthony guessed.

"Gavin said it appeared as if he switched them around, not stole them."

"But maybe that wasn't his first time in the room. Maybe he stole them at a different time and brought them back here."

"I don't know. That's a lot of maybes. Why would he do that? Do you actually think an angel could have done this? Stole from heaven, then handed the vials over to demons?" Ang asked incredulously.

"Angels have fallen before. Isn't that what demons are? Fallen angels?"

The idea seemed preposterous, but Ang couldn't ignore the implications. If these crystals were for the beasts that were created here, she and Anthony could destroy them all without having to go near them. Simply break the crystals, releasing their essence, and they should all die. The monsters wouldn't see them coming or be able to retaliate. But what if it didn't work? It might instead alert them to their plan to escape, her presence in the castle, and infuriate them to the point of certain death. And another issue was still apparent.

"How do we know whose crystals these are? What if your crystal is here or the crystals of the prisoners down in the dungeon?" Ang wondered aloud.

"Maybe there's a way to check. How did Gavin know to find your crystal?" Anthony asked.

Ang searched her mind and remembered that all he had to do was think of her, picture her in his mind, and the crystal appeared before him. She told Anthony the method, and he closed his eyes, conjuring up an image of one of his brothers.

At first, nothing happened. Then, gradually the crystals shifted and cascaded like flowing water, finally resting with one crystal directly in front of Anthony's eyes. He plucked the vial from the contraption and upon it was the name of his brother—the one he had pictured in his mind.

"It worked," he said in disbelief.

Ang moved to the wall, closed her eyes and thought of Anthony. The wall didn't shift, move, or swell. A positive sign, she thought. She did the same with her sister's image, and again no response from the wall.

"Nothing happened when I thought of you or my sister," Ang said encouragingly.

"Well, what do you think? Should we try to destroy them?"

Ang paused, contemplating the consequences. She felt nervous, concerned it might hurt somebody innocent, especially Ronnie, or Anthony whom she was growing quite attached to. And there was also the possibility of alerting the evil spawn to their presence. If it didn't work, they would be in a heap of trouble.

"If we're going to do it, we need to be ready to act immediately." He checked his watch. "The women should be going into the main room for lunch right now, and they'll be there for half an hour. This is our best chance."

Ang felt unprepared. "What do we do once the crystals are broken? How do we know if it worked? We could end up running into the dungeon room straight to our own deaths if the monsters are still alive."

"Do we have any other choice?"

Ang exhaled sharply. "Not really. Okay, let's do it."

"So, the plan is to break the crystals, run to the dungeon through the tunnels, grab your sister and escape back into the tunnels leading all the way out to the plateau by the river, the one I told you about."

"Sounds like a plan. And the other women? We can't leave them here."

"You're right, how could I forget? It has shamed me all these years that I couldn't do anything to help them. If we succeed, and my father and all my brothers are dead, the women will finally be free. We can all escape. Are you ready?"

"As ready as I'll ever be."

Anthony took a deep breath. He retrieved the vial he previously held, the contents angrily swirling with greater intensity as if anticipating his intent. He raised it above his head, and quickly thrust his arm downward releasing the crystal.

It tumbled as if in slow motion heading towards the ground. Ang and Anthony stood motionless, not breathing.

The vial, after what seemed an eternity, finally hit the floor.

And bounced.

Ang and Anthony remained motionless.

Finally, Anthony broke the silence. "Wow, they're tougher than I thought."

Ang searched the room. She located a heavy metal bar propped in the corner of the room. Without hesitation, she grabbed it from its resting spot and swung with all her might at the crystals housed in the shelving unit. Metal connected with vials.

The crystals that were hit smashed instantly. Anthony quickly followed suit, gathering unbroken crystals from the wall and smashing them to the floor with more power this time. Stomping the remaining unbroken stubborn crystals rolling around with the heel of his boots.

They continued aggressively and urgently—Ang smashing with the heavy metal bar, Anthony smashing and crushing with his arms and feet. Occasionally, Anthony would have to picture one or several of his brothers in order to turn the shelving unit to expose more crystals.

They didn't spare one second, not wanting to give the remaining beasts a chance to notice anything was wrong, find Ang and Anthony and stop them.

An agonized wail pierced the air—distant yet audible—a male voice in agony but was quickly vanquished as more crystals were smashed. More groans ensued, men in torment. Ang thought it might actually be working. The floor was covered in black swirling essence and shards of glass. She instinctively drew her parka up over her nose and mouth, careful not to inhale the acrid fumes. She noticed Anthony did the same with his own sweatshirt, the warmest top he owned, not owning an outdoor jacket.

They continued until only one crystal remained on the shelf.

"Are you positive that's it?" Ang grilled.

"I've thought of everyone. The shelves aren't shifting anymore." He grabbed the last unbroken crystal from the shelf and smashed it with a vengeance. Now, every last crystal littered the floor in shards, angry black fumes snaking across the cement seeking refuge.

"I hope it worked," Ang said.

"Listen to their screams. It must have worked. Now let's go and get your sister."

He pulled Ang through the secret entrance back into the tunnels. Together, hand in hand, they raced through the twisting and turning pathways that led them down to the dungeon.

The anguished screams intensified as they approached the dungeon wall. Skidding to a stop directly before the crack they used the previous day to spy on the women captives, Anthony pressed his eye to the opening. "It did work! Look."

Anthony slid over so Ang could get her own view.

The dungeon room was pure chaos. The giants that had previously stood guard now lay unmoving, silent, on the ground. Only one still writhed in agony, moaning like a mortally wounded animal. Then he, too, lay still.

The women were scurrying back to their cells, unsure what was happening, not knowing if they, too, were in danger—retreating to their only vestige of safety within the castle walls.

Ang couldn't find Ronnie amidst the commotion. Had she run back to her cell, like the other women? Was she hiding? What if they were too late, and Ronnie had already been killed by these monsters?

"Are you ready?" Anthony asked, poised for action before the hidden door, prepared to slide it open on Ang's command.

"What if we don't make it?"

Anthony gazed deeply into Ang's hazel eyes, still breathing heavily from their run through the tunnels and the adrenaline coursing through his veins in anticipation of what was to come. He pulled her body against his. She could feel his heart beating rapidly. Warm hands now threading through her hair, cupping her scalp and pulling her face towards his. He pressed his lips to hers. Kissing her urgently, his tongue searched hers, and she responded automatically, melting into him, and for a moment time stood still. Intense heat passed between them, inside them, and she never wanted them to part, happy to stay in his arms forever. The world around them dissolved, along with her fear and anxiety. But, the moment they parted, it all came crashing down on her again. The harsh reality was that there was a huge chance they wouldn't survive.

Anthony stared longingly, deeply into Ang's eyes once more. "I'm not willing to lose you. We can do this. You saw in there… they're all dead. We're going to make it. All we need to do is get Ronnie and leave. Piece of cake, okay?"

Ang looked doubtful. Yet, knew this was their only chance of escape. She nodded her assent.

Anthony leaned over and gave Ang one more quick peck on the lips.

"Let's go."

Chapter 26

Anthony forced open the heavy panel that allowed them entry into the bowels of the dungeon. The chaos in the room was abating. Most of the women, succumbing to fear, had concealed themselves within the prison cells; only a few stragglers wandered the dim room in a daze. Their captors lay unmoving on the ground. Four in total, two of which Ang recognized from their spying session the previous night. The chimera, Wolframe, and the four-armed giant. The other two collapsed mutants were strangers. One of the creatures lay directly across the main entrance to the dungeon, preventing escape from that route. Thankfully, they were going to be using the tunnels.

Ang ran around to all the cells searching for her sister. Calling out her name and encouraging the women within each cell to flee, that this was their chance to escape. For some, a spark of hope returned to their sunken eyes, and they quickly followed her. Others remained hidden in fear and shock.

The cells stank of mould and urine. Lack of artificial lighting and windows made it difficult to see immediately which cells were occupied and which were vacant. And there were so many cells. It was delaying their rescue plan. Seconds ticked by. Minutes. Still no Ronnie. Anthony searched as well, but Ang hadn't heard any calls from him yet, so she assumed he hadn't found her either.

Finally, in the second to last cell, she found her sister curled up in a ball under a small cot. She was trembling uncontrollably, skin pale as milk. Ang attempted to pull her sister out from under the bed, but the frightened woman started thrashing, not realizing who was holding her, thinking it was someone trying to harm her. One of the mutants. Arms and legs punching and kicking, Ang took a few hits to her chest, one square in the jaw.

"Ronnie, it's me, Ang! I'm trying to help you! Look at me!" Ang reassured her, dodging another flying fist. She tried to grasp Ronnie's face, help her to focus and see that she had come to her sister's rescue. This caused the frightened girl to thrash more aggressively. Ronnie raked her nails at the skin on Ang's hands, trying to release her grip.

"RONNIE, IT'S ME, ANG!" More forcefully, shaking her.

Ang's screaming finally struck home. Ronnie studied her with wide, crazed eyes. Then recognition registered. She stopped thrashing and tears instantly streamed down her face. Then she threw her arms around her sister, probably for the first time in their lives, clinging to her like a drowning child.

"You won't believe what they've done to me," she sobbed. Ang shuddered, knowing only part of what probably happened, and felt such deep pity for her sister, her flesh and blood, yet practically a stranger.

"We have to go now," Ang urged and pulled her sister to her feet. As she spun around to flee the cell, she slammed into a wall of solid flesh. It was one of the largest creatures she had ever seen. His bulk completely blocked their only exit. Unlike the other mutants, this one was very much alive.

And he was pissed.

Well over seven feet tall, his hands were as big as clubs. Six arms sprouted from his torso, two of which were robotic prosthetics. Razor-sharp fangs lined his mouth. One eye was missing, hidden by an electronic metal patch embedded into his flesh, the other eye black as pitch. From the description Anthony gave her when they were in the library, this had to be one of the triplets, the giant with comic-book-villain strength.

Friedrich.

He reminded Ang of the guard with multiple appendages she had seen the previous night, but who now lay dead. This behemoth was deadlier, displaying an extra set of arms, two of which were capable of major destruction, and added height and musculature. Ang shrank back in fear.

Why wasn't he dead on the ground like the others? The only explanation for his standing in front of her was that his black crystal wasn't among the ones they had destroyed. Was it possible some crystals had been removed from the storage case? Stored elsewhere? How many others had survived? They had to get out of the castle! Now! Before they had a chance to find out!

"Anthony!" Ang yelled, hoping he was close enough that the monster's supernatural abilities would be blocked. She assumed that even without his powers, Friedrich's strength would far surpass that of any average human man. Each of his six biceps, metallic or flesh, was larger than her head. The only advantage they had over the behemoth was their speed of movement, for he moved slowly in the small cell due to his enormous bulk and lack of space.

One huge robotic arm, clenched in a fist, swung down missing Ang's skull by millimetres. Splinters of wood sprayed her face as the metal prosthetic connected with the cell's wooden door frame. Sparks flew, and Ang could smell burned wood, instantly realizing the arms were full of pulsing electricity. One touch from those arms would deliver a shock she most likely couldn't survive. His fist lodged within the frame, allowing Ang and Ronnie to duck underneath the giant's extended arm as he attempted to disengage his bodily weapon. Muscles rippled in his extra arms as they wiggled the prosthetic back and forth until the steel finally released in a shower of wooden splinters and sparks.

Out in the main dungeon room, Ang and Ronnie slid behind a large supportive beam that connected from ground to ceiling. The giant charged after them, the floor vibrating with each step.

Swinging the prosthetic fist again, he bludgeoned the pillar that sheltered the two sisters, cracking it in half. Both halves folded in on themselves, toppling away from the girls, crushing one of the panicked pregnant women who had been running by at that moment. The woman's eyes glazed over. Blood issued from her mouth.

"Marcy, no!" Ronnie screamed hysterically. She flew over to the mortally wounded woman, her only confidant in their prison.

Another pregnant woman—brunette, short with a bulging belly—had been watching cautiously from a nearby cell. She rushed over to help free Marcy. Their combined efforts were futile, the beam too heavy, the crushed woman's injuries fatal.

Ronnie sat frozen; sight fastened on Marcy's bloodied body— her face now a death mask. Desperately tugging her arm, Ang urged Ronnie to move, to continue fleeing.

The giant was winding up again.

The pregnant brunette scurried back to her cell, concealing herself within.

"RONNIE, WE HAVE TO GO!" Ang shrieked, now pulling her sister to her feet. The electrically charged fist raised again directly over their heads, poised in a death strike. With every ounce of strength that she possessed, Ang yanked Ronnie and herself out of the fist's path at the very last second. It came so close she could feel the wind from the weapon's movement ruffle her hair.

But now they were trapped between the fallen debris from the beam and the six-armed mutant, with nowhere to flee. Two fists rose over their heads in a double strike pose. The mutant's gruesome features contorted into what must have been a smile. He knew they were trapped. Ang closed her eyes, arms shielding her head to thwart the blow.

It never came.

Instead, a sharp clattering forced her to reopen her eyes. A mahogany dining chair was being shattered over the giant's head, showering her and Ronnie with slivers of wood.

Friedrich swayed unsteadily on his feet then fell heavily to the floor, revealing a very proud and relieved Anthony on the other side.

"I've always wanted to do that."

"Well, you might get your chance again," Ang blurted as the giant got back up onto his feet, unharmed. "Hurry, we have to go now!" She grabbed her sister, still unresponsive from shock, and they raced towards the tunnels to complete their escape plan. Ang was more than aware of the other women still trapped there, and only hoped they would follow them. If not, she planned on contacting the authorities as soon as possible to come to their aid. But, for now, she could only concentrate on rescuing herself, her sister, and Anthony.

As they reached the entrance to the tunnel, Anthony rushed in, followed by Ang, but as her sister made it to the opening, the six-armed giant grabbed her from behind with his real arms, which were better able to grasp than the metal ones. He spun her around so quickly that it caused her to lose her balance. She fell heavily to the floor, head smacking backwards. Stunned, she lay there for a moment. But, as the giant descended upon her, survival instincts finally kicked in. Struggling to crawl back towards the tunnels, she scooted like a crab, kicking and flailing as much as she could to dislodge the hold the giant had on her ankle that prevented her freedom. One of Friedrich's free robotic arms reached forward and nudged her in the shoulder, emitting a muted shock that temporarily stunned her. Her body went limp. It was as if he were trying to incapacitate her without causing her harm. Was he trying to spare her, keep her unborn child safe? Preserve the fetus that grew within her sister's belly, one of his own siblings? Or was it Anthony's nullifying effects making the robotic arms less powerful?

Ronnie instantly regained her strength and capacity to move, and she continued to persistently kick and flail at her captor. At times she would almost get free, but then the giant would effortlessly slide her towards him again with his arms like she was as light as a pillow. It was a game of cat and mouse. Finally, he tugged her leg more roughly, causing her to skid forward at an accelerated rate, head slamming back against the cement once more.

The eerie sneer resurfaced on Friedrich's face. He was enjoying this struggle. Like a real animal.

Ronnie's head cleared enough to resume kicking, focusing on his groin, arms and legs, whatever her feet could reach while Ang and Anthony pulled her by the arms to free her from the monster. Ang only hoped they didn't tear her in half in the process.

Finally, their joint efforts paid off. Ronnie's ankle slipped free from the monster's grasp. Anthony pulled her into the secret passageway and helped her to her feet. The three escapees rushed through the tunnel following Anthony's lead, heading ever closer to the castle's hidden exit—the mountain plateau by the river. They kept glancing back over their shoulders to see how close the giant was, the distance getting progressively smaller. Friedrich was right on their heels.

"It's no use! We'll never outrun him!" Anthony yelled. He skidded to a stop. Ang and Ronnie almost crashed into him. He ushered the terrified girls behind him, turning to confront his evil brother.

The click of a gun hammer being cocked caused Ang to peer over Anthony's shoulder. Hands shaking, he clutched a pistol aimed directly at Friedrich's head.

"Freeze, you bastard!" Anthony commanded.

"Anthony, what are you doing?" Ang whispered in his ear. "Do you know how to use that thing?"

"Let's find out."

Ang watched in doubt. Where had Anthony found the gun? It looked like an antique, rusted and worn. Would it even work?

Friedrich kept charging towards them. Anthony closed his left eye, carefully aiming the barrel down his line of sight and bore down on the trigger. The earsplitting crack of the pistol filled the tunnels, echoing off the walls. Smoke puffed out the end of the weapon, and then slowly dispersed.

The giant yelped in pain, one of his left flesh-made arms was struck by the bullet and kicked back by the impact.

"You got him!"

"Actually, I missed. I was aiming for his head."

The giant slowed his gait, clutching his injured arm, leaving him with five working arms. He continued heading towards them, a sinister smirk mocking them. "Nice try, brother," Friedrich growled.

Anthony fired another round, this time hitting the giant's leg. The giant went down hard, cursing them with garbled words.

Taking advantage of the chance to get ahead of their pursuer, they ran ever faster through the myriad of tunnels. Ang's breath was ragged from the combination of physical and emotional exertion. Her sister kept pace but seemed on the verge of a breakdown. Ang only hoped Ronnie could hold off until after they were out of harm's way—if that ever happened.

They turned a corner in the tunnel, a slight glimmer of sunlight ahead urging them forward. But the light was swiftly diminished as another creature appeared directly in front of them, obstructing their path to freedom. He wasn't as tall as Friedrich but taller than most men, and his entire body bulged with striated muscles featuring pronounced vascularity. He wore a black top hat, black, leather vest over a T-shirt and form-fitted jeans. His beard was smoking as fissures cracked open in his skin underneath, issuing thin streams of smoke quickly followed by burning amber light. His eyes were pure black and filled with hatred, pouring out of him like a tangible entity.

Tomas.

Chapter 27

"Anthony, my dear brother," Tomas hissed. "Where do you think you are going?"

The threesome screeched to a halt, then shrank back from the fiery triplet.

"You wouldn't be trying to escape now, would you?"

Anthony remained frozen. Somewhere, not too far behind them, Friedrich would be getting to his feet ready to continue his pursuit.

Tomas raised his arm, revealing a metal contraption embedded in his wrist. It glowed with orange brilliance. "It's a pity this won't work properly yet. It would be so much easier getting rid of you this way, but soon enough, you won't be able to thwart my powers anymore."

He stomped towards Ang, who stood trembling behind Anthony's back. She instantly remembered him from the camping party, the night she almost died. It was Bushbeard. The drug dealer that had given Taryn the tainted magic mushrooms. Bushbeard was Tomas all along.

"And who do we have here?" Tomas reached over Anthony's defensive posture and caressed Ang's cheek with his fingertips. It felt like he was tracing hot coals along the surface of her skin. "You're not one of ours. Aren't you supposed to be dead?"

"Don't touch her." Anthony swiped Tomas' hand away.

The fiery mutant chuckled. "Are you fond of this one, my brother? I'm sure I can use that to my advantage." Staring past Ang, he focused his attention on Ronnie. "Now, you are definitely one of ours. Do you know that father has taken a fancy to you? He believes you are special. And the child that grows in your belly will also be special. At least that's what he thinks. I guess time will tell." Laying his hand flat against her abdomen, he tried to feel what grew within, but without his powers he could see nothing.

"Get your hands off of her!" Anthony lunged at Tomas, who deftly stepped to the side, spinning Anthony around and tucking him under his muscular arm where he secured him into an inescapable headlock.

Ang watched helplessly as Anthony desperately pulled and tugged at Tomas' muscular arm, trying to release his steel hold. Face now turning red, gasping for air.

"What do you think you're doing with these women, my dearest Anthony? You didn't really think you could escape, did you?"

"Angel...run...get out of...here!" Anthony gasped, face turning scarlet.

Shuffling sounds from behind reminded them that Friedrich was closing in on them from the rear, his heavy footsteps getting progressively louder.

They were surrounded.

And what of the third triplet? Did he survive as well? How long was it before he showed up, outnumbering them, making their escape less likely?

The exit beckoned to her, so close now. The cool wind from outside gently ruffling their clothes, their hair. She felt that if they could get outside, they might have a greater chance to survive.

Grabbing her sister's arm, Ang stared directly into her eyes. "Follow me," she mouthed. She darted past the massive fiery triplet, too busy strangling Anthony to react or stop her from getting by. But, by the time Ronnie was running past the mutant, he shot out his foot, tangling her steps. Sprawling to the ground, her cheek scraped the hard-packed earth. Ang quickly hauled Ronnie to her feet. Dirt and blood now smeared her face, and together they scurried further towards the exit. It was so close now; she could smell the fresh mountain air. The temperature suddenly plummeted below zero, their ragged breaths condensing into plumes of mist with each exhalation. The earthen ground became more treacherous, coated in shallow pools of ice. The girls zigzagged past the slippery patches to avoid skidding. Regardless, Ronnie hit a patch, foot slipping sideways, bringing her crashing to her knees. She yelped in pain as her foot twisted at an odd angle. It was difficult for her to stand after that, unable to walk independently. Ang threw her sister's arm around her neck and helped her limp and hop towards the exit. Their progress now slowed, the gap was quickly closing between themselves and Tomas. She chanced a glimpse behind her.

Tomas pursued them, blood rage in his eyes, and still not relaxing his grip on Anthony's neck like Ang had hoped, he dragged his brother along, face now bordering on an unhealthy shade of plum. Anthony was on the verge of passing out. Eyes glazing over, half-lidded, unfocused.

Up ahead, dappled light welcomed the two girls. As they reached the light source, they realized it was a porous wall composed of branches and leaves. Tearing the foliage aside, blinding sunlight announced they had finally reached the plateau. The crisp mountain air blasted them, reminding Ang that they were fleeing into unrelenting winter conditions, Ronnie garbed only in a light shift. How long could she last in this climate?

But, right now, they had other pressing matters.

As they stepped out into the clearing, two men awaited them. Ang now knew the psychotic doctor to be Renner Scholz, Anthony's father, and Gregor—the third triplet. Renner wore a scowl of murderous hatred on his face. Gregor's metallic face was lit up in cerulean light.

Tomas dragged Anthony along, slipping between the branches and leaves and out onto the plateau to reunite with his sibling and father, sandwiching the petrified girls.

"Tomas, it appears you were right. Anthony can't be trusted after all." Renner's voice was eerily calm, black eyes boring through his untalented son. Anthony started to say something, but as if on cue, instead, he lost consciousness. He slumped in Tomas' grip, and dangled, unmoving.

The ground heaved. A tremor could be felt in the firmament, like an earthquake. The air popped loudly with a sudden change in air pressure. Wind crackled around them, suffused with electricity.

"What the hell was that?" Ang whispered to her sister, staggering as the earth shifted beneath their feet.

Tomas dropped Anthony to the ground like a sack of garbage. Raising his arm where the contraption was embedded, he eyed it eagerly. "It's back."

A rope of fire erupted from his extended arm, circling dangerously close to where the girls huddled. The cracks in his face now blazed with fiery light, his right eye a burning ember.

What's happening? Ang searched the plateau for a means of escape, but they were surrounded. And she couldn't leave Anthony behind. He was totally helpless. Unconscious.

As her eyes panned her surroundings, she noticed a familiar face, one she hadn't seen in a while, sparking in her a glimmer of hope.

"Gavin?"

Appearing out of thin air, her guardian angel hovered above the ground, his iridescent eyes and sparkling form more wondrous than ever. Gaze panic-stricken.

Realizing Ang could finally see him again, Gavin became frantic, gesticulating wildly.

Angel, you have to get out of here! Now!

"I kind of figured that out on my own. Do you have any ideas that might actually help us? Where have you been all this time?"

"I've been with you the whole time. You couldn't see me for some reason. Look—it's him. Do you see?" He pointed at Renner and the mutant triplets. "It's the angel that possibly switched your crystal."

Ang turned to see what Gavin was pointing at, what had him so disturbed.

And then she saw it with great clarity. There was another being among them—one that wasn't visible before Anthony lost consciousness. It was draped over each of their bodies like a man-shaped cape.

Was this the other angel? He certainly didn't have the appearance of one, not beautiful and glowing like Gavin but rather the antithesis of light and love. Skin a pale mottled grey with angry purplish veins drawn tight over his skull. Dark circles ringed his black, hollow eyes. His teeth were sharpened points, his tongue swollen and black. Onyx wings with pointed tips dripping an oily ichor sprouted from his back. Yet there were some noticeable similarities between this vile creature and her guardian angel... the way he carried himself with a profound presence that made you feel as if you should bow before him. Give him great respect for he was one of the most powerful creatures that roamed the Earth. If this creature was once an angel, was he now fallen from grace? A demon? Yes, that fit. The creature's likeness hung over Renner and Anthony's brothers as if they wore him like a cloak and controlled their every move. The hairs stood up on the back of Ang's head, and her face blanched.

They *were* possessed. Milena was right.

The fallen angel watched the exchange between Ang and Gavin with great fascination.

"Well, do you see him?"

"I do."

The demon's words came through Renner's mouth like a ventriloquist's dummy, both the demon's mouth and Renner's moving in unison. "My, my, what do we have here?" He scrutinized both Gavin and Ang, trying to understand the strange dynamic. "Gavin. How long have you been here? And how is it that she can see you? See me, for that matter?"

"Don't tell him!" Gavin yelled as if Ang would ever share her secret with this monster. Besides, she didn't understand yet herself.

"You're not supposed to be here. Tomas, weren't you supposed to take care of her?" Renner flashed an expression of disappointment his way. Then back to Ang. "I got rid of your other guardian angel…how is it that you have another one?"

"Sorry to thwart your plans to kill me. Now, there's a new plan…getting my sister back."

The demon turned his attention to Ronnie, and his temper flared.

"I see that! You may think that you can save her, but you can't! She's mine! She will always be mine!"

"Philip," Gavin intercepted, "I watched you change the crystals. Why? What are you trying to achieve here? You can't get away with this."

"You still think I am Philip," the demonic voice snickered. "Yes, yes, I have taken his form, the beautiful version to help get me into the crystal room, and this more appealing darker form for now. You could only wish that I *were* Philip. Then you would have had a chance against me. I used his form to get into the crystal room to do my work without anyone being the wiser. And the form of other guardians as well, getting them kicked out of the heavenly realm for their apparent insubordination, which made it much easier to dispose of those they were guarding…their clients. It made my job a little easier, so there wouldn't be anyone to come searching for the missing women. And I assure you, I will get away with this. In fact, I already have."

"If you are not Philip, then what is your true form?" Gavin asked.

His image transformed from that of Philip into the most wretched creature that ever lived. Thickly coiled horns sprouted from his skull, his eyes glowed deep red, teeth sharpened into finer points, and his body tripled in size while his wings grew talons at the tips. The darkness that he exuded was all-encompassing, and Ang felt the deepest despair and fear in his presence.

"Lucifer!"

"Yes, Gavin. And I'm a little insulted that you don't bow down to me like you should. In time, that will happen. In time."

He gestured to Tomas, who had his flame at the ready. "What are you waiting for?"

Swinging the fiery rope at Ang's head, it flicked at the air as she ducked in the nick of time. But then it quickly returned, burning brighter and hotter than before.

Dropping to the frozen earth, again she barely escaped the flame. Rolling out of harm's way, she intentionally angled her body towards the cave entrance, trying to get closer to Anthony. If she could only reach him and wake him up, she believed the mutant's powers would again be blocked.

Springing to her feet, she raced towards the cave's entrance where Anthony lay in the fetal position. Too still. Was he alive? The plum tinge of his skin had transformed back to its original pale shade. She hoped that was a good sign.

He had to wake up. As she raced towards him, her mind churned with questions. Was the reason she could see Gavin again due to Anthony losing consciousness? Did his unique ability also block her from seeing her guardian angel? And the demon, the devil, that possessed Renner and the triplets? Would his image also disappear once Anthony regained consciousness? And why could she see the devil at all? Was it because he, too, had tampered with her crystal? That's why he knew she should be dead. It was Gavin's hunch, which also meant he may be able to exert control over her if he so desired, just as Gavin had demonstrated with the bear.

It made sense. It was what they had thought all along. But now they knew who they were up against. Not some random gang of human or mutant psychopaths but the original fallen angel, Lucifer himself.

"You are a determined little girl, aren't you? Cheating death, not once but twice now. But, don't worry, we won't fail again. Gregor!" Renner spat. "Stop her!"

Gregor's robotic gaze locked on Ang.

Anthony's supine form was within arm's reach. But, before she could touch him, her body involuntarily collapsed. Every inch of her was instantly paralyzed. A dark presence pervaded her mind. Like fingers probing, prying, poking around, trying to take purchase. Her brain felt violated, like worms were crawling through her head. Squirming, writhing within. She was unable to fight the debilitating sensation, her body useless, her mind slowly being corrupted. Darkness swam at the edges of her vision, pressing in on her thoughts, drowning them. Her body felt cold.

A humming sound erupted from her chest, a high-pitched vibration. The amulet she wore on her neck turned snow white and ice cold.

The humming grew louder, and Ang all at once felt the ability to resist. Not fully, but more so than before. Her body twitched as she tried to move. A spurt of strength fuelled her muscles, and she struggled to sit up as if she had been tied down by tiny Lilliputians and was finally able to burst out of her bonds.

"It's not working! There's a block preventing me from fully controlling her mind," the sightless triplet's computerized voice system expressed, sweat beading his brow despite the chill in the air. The steel visor embedded over his empty eye sockets reflected the sunlight into Ang's eyes, temporarily blinding her. She raised an arm to block the light, revealing the amulet.

"Look, it's the necklace!" Tomas noticed, pointing at the amulet resting against Ang's chest. The white glow pulsed in sync with the humming vibration.

Ang panicked as Tomas charged at her. Now sitting upright on the frozen ground, she tried to scoot backwards, but all functioning had not yet returned, like she was trying to move in a vat full of molasses.

When he reached her, Tomas bent over and snatched the metal from her chest and yanked hard. The chain snapped. Winding up, he launched the medallion back into the entrance of the tunnel, past Anthony's body, and deep into the shadows beyond. If Ang wanted to run after it, she would be going back into the castle. Easier to subdue. As if running after it was an option at this point as her body struggled to obey.

With the amulet now removed, Gregor's power was unhindered over her.

The finger-like sensation resurged ten-fold, probing her defenceless brain with other-worldly strength. Energy waning, the darkness closed in around her all over again. She could fight no longer. Is this how it ends? Numbness filled her along with the darkness. Her vision fogged over.

Through ears stuffed with cotton, she managed to hear a distant grunt. Suddenly, like a blanket lifted off her mind, her head and vision cleared, and her full strength and movement returned with a surge.

Gregor lay on the ground, a trickle of blood leaking out of a gash on the side of his forehead. Ronnie stood over him clutching in both hands the weapon she had used to knock the giant to the ground—a chunk of rock.

It gave her the advantage to escape.

She scrambled over to Anthony, still splayed unmoving on the ground and violently shook him. He moaned but still no recognition. At least she knew he was alive.

"Anthony, wake up," she yelled shaking him more vigorously.

Gregor staggered to his feet, static flitting across the metal mask, then clearing into the fixed cerulean orbits of light that represented his eyes. "Why fight? It's futile, can't you see that? You are powerless against us!" the robot voice taunted as he swiped at the blood on his forehead, smearing it with the back of his hand.

"I wouldn't be so quick to think that. We destroyed your other brothers!" Ang turned to Renner. "Your sons!"

Renner's expression was murderous. "But you were never close to destroying me or my three sons here. You didn't think I would be stupid enough to leave our crystals lying around?" Renner responded. "Now, for my other sons, yes, for that...YOU WILL PAY!"

As if summoned, Friedrich finally emerged from the tunnel to join his father and brothers. Blood leaked from the bullet wounds in his arm and leg. Had they nicked an artery? His face was colourless, his movements sluggish.

Despite his wounds, his robotic arms were fully charged and functioning; occasional bursts of electricity writhed over the metal, audible. They were outnumbered. Then Ang suddenly remembered.

The gun!

Anthony had tucked it into the waistband of his pants. But the realization came too late. With a flick of his finger, Renner commanded Tomas. "Kill her!"

The dark angel hovered over Tomas' shoulder as he bore down on Ang, the mere sight of it stealing the air from her lungs.

She shrieked in pain as he grabbed her roughly by the hair. Her attacker then raised the weapon of fire embedded in his wrist and controlled the flame, multiple tongues of fire now reaching forth, teasing her, licking and gliding across her exposed skin.

"ANTHONY!" she screamed.

Anthony's eyes flew open.

Instantly, the fire that lapped at Ang's skin was extinguished. Surprised, Tomas noticed Anthony, now struggling to stand. Fury overcame him. "NOOOO!"

Ang kicked and screamed, trying to free herself from Tomas' impossible hold. It was no use. Despite the fact that he was distracted, his hands were like iron manacles, solid and indestructible.

"Always you!" Hatred dripped from every one of Tomas' words. "You have thwarted me for the last time, BROTHER!" Looking at Renner, he added sarcastically, "With your permission, Father."

"Wait! Give me a moment." Renner stalked over to Anthony. "I had such high hopes for you, Anthony. I stood up for you, protected you for all these years. And this is how you thank me?" his voice elevated in anger until he was screaming in Anthony's face. "First, my beloved Milena. And now...her." He swept his eyes over to Ronnie, who was cowering behind a snow-encrusted boulder. "You're always trying to steal away the most important things in my life—take them away from me. I will never forgive you for taking Milena away from me."

"You killed her yourself, you sick fuck! It's your fault she's dead!" Anthony barked back.

Renner was taken aback, whether it was from the shock and denial of Anthony's words or the fact that he had stood up to him. He poked a gnarled finger at Anthony's chest, hard enough to bruise. "Your mother tried to make you feel special, like you were somehow different from the rest of my offspring."

He paused.

"But you're not. You were made the same way as your brothers and if anything, you are the *least* special of them all. You don't even have any power. You are useless to me. I should have killed you a long time ago. The day you tried to escape. Now, I'm wondering why I ever spared you. I should have listened to you, Tomas. You were right all along. Now, it's time to make things right."

"Father, let me do the honours. I owe him."

"Tomas, although I owe him as well, I am a gracious father. The honour is all yours. Do as you wish."

Anthony's eyes filled with terror.

"But, what about the prophecy? You need him!" Ang yelled, rallying for Anthony's life.

Renner spun towards Ang, who was stuck in Tomas' unrelenting hold. "What do you know of any prophecy?"

"He's linked to it. And you know it. Gregor had a vision the day Anthony was born, and again the day he tried to escape. He had one yesterday, didn't he? Anthony is linked to the prophecy, and if you harm him, none of it will come to pass." Ang didn't want the prophecy to come true. What she had overheard from the mutants in the hall foretold of world destruction, but she would do anything to buy time for Anthony.

And it was working. Contemplating her words, Renner hesitated long enough.

"Does it have this in the prophecy?" Anthony asked.

Renner turned to face Anthony, eyes growing wide as he saw the gun cocked in his son's shaking fists. The shot rang out, echoing for miles in the mountainous terrain. Renner glanced down in shock. A red circle blossomed in his abdomen where the bullet had entered, passing straight through his body and exiting out the back, black trench billowing outward as it punctured the thick material. The circle of red on the white shirt he wore beneath the open trench coat quickly spread outward.

"FATHER, NO!" Tomas howled. "WHAT HAVE YOU DONE?"

Renner pressed his hands against the bullet wound, trying to stanch the flow of blood as he collapsed to his knees. "Get them!" he ordered.

The triplets immediately sprang into action at their father's command.

Tomas threw Ang to the ground, focusing his rage on Anthony, his nemesis. Finally, he had been granted permission to kill him. And nothing would stop him. He charged at his ungifted brother, who still held the smoking gun in his hand, the one that had shot their father. Anthony drew the weapon up, aiming it at Tomas' face, but he was too slow. Tomas' huge fist punched him square in the jaw, sending him and the pistol flying backwards. A spray of blood decorated the snow.

Ang scrambled over to where the gun had fallen, grabbed it and trained it on the fiery triplet. Before she could shoot him, Friedrich seized her from behind with his metallic arms. Short bursts of electricity coursed through her body, and she convulsed uncontrollably, all her nerves exploding, burning. Was Anthony bordering on losing consciousness again? The prosthetic arms were almost functioning, thankfully not at full capacity or she surely would be dead. The electricity ebbed, and a high-pitched squeal could be heard as the arms recharged.

Taking advantage of the brief reprieve, she lifted her arm that miraculously still held the gun despite her muscles being incapacitated moments before, turned and discharged a bullet straight into Friedrich's head. His face exploded on impact, brain matter splattering all over her. She dropped heavily to the ground and retched into the snow.

Friedrich slumped to his knees, and then flopped face first to the ground, dead.

"NO, NO, NO!" Tomas shrieked again. He abandoned Anthony and charged back at Ang.

Ang scampered away from Tomas, quickly snatched up a heavy branch from the ground and wielded it as a weapon. Using all her strength, she swung at him, but her efforts only seemed to amuse him. "You think that's going to stop me?"

"No, but I will." Anthony ran up behind Tomas, jumped on his back, and began showering him with fists to his head. Successful in bringing him down, they continued to wrestle on the ground, rolling, slamming, fists flying, and blood spraying. Anthony suffered most of the damage, bruises and blood now covering his face.

Meanwhile, Gregor had located Ronnie and had pinned her beneath his massive weight, crushing her, holding her hands immobile above her head in one fist. Without eyes, he sensed the tragic death of his triplet brother, Friedrich, which fuelled his anger, and he threatened to unleash it on Ronnie, who thus far seemed mostly undamaged, despite her twisted ankle. She thrashed below his weight, appearing like a tiny child compared to the giant.

Ang stood frozen between the two struggles, unsure of how to help either of her companions. Renner helped make her decision.

The mortally wounded doctor was lying on his side, doubled over in pain, slowly dying, yet he noticed Gregor's violence escalating. "Don't harm her, Gregor! Whatever you do, you must keep her alive! Protect the unborn child!"

Even though the triplet was instructed to protect Ronnie, Ang knew she needed to help her sister. Rushing over to them, she smashed the branch clutched in her fists over Gregor's head. The monster was momentarily stunned, allowing Ronnie to wriggle free from his grip and scramble out of harm's way.

The sound of a sonic boom shattering the atmosphere drew all their attention back to Anthony. He was lying on the ground, immobile, unable to withstand all the blows he had sustained to his skull. Unconscious, again. The earth shuddered, felt like it was splitting apart, and there was a distinct change in air pressure.

Immediately, Ang felt fingers probing at her brain, the precog's powers once more returned. The amulet lay beyond her grasp, hidden somewhere in the tunnel's shadows. Without it, how would she survive his attack? With the darkness that closed in around her came visions of evil spirits, usurpers, wanting to suck away her soul. Greedy, little spirits, fighting over her essence. Fires raged behind her eyelids, death and decay filling her thoughts, her entire being. In that moment, she believed she glimpsed a part of hell.

And then, another shot rang out. The precog staggered forward. A bullet had punched through the middle of his chest. Toppling over, Ang broke his fall, lying crushed beneath his massive girth. As he slowly lost consciousness, his weight quadrupled, now dangerously squeezing the air out of her, lungs on the verge of collapsing. Suffocating her. She could feel the warmth of his blood saturating her jacket, right through to Milena's tracksuit she wore underneath. *I need to get him off me!*

Using a rocking motion, she was able to gather enough momentum so that gravity could take over, Gregor finally rolling off her body to the left. Blessed air seeped back into her lungs. She checked around to see who was her saviour shooting the mutant at the perfect moment.

And was surprised to find it was Ronnie, still lying on the ground, holding the shaking pistol in her hands.

Tomas' fury escalated, another brother down. "THIS STOPS NOW!" he bellowed; lisp fully noticeable.

A massive boulder, the one Ronnie had previously been hiding behind, lifted of its own accord. Earth, snow, and dried grass fell from its undercarriage as it hurled through the air, directed right at Anthony's lifeless body.

Without a moment's hesitation, Ang crawled over to Anthony, draping her body over his. She didn't think of what she was doing, a useless sacrifice, her tiny body incapable of protecting the man she just met. But her feelings were bordering on love, and she felt as if she couldn't live without him.

She waited, breathless. Certain death approached. Images flashed before her eyes. She would never see Babka or Taryn ever again. This was it, her final moments.

Bracing herself for the impact, she unexpectedly felt a pure light energy course through her body. The boulder crashed onto her back, and upon impact, instantly burst into thousands of tiny pebbles, raining down around her and Anthony without any damage. Her back was completely unscathed.

Glimpsing back over her shoulder, she saw Gavin, pure relief on his face.

★ ★ ★

Watching, with lids half closed, death now imminent, Renner's last thoughts were of fascination. What he witnessed had profound implications. But, could he make sense of it in time.

"Tomas!" he called his son to his side.

Tomas loped over to his dying father, frustrated at another thwarted effort to dispose of his brother and his new annoying friend. Livid over the death of his brothers from their destroyed crystals and the fatal wounds inflicted on his father and Friedrich.

"Did you see that?"

"Yes, father. How is that possible? Does she have powers of her own?"

"No, not powers of her own. This power came from him—the angel." Tomas leered at Gavin. Tomas could see the guardian angel through the eyes of the devil that controlled him.

"But, how?"

"I don't know. But you need to figure it out. Figure out how his power was able to course through her body, without having to possess her. It was all the angel's doing. The girl had no control over it. I've never seen anything like it. This may be the answer we're looking for." He coughed, an awful gurgling sound. "Gregor still breathes. You need to get him out of here, make sure he is healed. Together, you must finish my mission." More gurgled exhalations and choking followed. "Figure...it out." Bubbles of blood sputtered from his lips. Then his eyes glazed over, lifeless.

★ ★ ★

Renner lay limp in Tomas' arms. No longer breathing. No longer living.

Tomas wanted nothing more than to exact vengeance for his brothers and father. But his father's dying wish took precedence.

Storming over to Gregor, he hoisted his dying brother up into his arms, then turned and focused his eyes on Ang and Anthony.

With the voice of the darkest angel, he cursed, "I will be back to finish this! You will both pay!"

It sounded as if the Earth itself cracked in half. The air rippled and warped. And then, they were gone.

Where the castle, Renner, and the triplet brothers once stood, now there was nothing left in their wake, save for the dirt and snow of the mountainous terrain.

Chapter 28

The air was sucked out of Ang's lungs. Gasping, she waited for the air pressure to equalize after the sudden disappearance of the castle, Renner and his mutant sons. One moment they were surrounded by the threat of violence and certain death, and the next moment…the threat was gone.

The ensuing silence felt almost peaceful. The amber sun perched high in the clouds, rays like long, delicate fingers reaching down to mollify the Earth. A snowflake swirled in the wind, landing softly on Ang's shoulder. More flakes followed suit, dusting her toque and jacket like icing sugar. She was so cold, beaten, and bone-tired, she couldn't move, lying there prostrate on the blood-soaked snow, a part of the earth.

And then she felt it.

A tremor at first. Only slight, against her back. Then, the ground shuddered so violently she feared it would swallow her whole.

Were they back? Had Tomas returned, ready to follow through with the promise to get his revenge?

Propping herself onto an elbow, she searched the landscape. Small pebbles trickled down the rockface nearby, coming to rest against her boot. More pebbles, larger, followed suit, some bouncing high enough to strike Ang on her arms and legs. Springing to her feet, realization struck home.

"Ronnie, we have to get out of here! It's going to collapse!"

Lying a few feet away, her sister slowly stirred, and with agonizing slowness got to all fours, attempting to stand. Anthony was still unconscious and would need all of Ang's help, so Ronnie was going to have to take care of herself.

"Hurry, you have to get out of here!" Ang hollered as she grabbed Anthony by the heels and slid him over the slippery snow, away from the avalanche of small rocks and chunks of earth towards ice-covered bushes for safety.

Another massive tremor, the likes of an earthquake, and as Ang peered up at the mountain, she could see a clear view of the cave—the one that had once housed the immense Gothic castle—completely fold in on itself. When the castle vanished along with Tomas, a vacuum-like effect must have been created, pulling the roof and walls of the cave inward. Unable to withstand the suction, the cave collapsed, the entire rock face and secret tunnels now collapsing as well. The earth shuddered and groaned. The steady trickle of pebbles transforming into a deluge of rocks—boulders the size of basketballs now bounding treacherously down the mountainside towards them.

"Ronnie!" Ang screamed. "Look out!" Her warning was too late. Ronnie, because of her injured ankle, reacted too slowly to avoid the danger. A large chunk of limestone crashed into her, instantly crushing her already-injured leg.

"I can't get it off!" Ronnie, panicked, struggling to dislodge the boulder. Ang rushed over to help, but the rock felt like it weighed a thousand pounds, refusing to budge. Other rocks continued bounding down, forcing Ang to dart back and forth to evade being struck herself. Pinned beneath the boulder, Ronnie was unable to move, a sitting duck, only a matter of time before she would be struck again. Ang had to move fast. She heaved on the rock and finally felt it move an inch. However, the slight movement caused Ronnie to shriek in pain, tears now coursing down her cheeks.

"Ah, shit, Ronnie. I'm so sorry. But I don't have a choice. I have to try again."

Ronnie nodded. Braced herself. Ang heaved on the rock again, noticing more movement. But, not enough. If only Anthony would awaken, she would have two more hands to help her gain purchase and move the heavy boulder off her sister. But a quick glimpse told her that wasn't an option. He was still down for the count.

A jagged chunk of shale, sharp as glass, flew down the mountain wall, bounced off a jutting portion of rock that blocked its pathway, sending it careening through the air directly towards Ronnie's exposed face.

Slicing through her right eye, it gashed across her face and down her left cheek. Blood gushed down her face, mixing with her tears. Ronnie's tortured scream sheared through Ang's soul. Her sister would never see out of her right eye again, and if Ang didn't move quickly, more damage was likely to come.

The branch she had used to fight off Tomas and smashed over Gregor's skull lay discarded a few metres away. Its tip, bloody and cracked.

"Hang in there, Ronnie." Her sister had a strange far off look in her undamaged eye.

Ang scrambled over to the branch, hefted its significant weight into her arms, and fled back to her sister. This time, the branch became a lever. She wedged one end underneath the boulder and applied her full weight to counter it. The boulder moved high enough for Ronnie to drag out her crushed leg using both of her hands to do the job. Ang released the boulder, and it rolled back into place.

Now that Ronnie was free, Ang helped her to a standing position. Face wan, eyelid flickering—warning for Ang to brace for her sister's full weight. As Ronnie's good eye rolled back in her head, Ang caught her sister's sagging body, and then dragged her to the safety of the bushes, laying her gently in the snow beside Anthony.

"That was *all* you that time."

Ang jumped, realizing that Gavin was back. "Well, I'm afraid that was the last of it." She plunked heavily on the snow beside Ronnie, her energy completely spent. Gavin came over and sat down beside her. "Do you think they're alright?" Ang asked. Her eyes flicked down to Anthony's injured skull, Ronnie's crushed leg and mangled face, and then back up to Gavin.

"I can sense their hearts beating strongly. I think they will survive. Look, she's already struggling to wake up."

He was right. Ronnie's eyelid flickered. Ang smoothed the hair away from her sister's face, now soaked in blood. The earth continued to rumble beneath them, but at least they were out of harm's way.

"How are we going to get everyone out of here and back to the car? The climb up here was treacherous enough without having to assist the injured. We're a bit lower down now, thanks to the secret tunnel, but there's still a long way to go." Ang's shoulders drooped. Mittens soaked from the snow and blood, her fingers were so numb, they felt separated from her body. While she fought for her life it was easy to ignore the chill, but now it gripped her fiercely.

"Perhaps they can help?" Gavin pointed back further on the plateau where a denser copse of shrubbery grew, where once, many years ago, they had been burned by a young boy's searing rope of fire.

Three young women, wearing only paper-thin shifts like the one on Ronnie, stood trembling, afraid to come out of hiding. One girl Ang recognized—the missing woman from the news report the morning Taryn came by to announce the camping party. The other two were both blonds, arms locked around each other, stark fear in their eyes.

So, some of the women had escaped. But where were the others? Had they been transported with the castle to wherever Tomas had fled? Or were they trapped in the tunnels as the walls collapsed on top of them?

Ang shuddered. Both fates were dreadful.

"You can come out," Ang invited. "I think it's safe." They didn't stir.

"*Are* we safe?" Ang directed her question back to Gavin. "Or, will they return?"

Gavin shook his head in frustration. "I wish I could answer that. All I know is that they are gone for now. Attending to Gregor's wounds, I'm assuming. That should buy us some time."

Some time. It sounded bleak.

"Without Renner to guide them, perhaps they will simply disappear forever," Gavin said.

"Or, return to avenge him. You heard Tomas' parting words."

"Let's focus on getting you out of here for now."

"But, I have so many questions. You called the demon, Lucifer. Like, *the* Lucifer, as in Satan? Was it really him?"

"The dark one himself."

"But you said it was Philip who had switched the crystals."

"Lucifer is a shape-shifter. He can take on any shape or form he desires, whatever will serve his purpose. Like the serpent that tempted Eve in the Garden of Eden. He must have taken on Philip's appearance to gain entry into the Crystal Foundation, undeterred. The other guardians I had noticed gone missing over the past several years...that must have been his doing as well. He admitted as much. But, how has he gotten away with it for so long? I need to alert my boss and the other angels in the Crystal Foundation, but I don't know how."

"How could Lucifer even get into heaven? I thought he was banished to Earth."

"He was. After attempting to steal God's throne for himself, he was punished. Cast down to Earth. But he still has access to the second heaven, the space in between. The Sea."

"The Sea?"

"There are three heavenly realms. The Earth, which is the first heaven, is where you dwell, and where Satan is permitted to rule. The third heaven is where God's throne is held. And then there is the space in between: the Sea, or the second heaven. A place where the angels, spirits of the deceased that have not yet ascended, and other entities abide. Lucifer has access to the first and second realms, although of the second realm he is not usually welcomed. The third realm is not accessible to him anymore unless summoned there by God himself."

"And I could see him because he touched my crystal? Tampered with it?"

Gavin nodded. "I think so."

"Am I always going to be connected to him?"

"I hope not. But I am not certain."

Ang nervously scanned the plateau, fearful of the demon's return.

Gavin closed his eyes, sitting impossibly still. Reopening his eyes after a moment, long, black lashes fluttered upwards like butterfly wings. "I don't feel their presence anymore. Not a remote inkling. They must be far, far away."

Still, Ang knew they could materialize as easily as they vanished. As long as Anthony was unconscious.

"Do you think when Anthony awakens, they won't be able to come back? If he blocks their powers?" Ang asked Gavin, hopeful.

"I believe so."

"Then he needs to wake up. And, thanks, by the way. For saving my life. Again." She pictured the massive boulder hurtling towards Anthony and her miraculous ability to protect him with her own fragile body, the way it exploded on impact, leaving them both unharmed. They would have been killed had it not been for Gavin transferring his power into her body.

"I'm still not comfortable interfering with the laws of nature. With the flow of life. But I couldn't let you and Anthony get crushed." He paused, pensive. "I have a bad feeling…"

"What kind of bad feeling?" Ang encouraged.

Gavin tried to scuff the snow with his hand, make trails through the cold flakes. It remained smooth beneath his touch. Only through Ang was he able to move anything on Earth.

"I worry that the devil may be able to influence you, control you, like I can. And is he able to control the people attached to the other crystals he has touched? What then?"

Ang shuddered. The thought of a demon controlling her petrified her very soul. She recalled the feeling of Gregor's probing, trying to take purchase of her thoughts, her conscience, her whole sense of self. She assumed that is what it would feel like. She wished she had the amulet that Milena had left for Anthony. It now lay buried within the collapsed tunnel, out of her reach forever. Her body trembled.

"I'm probably wrong," Gavin regretted venting his worries, upsetting Ang in the process. But perhaps it was better for her to be aware of the prospect. "That type of power would be too tempting for Lucifer to pass up. That's why I told you not to mention the crystals while in his presence. He must never know of the possibility."

"What do we do now?" Ang surveyed the area around her, at the destruction of the mountainside, the women hiding in the bushes, her injured sister, her new friend and potential love interest lying unresponsive on the ground. Ang shifted over to Anthony and cradled his head gently in her lap. She ran her mitten down his cheek, the porcelain skin now streaked with a trail of pink bloodied water.

"It's time to go home." Gavin's body shimmered, his image becoming diaphanous. Ang could see right through him until she couldn't see him at all.

Anthony moaned as he regained consciousness. Ang stroked his raven-black hair, urging him to awaken. The gash above his eye where the giant had struck him would surely need stitches, but at least the blood had started to clot.

Ronnie would also need medical attention for her ankle, crushed, twisted at an odd angle. The deep gash on her face had turned puffy and red. Her eye, lacerated, would most likely need to be removed. And then there was the possibility of frostbite. But what worried Ang the most was her sister's psychological state. She, too, had regained consciousness, but Ang hadn't noticed. With her need to fight for her life now gone, Ronnie lay on the snow, eyes glazed over, staring up at the sky.

Ang assisted her into a seated position. Ronnie wrapped her arms around her legs and swayed gently in the breeze—back and forth, back and forth. Still staring off into the distance. Oblivious to the cold even though she was only garbed in the hideous smock the mutants had given her and the others. Ang unzipped her parka and draped it over her sister's shaking shoulders.

Anthony finally sat up, seizing his head and grimacing from the pain. He gazed at Ang with pure relief in his eyes.

"You're okay."

Ang nodded. "That's more than I can say for you. How's your head?"

Gingerly, he touched his scalp. Winced. "I think I'll live." He searched the empty land in awe. "We did it? Are they gone?"

"Well, sleeping beauty, you missed a bit of action while you were out."

"What happened?"

"After you blacked out, Gregor tried to take over my mind again, but thankfully Ronnie shot him. Whether he died or not, I don't know. In the meantime, Renner finally succumbed to his injuries but not before telling Tomas to save Gregor. Tomas obeyed, threatening to return and make us pay for our deeds. Then he vanished, along with the castle and Renner and Friedrich's body. All of them, gone. That's when the cave and tunnels caved in." She pointed at her sister. "That's how Ronnie got hurt."

Anthony gasped when he noticed the extent of her injuries.

"She's in shock."

"And me? How did I get over here? Did you save me?"

She humbly faced away.

"Thank you." He kissed her gently on the lips. "Well, I'm going to call this a victory."

"But we still have to find a way to get us all out of here."

She looked at Ronnie again. Her damaged sister, rocking in the snow, emotionally unresponsive. It was obvious her ordeal was far from over. Would she ever get past this?

The concealed pregnant women finally emerged from their shelter. With bare feet, they cautiously approached their rescuers, trying to avoid the sunken earth where the tunnels had collapsed in on themselves. The two blonds still clung desperately to each other, holding on for dear life as they walked nearer. Minor scrapes and bruises dotted their faces, arms, and legs, but other than that, they seemed to have avoided any life-threatening or debilitating injuries.

"Could someone help me?" Ang asked the frightened pregnant women. She wanted to get out of there as soon as possible before the twisted creatures could return.

Leaning over Anthony, she grabbed him under the arm while the woman from the news report rushed to grab the other side.

"I'm Leah," she stated, and they at once hoisted Anthony to his feet. He sagged a little, clutching at his pounding head again.

"I recognize you. There was a missing person's report on television," Ang said.

"I gave up hope that we would ever be rescued. Now, I actually get to see Rob again. He must be so worried."

Ang didn't have the heart to tell her that her husband had disappeared as well, most likely facing a much worse fate. She would find out soon enough.

Now for Ronnie.

"Ronnie, we need to go now. Do you think you can move?" Ang asked, but her sister's stare remained blank, her swaying unceasing. One of the blonds came to help, and together they picked her up, swinging her arms over the back of their necks and half carried her over to where the others stood.

"The path to my car is this way—past the rock, down the mountain. It's a bit of a trek, so we might have to take a few breaks. Everyone ready?"

And, with all in agreement, except Ronnie, who was still unresponsive, they headed down away from the mountain cave that once housed the mysterious castle, now a heap of rubble.

As Ang kept pace with Anthony, she couldn't help contemplating all they had been through. A kidnapping, a near-death-experience, a heroic rescue, culminating into an epic battle against supernatural mutants. And an unexpected love interest, when Ang had all but given up hope of finding the right person for her, someone who could accept her as she was. Quirks and all.

And what did the future hold? Here, she had invited this total stranger to live with her and her grandmother, the man she was developing romantic feelings for. Remembering how they had lain in the library, side by side, watching him sleep, the steady rise and fall of his chest, the perfect shape of his profile. The passionate kisses, the lingering embraces. The yearning to be with him, this beautiful man, who came from the darkest of origins.

A man naïve to the outside world.

She would be his sole provider for the first while, until he could get established into society. She would have two dependents to take care of, and she wondered if she was capable. Yet, the past few weeks had demonstrated how courageous and self-reliant she could be, discovering a strength she never knew she had. Able to overcome her insecurities by coming to her sister's aid when she needed her the most. Fighting for both of their lives and rescuing Anthony in the process. And now they were returning home. Looking back, her usual day-to-day anxieties seemed trivial.

"Where do you think they went?" Ang asked Anthony.

Silence, except for the crunching of their steps on the snowy terrain.

Then finally, "I don't know." His answer sounded hollow and flat.

Did the mutants survive? Would they come after them, wanting revenge for killing their father, their brothers? Would the precog survive what appeared to be a fatal wound? Would they want to retrieve the unborn siblings the surviving women still carried… that Ronnie carried?

All disquieting questions, but Ang couldn't focus on them now. The main priority was to get everyone to the car and find the nearest house or building and call for an ambulance and the police. She knew the authorities wouldn't believe them. The things that they witnessed, what the women endured, it would sound completely insane. No evidence was left to corroborate their story.

But they had to try.

Ang angled the small procession of survivors towards her car. "Let's go home."

Chapter 29

The Alps' snow-capped mountaintops trembled, the threat of an avalanche a mere whisper away.

An ancient Gothic castle materialized out of the ether, the cause of the trembling. There was no worry of anyone noticing its sudden appearance—the location had been well planned-out for its solitude and ability to be hidden from sky and on land.

Tomas held the precog, Gregor, in his arms, his ragged breaths barely registering in the cold air. The fiery mutant wailed in loss and fury, his cries echoing through the mountainous terrain, again threatening the snowcaps to dislodge and spill down the jagged cliffs, an avalanche burying them all. But luckily the snow clung to the peaks with frozen, white fingers.

The fury within Tomas had dislodged, however, no longer within his control.

Within a heartbeat, he had lost many of his mutant brothers, one of his triplet brothers, Friedrich, and his earthly father. And Gregor, his last surviving triplet brother hung on to life by a thread. Death crept closer for him, vying for him, but Tomas refused to allow that to happen.

He would not lose another one.

Out of the side of the mountain, a door opened. The snow, once smooth and unflawed, now displayed a gaping hole from which severely disfigured, mutated beings trickled out in a stream to see what was causing such commotion in their usually tranquil, hidden retreat.

They were astonished when they were confronted with their "sister" castle, the one that was supposed to be lodged in the Rocky Mountains which had now materialized on their doorstep.

After laying Gregor gently on a cushion of snow, Tomas lifted his massive form to a standing position, storming towards his brothers, fury and hatred boiling in his eyes.

"We should have killed him a long time ago!" he roared at a dwarfish animal-like man that led the deformed greeters. He had a grey beard, sunken eyes, and a stubby tail. His tiny stature was deceptive. He was cunning, vicious, and nearly as deadly as the fiery triplet before him.

"Whom do you speak of, brother? What has happened?"

"The stupid prophecy! It's all because of the stupid prophecy! We couldn't risk killing Anthony. Father would never allow it!" Tomas yelled, spraying spittle with each word. "And the prophecy was wrong all along. It had nothing to do with Anthony, and now it's too late!"

"Whoa...back up, Tomas. What has happened to force you to uproot the entire castle and transport here? Are you speaking of Gregor's prophesy? It can't be wrong; his prophesies never are...why do you think that Anthony isn't the one? Please, calm down enough to tell us what has happened," the deformed greeter probed, anxious. He observed the injured brother, Gregor, on the ground. "He is dying."

"Yes, we need the healer, right away."

"And Father? Where is he?"

"He's dead." The news hit the others like a hammer strike. "And so are the rest of our brothers from our compound in the Rockies. It was all Anthony's doing."

The hatred that spilled out of Tomas' black eyes was worse than tears and filled the greeter's soul with dread. "It's up to us now. We must carry on Father's legacy."

"But what can we do?" the greeter implored.

"To finish this…what Father started. And I know now how we can do it." An evil smile spread across his burned flesh, more petrifying than the hatred in his eyes. He had heard the exchange between Gavin and the meddling blond who should have died. His telepathic abilities still in full strength before Anthony awakened. No distance too great to eavesdrop on the most interesting conversation he had heard in a long, long while.

"I know exactly how we can do it."

Epilogue

Darkness, rich with ill intent,
And always wanting more.
Reaching fingers dipped in black,
To caress and stroke and lure,
Back into the darkness.

Will you come, sweet child of mine?
Perhaps I waste my breath in asking,
Not because I fear you will decline,
But because you may no longer have an option.

Such revelations have been discovered,
Although riddled with despair.
A dark day for my family.
Gregor, wounded, but mostly on the mend,
My other sons, not as fortunate,
Their crystals destroyed, Friedrich destroyed,
The women destroyed, perhaps some escaped.
And Renner, ah yes, my dear pawn,
Could I have saved you?
Perhaps there was a way.
But you betrayed me, not once but twice.
For that, my son, you are here now with me.
In the darkness, in the Sea.

Do not fret, for we are still influential,
You still have a purpose for me, with me,
While Tomas takes over your job on Earth.

Losses we have suffered, but all is not lost.
The sister castle in the Alps,
Hidden all these decades, now the new hub
Where Tomas will take the reins.
Teeming with mutants,
Another crystal room with crystals undamaged.
Other women, bellies already distended,
Full of new life.

Build me my army, my true son of mine,
My time almost comes.
A score to settle, not yours, not mine,
But ours.
Free will no longer the deterrent it once was,
Or so it seems.

Now, there is a much better way.

−Lord of Evil

THE END

Acknowledgements

My heart is bursting with love and appreciation for my family and friends, who have not only helped shape me as a person but have inspired me in so many ways to push myself beyond what I thought I was capable. This book is based on relationships, especially on those between best friends and the often complicated yet precious one between sisters. Without these relationships I have had the joy of experiencing throughout my life, this book would be lifeless.

So, thank you to all my family: the originals (Mom, Oc, and Steph), the three amigos (Lee, Erik and Batman), and the extendables (my always supportive in-laws, beautiful Godchildren, and ever-constant friends). I would be a hollow shell without you all in my life.

As for this second book in the *Father of Contention* series, although the underlying basis of this story is Christian, I have taken some liberties in describing what I think life after death and the heavenly realms would be like, and remind you that this story is, indeed, a work of fiction.

Will Tomas return to exact his revenge
on Angelika and Anthony?
And what will become of Veronica and her mutant baby?

Find out in
SEA OF FORGETFULNESS

Book III in the Father of Contention series
COMING SOON!

About The Author

Lanie Mores has her Honours Bachelor of Science Degree and a Master of Arts in Clinical Psychology and is a certified hypnotherapist and personal trainer. She lives in Ontario with her husband, son, and forever barking Chihuahua, Batman.

CPSIA information can be obtained
at www.ICGtesting.com
Printed in the USA
LVHW091210230819
628717LV00001B/6/P